INTRODUCTION

FOR THE longest time I thought it was "Boo-SHAY." I'd seen the name "Anthony Boucher" a lot: On the masthead of *The Magazine of Fantasy & Science Fiction*, for instance, and I'd read his *Far and Away* and *The Compleat Werewolf* collections of SF and fantasy fiction. I was studying French in school, so it seemed natural to use the French pronunciation. Only when I attended my first Bouchercon did I learn to pronounce it "BOW-chur."

Bouchercon is an annual gathering of mystery readers, writers, and collectors, and I was confused as to why they'd name it after a sci-fi guy. But to these folks, Anthony Boucher was a mystery guy—he not only wrote mysteries, he reviewed them for the *San Francisco Chronicle*, *Ellery Queen's Mystery Magazine*, and the *New York Times*. Oh, and he helped found the Mystery Writers of America. So, yeah, he was a mystery guy too.

Rocket to the Morgue combines both these passions.

When Otto Penzler, the esteemed publisher of this line of classic mystery novels, emailed me saying he thought I'd be "a great choice" to write an introduction to *Rocket to the Morgue*, I wondered why. I'd never heard of the novel and I'm not known as a mystery writer. I started in science fiction, moved into horror fiction, and for the last quarter century or so I've busied myself with weird thrillers. But it was Otto, and it was Boucher, and the novel had "rocket" and "morgue" in the title, so I said I'd give it a read.

Am I ever glad I did.

A little background: the man born William Anthony Parker White did most of his writing under the name Anthony Boucher; in the early 1940s his Boucher pen name adopted the pseudonym "H. H. Holmes" (which is, in turn, the pseudonym of a late 19th century serial killer) to write mysteries, including *Rocket to the Morgue*. (Confused? Wait . . .)

Rocket is set in 1941 Los Angeles, less than a year before the USA entered World War Two. It can be categorized as a locked-room mystery, but it's so much more than that. It's a firsthand peek into the innards of what came to be known as the Golden Age of Science Fiction, written by a man who hung out with the writers who forged that age and became household names within the genre. Not only did he know those writers, he peopled the novel with thinly disguised versions of them.

But I knew none of this when I opened the copy Otto sent me.

Chapter one is a commonplace domestic scene that introduces the detective protagonist, Lt. Terence Marshall. He's soon faced with a locked-room stabbing that defies explanation. He turns to an unorthodox consultant,

But chapter two drops us, *in medias res*, into a clichéd space opera starring Captain Comet and his robot companion Adam Fink—

Hold on. Captain Comet sounded an awful lot like Edmond Hamilton's Captain Future from that period, and I remembered a whole series of stories by the Binder brothers about a robot named Adam Link.

Turns out Boucher has us watching over the shoulder of pulp

OTTO PENZLER PRESENTS
AMERICAN MYSTERY CLASSICS

ROCKET TO THE MORGUE

ANTHONY BOUCHER (1911-1968) was an American author, editor, and critic, perhaps best known today as the namesake of the Bouchercon convention, an annual meeting of mystery writers, fans, critics, and publishers.

Born William Anthony Parker White, he wrote with various pseudonyms including H. H. Holmes, the moniker, borrowed from America's most notorious serial killer, under which *Rocket to the Morgue* was originally published. Boucher also worked in a number of genres outside of mystery, including fantasy and science fiction. He served as the mystery fiction reviewer for the *New York Times* for over twenty years, writing a total of 862 columns for the paper.

F. PAUL WILSON is an American author primarily working in the science fiction and horror genres. He has written twenty-three novels and numerous short stories in the Repairman Jack saga, his longest running series. He lives in New Jersey.

AMERICAN MYSTERY CLASSICS

from

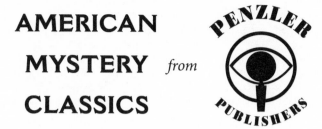

Available now
in hardcover and paperback:

ROCKET TO THE MORGUE

ANTHONY BOUCHER

Introduction by
F. PAUL WILSON

**AMERICAN
MYSTERY
CLASSICS**

*Penzler Publishers
New York*

Published in 2019 by Penzler Publishers
58 Warren Street, New York, NY 10007
penzlerpublishers.com

Distributed by W. W. Norton

Cover image: Andy Ross
Cover design: Mauricio Diaz

Paperback ISBN 9781613161364
Hardcover ISBN 9781613161357
eBook ISBN 9781613161371

Library of Congress Control Number: 2019933974

Printed in the United States of America

9 8 7 6 5 4 3 2 1

ROCKET TO
THE MORGUE

For
The Mañana Literary Society
and in particular for
ROBERT HEINLEIN
and
CLEVE CARTMILL

AFTERWORD:
By the Author

I'VE BEEN interested in imaginative literature all my life, but twelve years ago science fiction, in particular, up and grabbed me by the scruff of the neck with an intensive grasp that shows no signs of weakening with time.

The causes were two: directly, my acquaintance with the Mañana Literary Society, which existed in fact precisely (aside from murders) as it is depicted in this book; indirectly, the fact that pulp science fiction had, at that time, just reached maturity both in thinking and in writing and was at a fine ripe stage to make converts easily.

One of the first results of my conversion (beyond immediately reading all the good pulp science fiction I could lay my hands on) was this novel, first published in 1942. In one way it was very badly timed: the readers of hardcover books had at that time never heard of science fiction, and the whole subject tended to seem a little unbelievable to them. In another way the timing was precisely right: I had the opportunity to present a first-hand picture of an important stage in the development of American popular entertainment—a phenomenon of which the book-readers have become conscious only at second hand in the last couple of years.

I'm surprised on rereading *Rocket to the Morgue* to see how little its statements about science fiction have dated. Pulp rates for stories in the better markets are now about twice what is mentioned here (but then so is the cost of everything else—and some magazines are still paying 1940 rates). Science fiction is no longer restricted to pulps; it now flourishes in slicks, in books, in films, radio, and television. There are more magazine markets for adult thought and prose; when this was written, there were only the two magazines edited by John W. Campbell, Jr. (known in *Rocket* as "Don Stuart"), but recently *Life* bracketed as "the aristocrats of science fiction": Campbell's *Astounding,* Horace Gold's *Galaxy,* and *The Magazine of Fantasy & Science Fiction,* edited by me and J. Francis McComas.

But the reprint racket is still a problem; the lowest level of space opera is still very much with us; mimeographed fanzines and National Science Fiction Conventions have not changed; the top "name" writers in the field are largely still the same; and all of Austin Carter's explanations of the nature and technique of science fiction are as true now as they were then—and as they would not have been a brief five years before.

Actually, science itself has dated the book more than any changes in science fiction. In 1942 atomic fission was another of the peculiar notions the s-f boys kicked around, like time warps and subspace; rockets were something that only eccentric monomaniacs experimented with. To supplement the out-dated section on rocketry herein, by all means get hold of Willy Ley's magnificently authoritative and readable *Rockets, Missiles, and Space Travel* (Viking, 1951).

I'm not only surprised but amused to see that, in the best science-fiction tradition, I achieved some accurate on-the-nose prophecy. It looks as though I may have been tragically wrong in my hope that experiments for spaceflight would help world unity; but I did bring off two minor unconscious predictions. I used the title *Worlds Beyond* for a magazine (actually the unforgettable *Unknown Worlds),* and in 1950 there appeared on the stands a short-lived magazine with that title. I created a character called Captain Comet to parody all the inter-galactic supermen, and sure enough, there is now a comic book featuring the hyperspatial adventures of Captain Comet.

I think (as best anyone can judge his own work on rereading) that I've managed to capture a moment that has some interest as a historical footnote to popular literature. This is the way it was in Southern California just before the war, when science fiction was being given its present form by such authors as Robert A. Heinlein (still the undisputed Master), Cleve Cartmill, Jack Williamson, Edmond Hamilton, Henry Kuttner, C. L. Moore, and many others. (And this is as wise a place as any to add hastily that no character in this novel is based specifically on any actual writer—nor is any character quite devoid of some factual basis.)

I hope that some of the regular readers of whodunits may find this picture of the field provocative enough to make them investigate further—a much easier task now than when the novel was written. At that time there was no good anthology devoted to the best of science fiction—in fact, no such anthology, good or bad. Now you can start your investigations with the tastefully chosen collections of Groff Conklin, August Derleth, Raymond J. Healy (with and without J. Francis McComas), and Judith Merril;

you can go on to sample the three "aristocrats" mentioned above; and from then on I trust you'll have as satisfying and stimulating a time varying your criminous diet with the wonders of logical imagination as I have enjoyed for the past dozen years—and expect to continue enjoying at least until my sons radio me their greetings from the moon.

ANTHONY BOUCHER
Berkeley, California
December 12, 1951

writer Joe Henderson as he types out his latest novel while talking to his agent, M. Halstead Phyn, specialist in SF and fantasy.

Interesting . . . was this a tip of the hat by Boucher?

Then, in a progression of vignettes, we meet various pulp writers who all have a reason to hate a certain Hilary Foulkes, ruthless executor of his father's huge literary estate. All typical mystery fare until Boucher drops a bombshell:

It happens during the opening of the novel's second day when a character drops the name "Don Stuart," editor of two magazines, *Surprising Stories* and *The Worlds Beyond*.

I almost drop the book.

Don A. Stuart was the pseudonym of John W. Campbell, under which he wrote the timeless *Who Goes There?* (adapted into *The Thing from Another World* and John Carpenter's *The Thing*). In 1941, under his real name, he was editor of not one but two magazines: *Astounding Stories* and *Unknown Worlds*.

No question: He was talking about John W. Campbell—my mentor.

Decades later, when I was trying to break in, Campbell was also the only editor who told me *why* he was rejecting my stories. His rejections became my only writing course. I made my very first sale to him in 1970.

Imagine my shock to see Boucher's characters talking about this Don Stuart fellow—knowingly and with respect as the editor who was forcing science fiction to grow up. Which is exactly what Campbell did, starting in 1937, as editor of *Astounding*.

From that point on I started putting the characters under a microscope. Half the fun of the novel (at least for me) was sussing out who was who.

No question that one of the early major suspects, Austin Carter, is Robert A. Heinlein, known as "the dean of science fiction." The detective interviews him in Carter's office where the writer has a wall chart to keep track of all the interrelated stories he pens under his own name. Fact: In 1941 *Astounding* published a chart delineating the course of Heinlein's "Future History" stories.

The scene also gives insight into how the pulp writers played the game. The average pay rate was a penny a word, with an occasional bonus of a quarter of a cent to half a cent per word. Austin Carter explains his use of multiple pseudonyms:

"So whatever's outside the series is by Robert Hadley—that is, in a one-cent market or better. I don't like to hurt the commercial value of those names, so whenever I sell a reject for under a cent, it's by Clyde Summers."

Fact: Heinlein did just this with his pseudonyms "Anson MacDonald" and "Lyle Monroe." In fact, these pseudonyms have cameos in the novel.

Elsewhere, in conversation with the character named Joe Henderson—seen earlier writing Captain Comet space operas— someone mentions "annihilating galaxies left and right." Well, the writer who penned the deliberately juvenile Captain Future novels was Edmund Hamilton—or rather, Edmund "World Wrecker" Hamilton, as he was known.

As for agent M. Halstead Phyn, specialist in SF and fantasy, he might be Julius Schwartz, but I'm going with Forrest J. Ackerman, an agent and a fixture around the LA science fiction community at that time.

The only writer character I had no feel for was Matt Duncan. He may well represent a real person, but I know too little about him to make a guess.

So, Boucher has Heinlein, Hamilton, and Forry Ackerman on stage, with John W. Campbell in the prompt box.

But who does writer "D. Vance Wimpole" represent? He's got crimson hair and blue eyes and can dash off a thirty-thousand word novella like most people scratch out a shopping list. He's also a cad, a conniver, and a pathological liar.

There's only one answer: L. Ron Hubbard. Before he invented Dianetics and Scientology, L. Ron Hubbard was a redheaded, prodigiously prolific writer, known for the speed at which he could compose, who sold to a wide array of SF, fantasy, adventure, and western pulps. His reputation was that of a chronically broke womanizer who wouldn't know the truth if it bit him on the nose.

An amazing cast. *Rocket to the Morgue* made me very happy. In fact, it made me want to run up to every science fiction fan I know and shove a copy at them, shouting, "You have *got* to read this!"

The mystery element made me happy too. I'm usually pretty good at sussing out the perp, and I thought I'd solved the second murder (yes, there are two), but I was wrong. I like when a book fools me.

If you're not into science fiction, or if you think science fiction began with *Star Trek* or *Star Wars*, ignore all my backgrounding and simply enjoy *Rocket to the Morgue* as the murder mystery Anthony Boucher intended it to be. But if you're a well-read fan, or simply interested in the history of the genre, a double treat awaits.

F. PAUL WILSON
The Jersey Shore
Summer 2018

FOULKES, Fowler (Harvey), author; *b.* San Francisco, Calif., Jan. 15, 1871; *s.* Roger Clinton and Catharine (Livingstone) F.; A.B., Stanford, 1890; A.M., King's College, Cambridge, 1892; *m.* Mary Margaret O'Donnell, of San Francisco, June 3, 1893; I son, Roger O'Donnell (deceased); *m.* 2d., the Hon. Patricia St. John of London, England, May 10, 1903; I son, Hilary St. John. Teaching asst. in physics, Leland Stanford Univ., 1892-95; freelance newspaper work in San Francisco, 1895-1900; govt. propaganda bureau, 1917-19. Mem. Authors' League of America, Phi Beta Kappa. Republican. Episcopalian. *Author: The Lilting Lark,* 1897. *Legends of '49,* 1898. *The Last Coast,* 1898. *Beneath the Abyss,* 1899. *The Researches of Dr. Derringer,* 1900. *The Purple Light,* 1901. *Dr. Derringer Returns,* 1903. *The Intriguers* (play), 1904. *The Mission of Sorrow.* 1906. *The Missions in Twilight,* 1908. *The Further Researches of Dr. Derringer,* 1909. *Gold at the Mill,* 1912. *The Only Mrs. Foxley* (play), 1913. *Union Pacific,* 1916. *Derringer,* 1917. *Derringer at War,* 1919. *And the Earth Shook,* 1923. *The Unchallenged Theory,* 1924. *The Crimson Prism,* 1926. *The Last Researches of Dr. Derringer,* 1927. Life and Dr. Derringer: an Autobiography, 1928. Contbr. to mags. *Address:* care of Hornby and Fraser, 386 Fourth Ave., New York, N. Y.

—From *Who's What in the U. S. A.,* 1928-1929.

The essence of Fowler was that he was unique. There was a trick of contortion with which he used to amuse us in his rare but ever charming lighter moments; doctors who heard it described would pronounce it impossible until they saw it. Just so the man from Mars might say that it was impossible to create a character so real and vivid that he would become part of the consciousness of all mankind, from Peoria to Timbuctoo. But we who have read the glorious exploits of Dr. Derringer know that no proven fact could ever surpass in reality this magnificent creation of Fowler's.

—From *Foulkes the Man,* by Darrell Wimpole. New York, Hornby, 1931.

Eliminate the impossible. Then if nothing remains, some part of the "impossible" must be possible.

—From *The Researches of Dr. Derringer* by Fowler Foulkes. New York, Hornby, 1900. (And *passim* in other of the Dr. Derringer stories.)

THE FIRST DAY:
Thursday, October 30, 1941

LEONA MARSHALL stretched her long legs out on the bed and clasped her hands comfortably behind her red head. "Isn't it nice I couldn't nurse her?" she murmured. "Think how awkward it would be for you to take over a feeding."

Her husband took the bottle from the electric warmer and tested the milk on the inside of his wrist. "Handy-like," he agreed. He seemed satisfied with the milk and wrapped the bottle in a cloth. Then he lifted his three-month-old daughter from her bassinet and held her up high. The two beamed fatuously and gloriously at each other.

"No games," Leona warned him. "She has to learn that meal times are strictly business."

"We aren't playing games," Terence Marshall protested unconvincingly, settling his daughter into the crook of his arm and tenderly poking her plump stomach.

"No?" Leona's voice was suspicious.

"No. You know what, Leona; this is a fat little wench you've got here. Think she'll ever grow up to have her mother's figure?"

"Such as it is now . . ." Leona surveyed herself ruefully.

"It'll do. Come on, darling, open your mouth. This is milk.

1

Nice milk. You remember." The pink little lips parted reluctantly, then clasped avidly on the rubber nipple.

"Anything interesting happen today?" Leona wondered.

The baby released the nipple and turned her head vaguely toward the voice. Her father said, "Damn it, Leona, if I'm going to take feedings you might at least let me give them in peace."

"But did anything?"

"Here, darling. Nice nipple . . . Oh, nothing special. Just a murder. No," he cut his wife off hastily before she could speak. "Nothing up your alley. And why a lieutenant on Homicide should be cursed with a wife who loves mystery novels is one example of the ways of God to man that Milton forgot to justify. Nothing at all pretty about this one. No locked room, no mysterious weapons, no unbreakable alibis—the last mainly because we haven't even got a suspect yet."

"Still . . ." said Leona.

"All right—if you'll stay hushed, I'll tell you about it. She doesn't mind my talking. See: it kind of lulls her. No, this was just a bum in a Main Street rooming house. A floater. Name, according to the register, Jonathan Tarbell. Nothing on him to check that one way or the other. Been there a fortnight, according to the clerk. Just slept there, never around in the daytime. One visitor who called a couple of times—description too vague to help.

"Shot through the heart at close range. Thirty-five automatic. Weapon smartly, if extravagantly, left right beside the body. No prints, which together with the man's bare hands rules out suicide. Somebody, presumably the murderer, had searched the room, but hadn't bothered to take over three hundred dollars in cash.

"So it shapes up like this: Tarbell's clothes were new and fairly good, and he had plenty of cash—far too much for a man living in the lower depths. The murderer wanted something in the room, but not money. So in all likelihood Tarbell was tied up with some kind of a racket (blackmail, at a guess), pushed it too far, and got taken care of.

"That much is clear, and the obvious next step—"

"Aren't you ever going to burp her?" Leona asked.

"Now look. If I don't tell you about what I'm doing, you plague us with questions. If I do try to tell you, you start interrupting me and—"

"Go ahead and burp her."

"All right."

"And don't forget the burp cloth. We can't go having your suit cleaned every day."

"All right. And anyway I hadn't forgotten it." Lieutenant Marshall spread a diaper over his shoulder and hoisted his daughter up. "The trouble with you, madam," he went on, patting the infant's rump, "is that you haven't any real interest in crime itself. All you care about is the fancy frills and furbelows of romanticism that the whodunit writers trick it out in. Crime itself is essentially flat, dull, drab, and infinitely important." He spoke in the grave orotund tone into which his usual colloquialism occasionally lapsed, and his daughter answered him with a burp equally grave and even more orotund.

"I know," Leona chortled. "She's going to grow up to be a critic."

Marshall grinned at the baby. "Let's throw your mother a bone, huh?" With his free hand he fished out of his pocket a string of beads and a scrap of paper and tossed them over to the bed. "See what you make of those while we finish our dinner."

"Clews!" Leona cried gleefully.

"No, Ursula." Marshall resolutely turned his daughter's face away from her mother. "You can play with clews when you're a big girl. Right now you drink your milk."

"She took the whole bottle," he announced proudly ten minutes later. "Now you can talk."

"Where did you find these? Is she wet?"

"To the second question, what do you think? To the first, that bit of paper was in among the unstolen currency. The rosary had slipped down through a hole in the lining of his pocket. Indicates the body was searched by an amateur—always beware torn linings. And those two items are the sole damned leads we've got to go on."

Leona looked at the two letters and five figures scrawled on the paper. "A phone number and a rosary . . . I suppose you've checked the number?"

"It's an apartment hotel out on Rossmore near Wilshire. Veddy veddy swank. Not what you'd expect to be in communication with a corpse on Skid Row. Some twenty-odd apartments, though. It's going to be a job checking 'em all." He folded back Ursula's nightgown and began taking out safety pins.

"And a rosary . . . Just what does that prove? Supposing a blackmailer does have his religious moments—how does that give you a lead?"

Marshall stuck the pins in a cake of soap and went to work deftly on the diaper problem. Ursula decided she was being tickled and liked it. "Look at the rosary closer."

"It's nicely carved, probably quite an expensive one. Hand work, and good. Aside from that . . ."

"A zero on today's recitation, my sweet. You're the clew-addict, but on this you flop badly. How many sets of beads are there?"

"One . . . two . . . Seven."

"Exactly. And that's all wrong. I've noticed the rosaries that the nuns carry. There should be five sets. So there's something strange about this one, and I've got to check up on it." He finished pinning the extra diaper for night wear, pulled the baby's gown down, and fastened the drawstring.

"With Sister Ursula?"

"Uh huh." Marshall looked not too happy. "The last time I was mixed up in a case with Catholic religious clews, the goddamnedest things happened I've ever heard of in the history of homicide. Since then life's been peaceful. Just nice ordinary routine restful murders. And now this rosary crops up . . ."

Leona rose. "It's been swell having a few minutes' rest. Thanks, Terence. And now I've got to finish getting dinner ready. The Duncans'll be here any minute.

Lieutenant Marshall held his daughter in one arm and put the other around his wife. "I love you," he said.

"Which of us?"

"Both of you. And Terry too." He jerked his head toward the next room. "Is he asleep?"

"Probably not." Leona leaned over and made a face at the baby, who appreciated it. Then she put her lips firmly and warmly against her husband's. "I'm lucky," she said.

While Leona bustled competently about the kitchen, Terence Marshall assembled whisky and soda and glasses on a tray. He glanced at the clock and at the door, and then settled down for a moment with Dudley Fitts' latest volume of translations from the Greek Anthology. Occasionally he referred to his worn volume of the original and nodded with pleasure at the translation.

It had been agreeable, in the cool walks of Oxford, for Rhodes Scholar Marshall to speculate on the possibilities of continuing the scholarly life—the contemplation of chaste and ordered beauty, the strict rigor and infinite flexibility of the scholastic mind.

Then had come his chance acquaintance with young Southey and his introduction, through Assistant Commissioner Southey, to the methodical wonders of Scotland Yard.

Here, he realized, in the police work so damned and scorned by the man in the street, was the one perfect career for the individual who combined good will, a well-trained mind, and a body which had brought him All-America honors for two years running. And he had succeeded in the career, though only by dint of keeping his mind and his good will as much under wraps as possible. If any of the boys were to see him now, his eyes coursing over Greek minuscules and his lips curved in quiet contentment, nothing but the fear of his athletic prowess could prevent mayhem.

The doorbell rang, and he set the Greek Anthology aside.

"Be there in a minute," Leona called from the kitchen.

Lieutenant Marshall opened the door to admit the Duncans. He had met them on the Harrigan case (that case of the Nine Times Nine in which "the goddamnedest things happened" and through which he had met the amazing nun whose name he had given his daughter), and their hesitant and confused romance had been the one note of happiness in that murderous business.

Six months of marriage had changed them. Concha (Maria de la Concepción, to give the full name bestowed on her by her Spanish mother) was no longer a frightened and groping child, but a young woman beginning to feel for the first time sure of her place in life. And Matt Duncan was losing his bitter touchiness and slowly becoming willing to admit that people sometimes did like him and might even mean well by him.

"Sorry we're late," Matt said. "Believe it or not, we were waiting for a streetcar."

Concha nodded. "And we have, by the latest statistics, the coldest corner in Los Angeles to wait on. I'm frozen."

"Until you're twenty-one," said Lieutenant Marshall, "I am strictly violating the California law by giving you a drink; but that makes it medicinal. I don't think I'll report myself."

Concha handed her host her coat and accepted a highball. "If we only had a car . . ." she murmured.

Matt Duncan downed a quick straight one and refilled his glass. "If Stuart likes this novel I'm working on, we'll see what can be arranged. Though if we get into the war, God knows if they'll be selling cars. Or novels either."

"If?" said Marshall quietly.

"Only I don't see," Concha insisted, "why we have to wait for any old novel. If you'd only—"

Matt set down his glass. "Look. We are *not* going into that again."

"I only said—"

"Let it go."

Marshall grinned. "Children . . . !" he said chidingly.

Matt Duncan turned to him. "Terence, I like the touching story of your marriage. Arresting a girl in a vice-squad raid on a burleycue, and proposing to her while she was serving her jail sentence. You were a smart man to marry a woman with no money of her own."

"I don't know about that. I'm certain neither Terry nor Ursula would object too strongly to having a mother who was an heiress."

"And it isn't my own," Concha argued. "It's ours now, and why you shouldn't use it to buy a car if you wanted to—"

"Mary!" Matt's voice was quietly grim.

Concha shuddered. "You're going to have to shelter me,

Lieutenant. He never uses my real name unless he's mad as any-thing."

"And I've got a right to be mad. Here I—"

Terence Marshall sighed relief as his wife came in.

"I won't ask you do you want to see the children sleeping," she greeted the guests, "because you've always been such perfect lambs about it that I feel you ought to be let off for once. And besides dinner's ready."

The Duncans looked pleased at both announcements.

"I want you to do me a favor, Concha," said Lieutenant Marshall as he served seconds of the rabbit.

"Do it," Matt advised his wife. "There isn't any favor could re-pay Leona's cooking."

"I'm jealous," Concha pouted. "What I cook he just sits down and eats and never says anything about. Only maybe that's just as well . . . What's the favor, Lieutenant?"

"I do wish you'd get around to calling me Terence. I hate to seem official off-duty. But this is an official favor at that. I need Sister Ursula's advice on something, and I want you to drive out to the convent with me."

"Why?"

"Why? Hell, I don't quite know. But I can invade the Stately Mansions of the Rich with the greatest aplomb, and I can even manage not to look too out of place in a queer dive; but the one place in the city of Los Angeles where I feel like a peculiarly sore thumb is that convent. Come along and hold my hand."

"On one condition: Leona has to give me the recipe for this rabbit."

"Fair enough. Mind if I steal your wife tomorrow afternoon, Matt?"

"He won't even notice. He's in labor with a fantasy novel."

"Oh. More rabbit, Matt? Sympathetic magic for fertility?"

Matt Duncan looked up startled and brooding. "Thanks. Look, Terence. From all your experience, what is the one safe and certain way of committing murder?"

"At an offhand guess, the only sure way I know is to take your victim to Washington. I think it's fifteen years now since the capital police got a conviction on murder. Would that fit your plans? Only of course if it was a woman they could get you on the Mann act. I suppose murder is an immoral purpose."

"It's a man," said Matt darkly. "A male at least."

"Fun," observed Leona. "We have murder at the dinner table all the time, but it's always after the fact. This is a new approach. Who's the victim?"

"My darling dearest Hilary. Hilary St. John Foulkes, to you."

"Foulkes?"

"The only son and heir of the late great Fowler Foulkes, whose demise is mourned by none so much as by the poor bastards who have anything to do with his son."

"But who is Fowler Foulkes?" Leona asked.

Marshall laughed. "My wife! She loves mysteries, but get her on the truly important matters of reading . . . Hell yes, I grew up on the Dr. Derringer stories, and there's never been anything to touch them. Sacred, that's what they are. But why murder Hilary?"

"Meet him," said Matt. "Just meet him once. That's all. You don't need any extra motives. In fact, I haven't even got that far, and look at me."

"Murder in the absolute and altruistic?"

"Not quite. But what's your recommendation on method?"

"Introduce me to him some time and I'll diagnose. You've got to pick the method for the individual. Artistry in Crime; that's the Marshall motto."

"Let them talk," Concha conceded tolerantly. "But Leona, about this rabbit—"

"Oh yes. It's simple as anything, that's the nice part of it. Have your rabbit all cut up and jointed and put in a baking pan. Over it you slice up onions and green pepper and salt pork, and sprinkle it with paprika. No salt, remember; the pork takes care of that."

"Our wives can exchange recipes far more easily than we can," Marshall went on to Matt. "Murder doesn't reduce itself to formula so readily. You have to grasp the inexorably right but fleeting instant."

"Pour a cup of boiling water over it and bake it in a medium oven for an hour (that's usually enough) or maybe an hour and a half. About half way through you can take off some of the liquid; the rabbit sort of melts. And make your gravy with that and what's left in the pan when you're through."

"That's the easiest way to cook rabbit I ever heard of, and" Concha set down the bone she had been gnawing and wiped her fingers, "far and away the best. Got a pencil, Matt?"

Matt fumbled for his pencil and looked across at the Lieutenant. "About that murder, Terence. You think I'm kidding, don't you?" His smile was set and harsh.

2.

With lightning decision Captain Comet switched off the televisor and pressed the synchrosynthetic seleni-chromium mesh on his space-tanned wrist.

Adam Fink, the androgynous robot, clanked into the room.

"Quick!" snapped the lithe but brawny Captain. "The *Cen-*

tauri III is even now leaving the space port with a cargo of contraband xurghil weed for Venus. Take Gah-Djet, the mechanical brain, and travel at once to X-763, the maneuverable asteroid. Intercept the *Centauri* at the point marked Q prime on this orbit."

The electronic pattern-grooves of Adam Fink's metal mind recorded his master's orders. He turned clanking to go.

"And remember that Princess Zurilla of Neptune is aboard. No harm must befall her!"

The robot's head clanked in a jerking nod, and he left the room. Captain Comet's tense muscles flexed as he switched the televisor on again and beheld the central control room of the Interspacial Patrol.

"Z-999," he barked.

Suddenly the machine faded and went dead. A pulsing arc of purple light grew in the middle of the room and forth from it stepped a green-bearded Centaurian.

"Xix!" Captain Comet gasped. "Xix, the xurghil-smuggler!"

Joe Henderson jerked the copy from his typewriter and looked at the stack of blank paper-and-carbon sandwiches beside him. "I've got the Captain in an awful fix now," he said.

The little man on the couch yawned. "Grensham wants that copy end of this week."

"He'll get it. I'm darned if I know quite what happens next, but he'll get it."

"In the last ten minutes," said the little man reflectively, "your typewriter pinged twenty-five times. It averages ten words to the line. That makes two hundred and fifty words. From Grensham that's two fifty. So in ten minutes of lying here on the couch, I've made a quarter. Life could be worse."

Joe Henderson's face in repose had an almost adolescent

blankness. His slow shy smile gave it warmth and charm. "I know, you old horse thief. All the time I'm typing, I think, 'Every ping, a penny for Phyn.'"

"Life could be worse," the agent repeated. "Like for instance there could be more than one Hilary Foulkes."

Henderson frowned at the pile of unused paper. "What's wrong with Hilary? I met him once with Vance, and he seemed harmless."

"Didn't I tell you about the deal I arranged with MacNamara?"

Henderson made a distasteful face. "MacNamara? I don't think so."

"We were going to launch a reprint mag called *Galactic Stories*. Signed up with the Foulkes estate for a Dr. Derringer reprint in each issue. All announced and everything. But that sonofabitch Hilary slips over a clause I don't read. It says at the rates we pay we've got to print *reprinted from* blank *copyright* blank *by* blank *by permission of Hilary Foulkes,* in type just as big as the title. Otherwise we pay five hundred smackers per story."

"I don't know as I'm any too sympathetic there. You know what a racket this reprint stuff is."

"How come a racket? We give the public good reading matter cheaper than it could ever buy it first hand."

"Sure, and cut the throats of us poor dopes that write it."

"Stuff and nonsense, Joe. You don't understand business. Writers never do . . . But who the hell's going to read a reprint story if it says *Reprint* on it? Not that I mean we sail under false pretenses, but you don't have to go reminding them like that. And who can pay five hundred sinkers for pulp rights? So that's how come *Galactic Stories* folded."

Henderson nodded, not listening. "Look! Gah-Djet the mechanical brain'll spot those androids of Xix's with his detecto-tendrils and then . . ." He fed fresh paper into the typewriter, poised his fingers for an instant, and set to work.

M. Halstead Phyn (Author's Representative—Fantasy and Science Fiction Our Exclusive Specialty) heard the first ping with pleasure and felt the round copper coin jangle into his pocket. "All the same," he muttered, "some day I'm going to take that Hilary bastard. And not for pennies."

3.

Austin Carter was waiting for the phone to ring. He sat in a chair and resolutely refused to pace. Calmly indifferent, that's what he was. He reread a paragraph for the fifth time and suddenly found himself wondering what book he was reading.

He looked at the spine. *Memories of a Useful Life,* by Nehemiah Atchison. He threw it down and shouted, "Where the hell did we acquire Nehemiah Atchison?"

Bernice Carter looked up from the portable typewriter. When her husband was working, he used the office model in the study and embedded himself in the cottonwool of a sternly enforced silence. Bernice had composed her first saleable story in the office of a weekly news-sheet, answering questions about local politics between sentences. Sometimes now her stories refused to go right unless she was shouted at occasionally.

"He's some sort of great-second-uncle of Matt Duncan's. Those memoirs were privately printed as an inspiration to his family."

Austin Carter pitilessly kicked Nehemiah across the floor. "Damned if that's the kind of inspiration I need right now."

"They're pretty funny, in a nice stuffy way." Bernice's voice was as cool and fresh as her skin and her eyes. "I read them the other night."

Carter grunted and stared around. "Where's my solitaire cards?"

"In the study, I guess. Look, sweet: you know everything about the market. How much sex will Don stand for?"

"In a word, none." Carter half smiled. "Remember that story where my mathematical genius liked to watch women's breasts because they were such beautiful fifth-order curves?"

"I remember. Don changed it to heads. But that sounded all right."

"The hell it did. Heads aren't fifth-order curves. I don't mind his improving my morals, but I do object to his bolloxing my mathematics. What sly obscenity are you planning to put over on the poor man?"

"No; I guess I'd better behave. But this one's an interplanetary romance, and I just couldn't help wondering about the physiological aspect. Pity . . ."

Carter had risen to hunt for his cards, but now he contented himself with merely pacing. "Something will happen," he muttered. "I know it. It can't help but go wrong. There's a jinx on this novel, and that jinx is our darling Hilary."

"But Hilary hasn't got anything to do with this now."

"He'll find some way. And all because I refused to pay him a hundred dollars. Can you tie that? So I wanted to use quotations from the Derringer stories for chapter-head quotes in the novel. God knows that's not infringing on his territory. It wouldn't cut in on his sales. If anything, it's just another free plug. But would Hilary see it that way? One hundred dollars to use that handful of quotes, and the most I could hope to get on royalties out of the damned book would be four, five hundred."

"Never mind," said Bernice soothingly. "If this film sale goes through, you'll be practically in Hilary's class yourself."

"In a class with *that?* Madam!" He glared at the phone. "Bixon says the trend is all of a sudden toward fantasy pictures now, and Weinberg at Metropolis is hot as hell on this."

"He says."

"They must be through conference by now. Bixon said he'd call me as soon as— What shall we do with our ill-gotten gains, Berni?"

"Pay income tax."

"There'll be some left. Every time you hear people complaining about how much they paid in taxes, just stop and figure out how much must be left if they had that big an income. We'll have some left; and what shall we do?"

"Save it for me to live on while you go to war."

"No. I don't doubt we'll be at war soon enough. But let's be mayflies and carp the diem before it dies. Anyway, you're practically self-supporting. You know what I'd like to do?"

"Charter a space ship."

"Of course. But failing that I'd like to take you around to the National Parks and Monuments. Especially the Monuments, and above all Canyon de Chelly. I don't know another spot that has the combination of absolute beauty and historical impact that that Canyon has. The sheer titanic walls and the peaceful green—"

"You're like Macbeth, sweet," said Bernice. "When you get to an emotional peak of tension, you go all lyrical. You—"

The telephone rang.

Austin Carter answered it. "Hello.—Oh yes, Bixon. Yes.— Yes.—I see.—Of course." His voice was trailing down from hope to resignation. "Yes.—Well, there's always another time.—Sure, let me know. 'Bye."

"They didn't like it," Bernice translated.

Carter's brown eyes glowed with fury. "They liked it all right. Weinberg was nuts about it, in fact."

"They just liked it too well to buy it?"

"No. It's—"

"It couldn't be Hilary?"

"It is. Metropolis is planning to produce a series of Dr. Derringer pictures. Hilary whispered that they'd never clear the rights if they bought that dreadful Carter novel."

Bernice looked him up and down. "The whisky's in the kitchen, sweet. And while you go and get manfully drunk, I'd better get ahead with this novelet."

"Hilary . . ." said Austin Carter between clenched teeth.

4.

Veronica Foulkes stroked the ears of her Pekinese with one languid hand and rang for tea with the other.

"Of course, my dear, I don't expect you to understand fully. You aren't a Wimpole."

The slim English girl smiled. "After all, I'm engaged to one. And I think I understand Vance a little."

"Yes," Veronica Foulkes conceded. "You can understand me somewhat through my brother. But is that kind of understanding enough? You're so different from us, my dear. So earthbound. And even understanding Vance wouldn't help. He is a man. He's free to roam as he will while I . . . I need something and I'm not even sure what it is. You never feel like that, do you, Jenny? Do you ever—I don't know—yearn?"

Jenny Green shamelessly cribbed a line from *Patience*. "I

yearn my living," she said. "At least I hope I do. Hilary's so generous to me as his secretary."

"Hilary!" In anyone less gracefully voluptuous, the noise
that followed would have been a snort. "Oh, yes. Hilary understands how to take care of himself and his family. But what does
all this mean?" Her sweeping gesture included everything in the
quietly luxurious apartment, from her own rose hostess-gown
to the maid bringing in the silver tea service. "What does all
this pampering of the body mean when the soul— Just set it
here, Alice."

Jenny Green spread marmalade on toast. "I think 'all this' is
very pleasant."

"Ah, éclairs! No, Jenny, it's just that you're not sensitive. You
don't realize how Hilary— Oh well, I often wonder if other wom-
en are really as sensitive as I am. If only Vance were here!"

"May I join you in that wish?"

Veronica Foulkes shuddered gracefully. "Don't ever marry,
Jenny. Not even Vance. Marriage means the end of everything.
Marriage is the destruction of the free individual. Marriage is—"

"You mean you'd like to divorce Hilary?"

Veronica gasped. "Heavens, no. I couldn't *stand* the scandal of
a divorce. And you know the views of the Church."

"Why should they affect you, Ron? To hear Vance talk, I've
always thought the Wimpoles were one of the oldest established
families of atheists in America."

"I don't know . . . Atheism is pretty thin rations. Sometimes I
think I have a vocation. If I could leave all this behind and devote
myself to the life of a nun—the beauty, the purity, the simplicity
of it . . ." Her words issued mushily through her third éclair.

"And Hilary?"

"Well, you can see I couldn't divorce him. I wouldn't think of it. But now if he were to die . . ." she added brightly.

Jenny Green stared at her with something like shock. "I *do* wish Vance were in town," she said soberly.

5.

"No, Vance." The woman shoved away his hand. "We've got to talk this out. A romp in the hay isn't going to solve the problem."

"I don't know." The man smiled. He had an oddly narrow and pallid face, which bushy crimson hair enlivened. His eyes were a pale blue, with a watery keenness to them. "I think fine that way. Best plot idea I ever had hit me in bed with an octoroon in São Paulo."

The woman said, "Ha, ha. You're fun, Vance, while it's all still fun. Now it's gone damned serious on us. He wants five hundred dollars, or he'll turn over the whole report to my husband."

Vance Wimpole frowned. "I don't see yet how he got on our track. I've been so careful. Nobody knows I'm in Los Angeles. Even my sister thinks I'm still wandering the seven seas."

"He did get on our trail. That's the point. I don't care how. And can you get the money?"

"I can get it in . . ." he calculated mentally ". . . a week. I've got two hundred on me. I can do a novelet worth three hundred in four or five days. Send it off airmail, and Stuart always mails my checks airmail . . . A week from today you'll have the five hundred."

"By which time," said the woman bitterly, "you'll have found somebody else to spend the two hundred on that you have."

Wimpole poured himself a stiff drink. "I've never been one of the rejection slip boys. I've always made money easy, even if it never sticks around very long. But to loll back and have a sweet regular income pouring in . . ."

"If only he'll stop at this," the woman said. "If we can somehow keep him from coming back for more . . ."

"One plump and worthless brother-in-law," Wimpole mused, "stands between me and the administratorship of the wealthiest literary estate in America." He lifted his glass in a wordless toast.

6.

Sister Mary Patientia, O.M.B., laid down her stylus and contemplated an immaculately punched sheet of Braille. This portion of her day's work was ended. She bowed her head and offered a brief prayer of thanks to the Virgin because there had been no mistakes in her transcription.

Then, alone out of all the people in Los Angeles and probably in the world, she prayed for Hilary Foulkes.

For Christ said on the mount: Love your enemies, do good to those who hate you, and pray for those who persecute you.

Hilary Foulkes had earned many prayers in his life.

7.

Among the readers of this narrative there may be a few of those pitiable people who have never read the Dr. Derringer stories, of that benighted handful whom Alexander Woollcott has called "as lamentable as a child who never saw a Christmas tree."

For those few, a word or two of explanation may be necessary. You others, who know *The Purple Light* and *Beneath the Abyss* as firmly and loyally as you know *Through the Looking-Glass* or *A*

Study in Scarlet or *Treasure Island,* may be patient with the author's attempt to frame wonders in words.

Fantasy fiction is a loose term to cover a broad field. It embraces everything from *The Lost World* to *The Sword in the Stone,* from *She* to *Caleb Catlum's America.* But it has its aficionados, as intense and devoted as the audience for mysteries or westerns or hammock-romances. And the most loyal, the most fanatical of these followers of fantasy are the devotees of the fiction of science—science fiction to its fans, or more simply s-f.

Like the detective story, science fiction can be traced back to dim and ancient origins. And also like the detective story, it blossomed in the nineteenth century into the form in which we know it now. Edgar Allan Poe was very nearly as influential in one field as in the other. But the true Poe of science fiction, and the Wilkie Collins too, was Jules Verne.

Neither Poe nor Collins, however, is responsible for the living popularity of the detective story. That honor belongs to Conan Doyle, who added nothing to the form itself, contributed no feature that was not inherent in the work of the pioneers, but created a character of such superhuman proportions that he transcended the bounds of any one type of literature and became part of the consciousness of the world.

What Doyle performed with Sherlock Holmes, Fowler Foulkes achieved a decade or so later with Dr. Derringer. The scion of an old San Francisco family, Foulkes dabbled for a time in the Bohemian literary efforts so popular in that city at the turn of the century. He contributed to *The Lark* and was an intimate of Gellett Burgess and of Ambrose Bierce. He wrote pageants for the Bohemian Club and had a volume of verses published by Paul Elder.

And then he hit upon Dr. Derringer.

Foulkes' verses (which some critics prefer to those of George Stirling, finding in them an interesting anticipation of Jeffers' awareness of the meaning of the California landscape) are forgotten. His two plays, once successfully presented by Henry Miller, are as dead in the repertory as are those of Clyde Fitch. His series of historical novels, from the founding of the Mission Dolores to the earthquake of 1906, are known only to collectors of Californiana.

But there is not a corner of the world that does not know the stumpy, bull-chested, spade-bearded figure of Dr. Derringer, with his roaring voice, his silver-headed cane, and his devastating mind. Leland Stanford University still receives letters begging scientific advice and addressed to

Garth Derringer, Ph.D.
Department of Physics

and whimsical scholars delight in visiting the Foulkes Memorial Library of that University to confound each other with variorum readings from the earlier texts.

The story is told of a seismographic expedition which attained after arduous months the supposedly unattainable upper reaches of the Kulopangu. The chief of the Ngutlumbi was entranced by the elaborate apparatus set up to record earthquake shocks. He inspected it from all angles and at last inquired, confident of the answer, "Dokka Derinja, him make?"

This particular tale may display a touch of fanciful exaggeration, but it nonetheless typifies the esteem which the world has wisely accorded to the masterly creation of Fowler Foulkes.

Of Foulkes' other creation, his son Hilary, you have already heard somewhat and are to hear much more. Indeed, you will be in at the death.

THE SECOND DAY:
Friday, October 31, 1941

"AND WHAT," Lieutenant Marshall asked Concha Duncan as they drove west through the fall sunshine, "what is Matt's particular grudge against Hilary?"

The girl frowned. "I don't blame him really. Only it isn't funny to talk about murder."

"Murder's like suicide. Or writing. The more you talk about it, the less apt you are to do it. Release mechanism. But what's the motive?"

"It was a nasty trick . . . I don't suppose you know who Don Stuart is? Anyway he was an important science fiction writer and now he's editor of *Surprising Stories* (that's science) and *The Worlds Beyond* (that's pure fantasy). He's bought some of Matt's stuff and seems to think he's a comer. So Stuart got the bright idea wouldn't it be fun to have some contemporary Dr. Derringer stories."

Marshall nodded. "That's an idea. Foulkes died over ten years ago, didn't he? And he was even then a little behind the times. There are whole fields of modern science the magnificent doctor never touched. Think what he could do with atom-smashing or Dunne's time theories. Let's see—how old is Dr. Derringer now?"

"You mean how long ago were the stories?"

"I mean how old is that great man. The first stories were around the turn of the century and he was then about forty . . . That'd make him eightyish now. He could still be going strong."

"You talk as though he were a real man."

"Isn't he? I mean, doesn't one feel that he is? But go on with your story."

"That's what Stuart said. About how people think he's real. So he wrote to Austin Carter and outlined this idea and said if he didn't want it he should farm it out to somebody else in the M.L.S., and so—"

"Whoa! Just to keep things straight, who's Austin Carter?"

"He's the biggest name in all Stuart's stable of writers. In fact, he's I think three of the biggest names. He's nice, too; he got Matt started in the field."

"And the M.L.S.?"

"That's the Mañana Literary Society. Austin Carter started calling it that because people always talk about the terrific honey of a story they're going to write tomorrow. Like you said about . . . murder. Only lots of them do really write them. The M.L.S. is all the people around here who work at fantasy and science fiction, and Carter is sort of a contact between them here and Stuart in New York."

"I follow. Though I've got a feeling I'm on the edges of a strange new world. Go on."

"So Carter farmed out this Derringer idea to Matt. Of course Matt was all excited because he says the three greatest men ever written are Dr. Derringer, Sherlock Holmes, and the Scarecrow of

Oz. So he worked out synopses for six stories and Stuart okayed them, and he wrote to the Foulkes estate and they gave permission for a nominal fee to be arranged upon completion, and he worked like anything and turned out the set.

"Only then Hilary announced the fee. It was fifty dollars a story, and you couldn't do any 'arranging' about it. Matt was getting a bonus rate of a cent and a quarter from Stuart on these, so that made it about sixty-two fifty a story for him. And by the time he gets through paying Hilary, that'll leave him a total profit of seventy-five dollars for six stories. And he's not through paying yet because we spent the money from Stuart most of it, and he says he's damned if he'll touch any of my money to pay his business debts."

Marshall grunted. "I don't much blame him myself. I mean for the murderous gleam. Hilary sounds sweet."

"And I haven't told you the worst. The very day that Matt got Hilary's letter and hit the ceiling, we read in a gossip column where Mrs. Hilary Foulkes had just bought a fifty-dollar fur jacket for her dog. Honest, Lieutenant, if I ever see that dog . . . Matt says he wouldn't mind so much if his honest sweat had bought Mrs. Foulkes a dress or champagne or anything humanly reasonable; but a fur jacket for a dog . . ."

"And I bet it's a Peke at that."

"It probably—Oh, you turn to the right here."

The convent of the Sisters of Martha of Bethany had originally been laid out as a rich and formal estate in the Westwood hills. At the depth of the depression, it was munificently bestowed upon the nuns by a wealthy and generous layman who could no longer afford the taxes and assessments.

To the nuns it was a beautiful white elephant, a never-ending source of worry and delight. The sun, the view of the ocean from the hilltop, and the unspoken but patent envy of the Mothers Superior of other orders made partial atonement for the mile-and-a-half walk to the bus line and the constant cares of upkeep. And the ornate swimming pool furnished a splendid treat for the Mexican children who came weekly in school busses from the north end of town.

The sister portress lowered suspiciously at Lieutenant Marshall (she enjoyed her own slightly heretical views concerning the importance of men, tending to visualize Heaven as a noble matriarchy where the Virgin generously conceded a certain position to her Son), but smiled at Concha, whose aunt was one of the most loyal supporters of the convent.

"You can wait in the patio," she told them. "Though there's another lady there already waiting for Sister Ursula."

Even on overcast days, this patio seemed greenly bright with that peculiar submarine greenness of growing things. Today, in vivid autumn sunlight, it was verdantly aglow.

"I like this place," Marshall confessed, "even if I don't feel I fit. I used to have strange ideas of a convent. Maria Monk stuff. Dank and dismal and silent, save for an occasional wail from a newly bricked wall. But all this is so fresh and clean. It's . . . it's like a hospital without pain."

"It is a hospital," said Concha. "And it cures the other kind of pain."

Marshall paused in filling his pipe. "What a solemn thought from you, Concha! And why do Catholics always like to talk in paradoxes?"

She blushed a little. "I didn't think that up myself. I heard Sister Ursula say it once. But you won't tell me what we're here for? What are you going to ask her?"

The Lieutenant lit his pipe reflectively. "Nothing spectacular.

Unfortunately. I just need some technical information." He took the seven-decade rosary from his pocket. "Ever see anything like this?"

Concha frowned. "That's a funny one. No. I thought Aunt Ellen had every kind of rosary and scapular and medal that ever existed, but I never saw one before with seven decades. Does that—is it a clew?"

"Maybe. I don't know yet. That's why I'm here."

"Sir!" a woman's voice demanded imperatively.

Marshall turned. The woman was not what one might expect to find in a convent. Her body was ripe with a fullness which comes from neither of those two ideals of the Church, virginity or motherhood. And her smart fall outfit must have cost—well, he knew nothing precisely about such things; but if he saw it on Leona, he'd certainly worry about their bank account.

"Must you, sir?" she said.

Marshall looked blank. "I beg your pardon. Must I what?"

"Must you smoke a pipe here in this holy spot?"

He grinned relief. "Sorry if it offends you, madam. But the nuns rather like it. Sister Ursula says the monks call pipe smoke 'the gardener's incense.'"

The woman raised well-plucked eyebrows. "But such levity! Even if I smoked myself, I should no more think of smoking here than—"

"Did I keep you waiting?" The robes of an order make most women seem to move either with undue bustle or with equally undue majesty. On Sister Ursula, however, they always seemed the only possible garments for her at once quiet and vigorous movements. Her voice, too, had neither hushed piety nor disciplinary sternness; it was simply a good and pleasing voice.

"I was helping Sister Patientia shellac Braille pages. You'll forgive me?" She smiled at Marshall, kissed Concha lightly, and glanced curiously at the strange woman.

"This lady was here ahead of us," Marshall said.

"Dear me, Lieutenant! You make me sound like a butcher shop."

"I do not wish to intrude." The woman dripped offended hauteur. "I shall wait in the chapel. Where the only incense," she added emphatically, "is that offered to the honor and glory of God." She swept away. Her walk was at once devout and dignified; but still you noticed the curving sway of her full hips.

"My!" Concha gasped. "Who is she?"

"I don't know, my dear. I don't even know her name. She simply came and told the portress that she was suffering and that she wanted to talk with a Bride of Christ. I think Reverend Mother was a little startled by such devout language, but she asked me to talk with her. After all, if she's in any sort of trouble and we can help her . . ."

"And," Concha added with kindly malice, "you are having trouble with funds for that baby clinic out by the Lockheed plant."

Sister Ursula smiled. When she smiled, she looked not much older than Concha. When she was serious, she was completely ageless. Lieutenant Marshall, and even his shrewdly feminine wife, had never dared venture a guess as to her actual age. "I am sure," she said reprovingly, "that no such unworthy thought ever crossed Reverend Mother's mind. At least, not consciously."

Marshall relit his briar. "She thought I was being sacrilegious to smoke here."

"Oh dear. I foresee troubles with her. It's hard enough as a rule to try to make people holy at all. But when they set themselves up to be far more holy than God or His Church ever intended them to be, then it's a really dreadful problem to bring them down to humanity again." She led the way to a sunny stone bench. "Is this your day off, Lieutenant, or are you calling on duty?"

"On duty, I'm afraid."

"You mean you want me to—" Sister Ursula had leaned forward, an almost imperceptible sparkle in her eyes. But abruptly she broke off and sat back. "Oh dear, there I go again," she sighed, "We Brides of Christ, as the lady rightly calls us (though I must say I find the expression far more comfortable in a devotional poem than in ordinary conversation), do have our faults. And you know mine and you keep pandering to it. But first tell me: how is Ursula?"

"She smiles now, and you know she's human. And she weighs two ounces more than Terry did at her age. Come and see her."

"I will try." She smiled as Marshall reached into his pocket. "Snapshots already?"

"No."

The smile changed to a perplexed frown as she saw what he brought out. "Lieutenant! I thought you were the staunchest of agnostics."

"I'm afraid I'm not carrying this rosary for devotional purposes. I just want to know what you can tell me about it."

Sister Ursula puzzled over the skillfully and elaborately carved beads. "Where did you get this?" she asked at last.

"What is it?" Marshall countered.

"It is a rosary," she said slowly. "But it is not the Rosary. That is, it is not the conventional set of beads with which one meditates on the mysteries of the redemption in devotion to our Blessed Mother."

"So? I thought a rosary was a rosary."

"Oh dear, no. The popular devotion revealed to the monk Dominic is certainly the most widespread of rosaries, but there are others. I know, for instance, of a rosary of the Infant of Prague; and I believe that there are indeed Tibetan and other non-Christian rosaries. The number and arrangement of the beads varies naturally with the prayers intended to be recited, and this has seven sets. The crucifix, of course, eliminates anything like a lamaic rosary. But what might seven symbolize. The seven sacraments . . . The seven dolors . . ."

"Or it might be a multiple of seven," Concha suggested. "The regular rosary has five decades, and you say it three times round for the fifteen mysteries."

"A multiple . . . Yes, thank you, Mary. I remember now."

"You know what this is."

"Yes. It is a rosary of the Stations of the Cross. There are fourteen of those, and you say this twice, meditating on a station with each decade."

"I never heard of that," said Concha.

"I am not surprised. A priest in San Francisco started the devotion some forty years ago, so that the many Californians who then lived near no church might still make the stations. But Father Harris was killed in the earthquake, and the devotion died out. I believe that it was never formally approved by the Holy See. Not, of course, that that means it's to be condemned. Any individual is free to say the proper prayers in the devotional form that most appeals to him."

Marshall looked disappointed. "You mean, then, that this is perfectly all right? It's orthodoxly Catholic?"

"Not precisely orthodox, perhaps, but certainly not heretical."

"Hang it. If it had belonged to some strange minor offshoot of a sect, it could have been a great help to me in narrowing things down."

"I should think you could narrow things down a good deal

even from this. This devotion flourished for only a few years and almost entirely in one city. The wood is unusual, and the carving is exceptionally fine; this rosary was probably made to order and cost a good deal. It doubtless belonged to one of Father Harris' wealthy patronesses."

Marshall nodded. "That sounds logical. And if the rosary's worth something on its own as an object of art, that might account for . . ."

"May I make a suggestion? Leave it with me, and I'll show it to Sister Perpetua, who knows more about religious art than I should ever have thought possible. I wouldn't be surprised if she could even tell you the name of the carver and in fact the period of his work to which it belongs."

"Thanks. We'll try that." He handed over the rosary.

"And Lieutenant . . . You wouldn't care to tell me anything about the . . . the circumstances?" There was that sparkle in her eyes again.

"Certainly. But there's nothing interesting about them. Not worthy of you, Sister. Just a matter of trying to trace a floater who got himself killed. This rosary's about the only lead we've got to check his identity.

"Go on . . . No! Oh, Lieutenant, I'm ashamed of myself, I've been good for a year now, haven't I? We've been good friends and I love your children and I've never once tried to interfere and solve your cases for you. I even shut my ears that night you tried to tell me about the Magrudei poisoning affair, and look how beautifully you solved it yourself."

"In three weeks," said Marshall, "and I'll swear you wouldn't have taken five minutes to spot the point of that unused match folder."

"Please. Don't try to flatter me. It's your business to solve crimes, and it's not mine. I want to be good. But I've been good so long that I—I've begun to itch."

"Madam, after the job you did a year ago, you're more than welcome to solve my cases any time you want to. If you itch so, why shouldn't you scratch it?"

"It's hard to explain . . . But look at it this way. You've met Sister Felicitas. She has a vice; it's loving sleep too much. You'd be—well, you might almost say an occasion of sin if you proffered her a nice feather bed. Or Sister—no, I shan't name names; but I can think of two or three that only the Devil himself should leave a box of chocolates beside.

"You see, the rules of the order, to say nothing of our own religious devotion, don't leave much scope in our lives for what the world thinks major and serious vices. So we come to realize the importance of the rest of the Seven Deadly Sins. Everyone admits the evil of Lust and most people include Avarice, at least on principle; but there are dangers to the soul in Gluttony too, and in Sloth. And in Pride.

"Before, when you were kind enough to say that I helped you— No, that's false modesty, which is the worst emblem of Pride. When I helped you, I took great pride in how clever I was being. I felt power. I even," she lowered her eyes, "I even exercised power over a man's life. And I won't do it again. I'll do all I can to find out what you need about this rosary, but I don't want to know any more. Or rather I want to, but I want not to want to."

"All right. But I've got a confession to make too. For the past year I've been hoping somehow to tempt you back where I think you belong. I needed the dope on this rosary, yes; but I welcomed that need because it gave me a chance to present you with a criminal case needing your specialized knowledge. It isn't much of a case, but if you'd hear me out and tell me—"

"No," said Sister Ursula firmly. For a moment they sat, the policeman and the nun, looking at each other as earnestly as unhappy lovers.

Then Marshall grinned. "All right. But if the Devil ever rides you unbearably hard, I'll always stand ready to take his side. The force lost a wonderful policewoman when you decided to take the veil."

"Thank you. And now I must try to console Sister Patientia— or no, there's that strange woman waiting in the chapel."

"What's the matter with Sister Patientia?" Concha demanded. To her the nuns, who had known her from childhood, were like so many aunts.

"I'm afraid she's rather vexed, and understandably so."

"What happened?"

"She was engaged in a Braille transcription of one of the Dr. Derringer novels, and wrote to the Foulkes estate to clear copyright. You know that such consent is always given free automatically; you simply have to secure permission as a matter of form. Well, the heir replied that he would be delighted to have the blind read his father's work, and that the standard commercial reprint fees would apply."

Lieutenant Marshall whistled. "That Hilary! I'm going to be investigating his murder yet."

2.

The chapel—the chaste new white-and-gold Rufus Harrigan Memorial Chapel, gift of Concha's Aunt Ellen—was empty save for the smartly dressed woman who knelt at the communion rail. As she heard the nun's footsteps she rose and crossed herself, slowly, as one for whom the gesture still has to be thought out step by step.

Sister Ursula genuflected before the altar. "You wished to talk with me?" She asked quietly.

"If you will be so kind to one who has suffered."

"We can go out in the patio. The irreverent man with the pipe has gone now."

"Thank you, Sister."

"What was it you wanted?" Sister Ursula asked as they walked along the corridor.

"I want to know all about what it is like to be a Bride of Christ."

The nun's hand toyed unthinkingly with the strange rosary. "That isn't an easy question to answer, you know. Sister Immaculata is working on a biography of Blessed Mother La Roche, the founder of our order. She says that any one who would attempt to put the true meaning of a nun's life into words must be either Saint Theresa or a simpleton."

"Saint Theresa!" the woman sighed. "That dear sweet little thing!"

Sister Ursula smiled. "I mean the other Theresa, of Avila, who—"

But the woman interrupted her. "I beg your pardon, Sister, but that rosary—"

"Yes?"

"Where did you get it?" For a moment her devotional manner had vanished, and she seemed alertly interested. "Where did it come from?"

"I don't know," Sister Ursula answered truthfully. "Why? Do you know anything about it?"

"Know anything? Why, I'm sure it's my—" The woman

paused. She raised her clasped hands to her full breasts and let her head sink pensively. "But we must not think of such things now, must we? No, Sister, it makes no difference. Tell me what you can of your life."

Sister Ursula bit her lip. That rosary came from a murdered man. If this woman knew anything about it . . . Though what connection there could be between such an expensive article as this and what the Lieutenant had called a "floater" . . . Still if she could try to find out . . .

The angel of Satan had rarely buffeted her so strongly. But she said only, "I think the best way I can explain is to show you a little of our work. We are called, as you know, the Sisters of Martha of Bethany, because Mother La Roche believed . . ."

3.

In the early days of Olsen and Johnson, long before Hell zapopped, they had a skit which took place in a hotel room. Among the manifold and wondrous inconveniences of this room was a drunk who wandered in from time to time trying to find the bathroom.

On his fifth entrance he looked at the two unhappy comedians and moaned desolately, "Are you in *all* the rooms?"

So Lieutenant Marshall felt now. He had dropped Concha off at the Duncans' apartment, refusing to interrupt Matt's work even for the laudable project of splitting a beer, and driven on to the very different and opulent apartment hotel whose phone number he had found on the Tarbell corpse.

On the way to the convent he had heard about Hilary Foulkes from Concha. At the convent he had heard more about Hilary

Foulkes from Sister Ursula. And here the first name that caught his eye on the mailboxes was

HILARY ST. J. FOULKES

". . . in all the rooms . . ." Lieutenant Marshall muttered.

A uniformed maid answered the door. To Marshall's, "I want to speak to Mr. Foulkes," she replied, "I will take in your card, sir."

"I'm afraid I haven't one on me. Just tell him it's the police." He was about to add some reassuring phrase to ward off the usual civilian terror of police authority, but the girl's face instantly brightened.

"Oh yes, Inspector, I'll tell him. He'll be delighted."

Marshall did not scratch his head. He was not given to the gesture, and in fact had never known anyone who was; but he understood the emotion which novelists mean when they write, "He scratched his head." He had never before encountered any individual who welcomed the police so eagerly; and he certainly should have expected Hilary St. John Foulkes, from all he had heard so far, to be the last to do so.

He seated himself gingerly on an exquisite and spindly chair. This living-room was a woman's room. There was no solid comfortable chair for leg-stretching and pipesmoking. The entire room was daintily and painfully neat. No trace of ashes or glasses or magazines or other normal signs of human enjoyment. The only reading matter was a small bookcase filled with admirably tooled leatherbound volumes. Marshall felt sure, even before he examined them, that they were the complete works of Fowler Foulkes.

He lit his pipe, looked about for an ashtray, and ended hopelessly by tucking the match into the cuff of his trousers. He was here, he admitted to himself frankly, because he was curious to see what the hell this Hilary was like. There was not a chance in a hundred—or to be more precise, there was just one chance in twenty-four—that Hilary had anything to do with the Tarbell corpse on Main Street. But, he assuaged his conscience, you had to start someplace in this apartment hotel.

"Inspector! But this is splendid!"

The voice surprised Marshall. He hardly knew why, but he had expected an effeminate piping. This voice, deeper and clearer and more rounded even than his own had been at the height of his debating career, hardly fitted his first rough concept of Hilary.

The man fitted better visually than aurally. He was a little under average height and a little over average weight. Not that he was fat; just that one might have preferred cheeks a trifle less plump and a neck that did not roll over the collar. He wore a beautiful red-and-gold dressing gown, which Marshall instantly coveted, over too tightly cut pin-stripe trousers and a shirt of delicate pink with stiff white collar, all of which Marshall wouldn't have worn to a masquerade.

There was a penguinish waddle to his walk, and the officer half expected a flipper instead of the soft hand that eagerly took his.

"The name," he said, "is Marshall. And the rank is just Lieutenant."

"Delighted, Lieutenant, delighted. Do sit down. Shall I ring for tea?"

"No thanks. I won't take up much of your time. I merely want to ask a couple of questions."

Hilary Foulkes sat leaning forward politely, his hand pinching the lobe of his right ear. Marshall faintly remembered a widespread publicity still of his father in the same pose. "Naturally, naturally. But I am amazed, Lieutenant, at such prompt service."

"Service?"

A tone of hurt doubt was apparent in Hilary's voice. "You *are* from Homicide, aren't you?"

"Yes, but—"

Hilary settled back relieved. "Go ahead. Go ahead. It was only that it seemed so rapid. It can't be an hour since I phoned."

"You phoned to Homicide?"

"Of course. Wouldn't you if someone were trying to murder you?"

Marshall preserved impassivity behind his pipe. "Of course, Mr. Foulkes. I only wish that more citizens had your civic conscience." If a notable visitor was going to think wonders of the department for its rapid service, why disillusion him? Actually, Marshall reflected, the call had probably been routed through to poor old Halloran, who had a way with cranks, and who might get around here some time in the next week or two.

"Now I don't know quite how to commence, Lieutenant. Perhaps if you were to ask me the usual formula questions—or do you have a formula for a man who's being murdered?"

"We're more used to dealing with him after the fact, I'm afraid; but it's a pleasure to get in ahead of time for once. First of all, Mr. Foulkes, who is trying to murder you?"

"Heavens! Heavens, Lieutenant, if I knew that, do you think I'd have sent for you? This is all a mystery to me so far. And naturally I'm curious."

"Then what was the nature of the attempt?"

"The attempts, Lieutenant. The attempts. There have been several. Let me see . . . The first was the car—or was it the brick? But both of those are so uncertain."

"Let me hear them anyway."

"Well now, the car. The car. That would be a week ago, more or less. I was taking Pitti Sing for her walk. We were crossing Wilshire Boulevard when a car made a left turn through a stop sign, going I should guess a good forty miles an hour, and bore down on us. We escaped only by the skin of our teeth. Skins of our teeth? No matter."

"That could have been an accident. Our Los Angeles drivers, I'm afraid, are notorious."

"I know. Once could be an accident, I know. So could the brick that fell so near me the next night, from an unfinished building where no workmen were in sight."

"You take these walks regularly?"

"Regularly? Frequently, at least. Yes, frequently. Usually about seven in the evening I take Pitti Sing for a walk."

"Pitti Sing is your dog?"

"My wife's, Lieutenant. A Pekinese."

Marshall managed not to smile, remembering the fur jacket and his now verified guess. "Notice anything about the car?"

"It was a convertible—I believe a Mercury, though I would not swear to the fact. I didn't notice the license, nor even who was driving. It all happened so suddenly . . ."

"Of course. Any further details on the brick episode?"

"Nothing."

Marshall puffed at his pipe. "I don't know that you need worry yourself, Mr. Foulkes. I realize that two such episodes on successive evenings are enough to perturb one, but don't you think—?"

"Oh, but I haven't told you about the chocolates. The chocolates. I had a birthday last week, and among various other gifts I received a box of chocolates by mail. There was no card, but I thought nothing of that. Stores do make mistakes in wrapping, you know. But when I took the first piece—how I thank Heaven that my wife was not with me then! If she had tasted first . . . But fortunately as I lifted this chocolate cherry, I noticed a tiny mark like a pinprick in the bottom. I had only recently read a novel concerning poisoned chocolates, and I must confess I trembled.

"Call me foolishly apprehensive if you will, Lieutenant. But the combination of the car, the brick, the missing card, and the novel frightened me. I took the chocolates to a chemist for analysis. Each of them contained quite enough cyanide to kill a half dozen people—providing, of course, that a half dozen people could eat one chocolate."

Marshall grunted. He had expected nothing but the recital of a pampered neurotic with a persecution complex, and the car and the brick fitted that pattern beautifully. The chocolates were different. He took the copy of the analyst's report which Hilary handed him. He knew the firm. Irreproachable standing. Damn it, he'd really happened on to something.

"I'll confess," he said, "that this puts a different complexion on things. Do you have the wrappings of that candy box?"

"No," Hilary admitted ruefully. "The maid had burned all the birthday wrappings before I made my discovery."

"You have the box itself?"

"It is still at the analyst's with the chocolates. I shall give you a note to him."

"Did you happen to notice where it was from?"

"Here in Los Angeles. It was one of the standard two-pound boxes of the Doris Dainty Shoppes, though I have of course no idea from which branch."

Marshall sighed. Try tracing the purchase of a box of standard mixture from any one of thirty-odd branches! "So," he said. "All right. Maybe we better approach this from the other end. Who would have any interest, Mr. Foulkes, in killing you?"

"Me? In killing me?" Hilary Foulkes spread his plump hands in the blandest of innocence. "That's what worries me. Who on earth could possibly want to kill me?"

Before Marshall could quite choke at this charming effrontery, a girl came into the room. She was slim and long-legged and carried herself with an easy and unobtrusive grace. "Cousin Hilary—" she began. "Oh, I'm sorry. I didn't realize you had—"

Marshall rose, but Hilary did not. He waved one hand languidly and said, "Yes, my dear?"

"I don't like to interrupt, but Alice wants to know if Veronica is going to be home to dinner. I don't even know where she's gone."

"Neither do I, my dear. Neither do I. But she will doubtless be home. You may tell Alice so." His eyes lit on the still uncomfortably standing police officer. "Oh, Jenny, this is Lieutenant Marshall. My cousin, Miss Green."

The girl's voice was light and friendly, with a trace of an English accent. "How do you do, Lieutenant. I hope Cousin Hilary is showing you proper hospitality. We can't do too much for those who may so soon have to defend us."

Marshall smiled. "Not that kind of Lieutenant, I'm afraid. Just police."

"Oh!" Her eyes widened. "Hilary, what on earth have you been up to?"

Hilary wriggled. "Nothing of importance, my dear. Nothing of importance. The Lieutenant was merely . . . was merely . . ."

Marshall took up the sentence. "I merely wanted to know if your cousin had ever heard of a man named Tarbell. Part of a routine check-up."

Hilary and the girl looked equally blank.

"Jonathan Tarbell," Marshall added. "Or," he went on, "whether a rosary with seven decades meant anything to him."

"That's sets of beads?" the girl asked. "Seven sets? Wasn't that—" There was no perceptible movement from Hilary, or at most a slight flicker of his eyes, but the girl broke off. "No," she said. "I'm thinking of something else."

Hilary smiled blandly and said, "And I fear the Lieutenant is not finding me very helpful. Mr. Tarbrush and the rosary are equally unfamiliar to me."

"I won't ask counter-questions," Jenny Green smiled. "I'll just leave you to plague Hilary. Oh." She paused. "Are you the Lieutenant Marshall who solved the Harrigan case last year?"

Marshall nodded.

"My! We were in New York then, but even there the papers were full of it. That was wonderful and don't try to say anything because I know I'm only embarrassing you. Sorry, and goodbye."

Hilary glanced after the girl as Marshall reseated himself. "You understand I didn't wish to mention these murder attempts in front of her. It would only worry her."

"Of course."

"And I'd like to congratulate you, Lieutenant, on the rapidity with which you picked up my hint. Most ingenious, those questions about the rosary and Mr. Tarpon. Most ingenious."

Marshall let it go at that. Those leads could be followed up later to better advantage. "But to return to our motives—" he began.

"And I am most fortunate," Hilary went on, "to have drawn the man who solved the Harrigan case. Most fortunate. That was a curious business, wasn't it? Locked room affair, as I remember."

"Yes," said Marshall tersely. "But to get back to our own case: It's nonsense, Mr. Foulkes, to say that there's no one who might want to murder you. There's never been a living human being of whom that was true. Surely you can make some nominations?"

Hilary puzzled. "Frankly, Lieutenant, no. Frankly. I lead a quiet, peaceful, and unobtrusive life. I have no close friends, and therefore no close enemies. My wife is faithful to me, and I to her."

"And you are a wealthy man."

"True. But need the fact necessarily mean that anyone wishes to kill me?"

"I'm afraid so. Sex and money are the two all-dominant motives for murder, and of the two I'll lay odds on money every time. So let me ask: Who is your heir?"

"My wife, of course. We have no children. Miss Green, whom you just met, will receive a comfortable income for life from a trust fund. Otherwise my wife inherits the whole of the estate."

"That includes your father's estate?"

"Naturally."

"And who will act as literary executor of the Foulkes properties?"

"My wife's brother, D. Vance Wimpole. He seemed a logical choice for the post since his father was something of a self-appointed Boswell to mine. Moreover he is himself a writer, though for the pulps," Hilary uttered the horrid word with ineffable disdain, "and is so very much part of the family. Not only is he my brother-in-law; he is soon to marry my cousin."

"Then by your death this Mr. Wimpole would secure a wife with a comfortable life income and the control over an exceedingly valuable literary estate?"

Hilary looked uncomfortable. "Nonsense, my dear Lieutenant. Utter nonsense. Vance is an eccentric, a madman if you will, but a murderer— Heavens! Besides, he is at present in Kamchatka or Kalamazoo or some such outlandish place. The chocolates were mailed in Los Angeles."

Marshall looked about hopelessly for someplace to knock out his pipe. "Mr. Foulkes, if you insist that you're being attacked, as this analyst's report certainly confirms, you must admit that someone has a reason for doing so. Obviously your wife, your cousin, and your brother-in-law stand to gain markedly by your death. What about others? Have you . . . Have you ever made any business enemies? Say through your administration of the Foulkes estate?"

Hilary resumed the lobe-pulling pose. "You seem a sympathetic man, Lieutenant. So many people will not understand the difficulties of my position."

"Yes?"

"If my father had invented Mr. Emerson's mousetrap, no one would question my right to collect fees from those who followed the beaten path to his door. If my father had built up some great and world-embracing business enterprise, no one but a Communist would begrudge me the income from it. But because my father enriched the world with a great character and a number of immortal narratives, some men sneer at me and assert that I have no right to this income.

"As you are well aware, I have every legal right. Our copyright laws protect an author's offspring quite as thoroughly as they do the author himself. And I have moral right too. In fact a moral duty. A moral duty to see that my father's work is respected, that it does not enter the public domain where any insignificant dolt may do as he will with it, that the works of Fowler Foulkes are as carefully guarded now as he would have guarded them were he still alive."

"In short," Marshall summarized, "you do think you might have made some enemies in administering the estate."

"It is possible. Possible, although it seems ludicrous that such petty enmities might lead to murder. But if you pin me down, Lieutenant, I can think of no one who might wish to kill me, Hilary Foulkes, an individual. These attacks must be directed against the son of Fowler Foulkes, against the administrator of the Foulkes estate."

"One point though. Your birthday. Timing it for that day made sure you'd open a box you might otherwise have regarded with suspicion. Wouldn't that point at some intimate?"

"My birthday is mentioned in my father's autobiography. In Wimpole's memoir too, I imagine."

"So." Marshall frowned and drew out his notebook. "All right. Now, Mr. Foulkes, if you could give me the names of any individuals who—"

The maid came in just then with a bulky package. "Excuse me, sir. This came by special messenger and it's marked RUSH. I thought perhaps—"

Hilary waved it away. "Set it down there. Well, Lieutenant, it's naturally impossible for me to remember the names of all those whose unreasonable requests I have at one time or another seen fit to reject. Possibly—"

"That package," Marshall interrupted. "Something you ordered?"

"No. I've no notion what it is. No notion. But that can wait. The most recent of these—"

Marshall leaned over the package and held up his hand for silence. The peremptory authority of the gesture hushed Hilary instantly.

In the silent room the ticking was clearly audible.

4.

"Where's your phone?" Marshall snapped.

"It ticks," Hilary observed. "How curious! It ticks . . ."

"Where's the phone?"

"It . . . Oh my heavens! Lieutenant! It's a bomb!"

"There is," Marshall admitted dryly, "that possibility. Now where's a phone?"

For the first time Hilary moved with rapidity. He leaped at the package, and Marshall had to counter swiftly to ward him off.

"But Lieutenant! We've got to go put it in the bathtub! We've got to—" His voice had gone up an octave.

Marshall held him by the arm and spoke firmly. "You called the police. All right. The police are here and in charge, and you're doing what I say. Leave that box alone and show me a phone."

"Leave it alone and show you the phone." Hilary giggled. "You rime, Lieutenant. You rime."

"The phone!" Marshall snapped.

"Right here." Still on the verge of hysterical giggles, Hilary removed the decorative flounces that had hid the instrument.

"Playing with possible bombs isn't healthy," Marshall explained as he dialed, automatically noting that Hilary's phone had a different number from the number of the building found on Tarbell. "And popping them in water is a popular fallacy. The only safe medium is lubricating oil, and I doubt if you've got a tubful of that handy.—Hello. Marshall speaking, Homicide. Give me the Emergency Squad.—No, Mr. Foulkes, we'll leave it to the experts. You can clear out if you want to and—Hello. Lieutenant Marshall speaking. I want to report a possible bomb. I—"

His attention had been distracted from his host, and Hilary Foulkes seized the opportunity to make a dash for the package.

What his intentions might have been was never to be learned. Marshall's long leg shot out across his path, and Hilary came down with a crash and lay still.

"No," Marshall went calmly on into the phone. "That wasn't the bomb. Just interference."

He gave the address, received the usual warning to do nothing until the squad got there, and hung up. He bent over Hilary, worried for a moment, but found nothing seriously wrong. Bump on the back of the head from hitting one of the spindly chairs. No damage, and Hilary would probably be less trouble if simply left on ice for a bit.

Marshall frowned, then nodded. Through two corridors he found his way into the kitchen. The maid, who apparently doubled in aluminum, was peeling potatoes. "Hello," he said. "Mr. Foulkes is expecting some visitors on very secret business. They don't want to take any chances in being seen. Would you please go for a walk?" He handed her a dollar bill. "Have a soda or see a newsreel or something."

"But I've got to get dinner and if it isn't ready on time Mrs. Foulkes'll—" she paused. "You're the police, aren't you?"

"Yes."

"I'll go."

"Please tell Miss Green too. Is there any one else in the apartment?"

"Only Pitti Sing, and she's asleep."

"She can stay," said Marshall grimly. "And who's in the apartment under us?"

"It's vacant, sir."

"Good."

The Foulkes apartment was large and multiple. The turning and the door that Marshall was sure would bring him back to the living-room led him instead into a chastely furnished bed-room.

"I'm blind as a bat without my glasses," he announced loudly. "Is that you, Mr. Foulkes?"

Jenny Green laughed, a laugh that was half embarrassment and half youthful pleasure: "You're a gentleman, Lieutenant." Her fresh pink and white skin disappeared into a faded wrapper.

"At times I regret it," Marshall confessed. "But look: Your cousin has secret affairs coming up and wants you should clear out for a half hour."

"Are you joking?"

"No. He seems to mean it."

"Oh. And when Hilary means something . . . I know. Thanks."

The second try worked and he reached the living-room. Hilary was still unconscious. And the package still ticked.

Marshall lifted a corner of the rug, shook out his pipe, and dropped the rug back over the ashes. He lit up a fresh pipe-ful and stared at the box. The temptation to investigate it was strong, but he remembered the cheering stories taught in the police training school of what happened to smart coppers who decided they were as good as the Emergency Squad. He copied down in his notebook the name of the messenger service and the cryptic numerals which presumably could help trade the order.

The box went on ticking.

He heard the maid leave, and a little later Miss Green. The apartment below was vacant. The ceiling was high. If the bomb did go off in the next ten minutes, it could injure no one—except, of course, Hilary Foulkes and the Lieutenant. He could probably arouse Hilary and carry him downstairs. But at the same time he should stay here and stand guard over the bomb. Mrs. Foulkes would probably be home soon. If she should come in and decide to investigate the package . . .

He puffed and tried to sort out what he knew so far. A car, a brick, poisoned chocolates, and a bomb. Somebody was decidedly in earnest, and at the same time curiously inefficient about it. And somewhere there tied into this a rosary and a phone number and a Main Street corpse. They had to fit in; there had been a marked reaction on that rosary question.

The box went on ticking.

The discrepancy of the phone numbers was easy to explain. This was probably an unlisted phone. Anyone trying to get in touch with Hilary would be unable to get it from the company and forced to content himself with the apartment house phone. But why should Jonathan Tarbell . . .

The ticking was louder now.

Louder than a jukebox at midnight, louder than a radio serial, louder than an air raid siren, louder than the world. It was the world, that ticking.

Marshall thought of the Tell-Tale Heart. But that was proof of Death Past. This ticking was proof of Death to Come, of . . .

He swore at himself, looked around the room, found a radio, and switched it on full blast. He never noticed what the sound was once it came over. He knew only that it drowned out the ticking.

It also drowned out the entrance of Veronica Foulkes. The first that Marshall knew of her presence was a loud scream, loud enough to top ticking and radio and all.

". . . to keep the loveliness of your hands soft and white in the hardest water . . ." a dripping voice was booming.

Marshall switched off the radio.

"You!" Veronica cried. "You're the man with the pipe in the garden!"

The Lieutenant bowed. "How nice to meet again. Now, madam, if you would kindly—"

"Hilary! What have you done to Hilary! He won't speak to me! He . . . he just lies there . . ."

"Your husband, Mrs. Foulkes, has had a slight accident. Everything will be all right. I represent the police and am in charge. Now if you will just—"

"I don't believe it. You're not a policeman!" Her bosom heaved, and she was just the guy to do it. "You've attacked Hilary, and I—"

"Please!" Marshall protested. "I'm trying to warn you. Will you kindly leave this apartment?"

"Warn me? So you admit you're a criminal! I knew it. Policemen don't smoke pipes in convents. Get out of here! And at once, or I'll call the real police!"

"But Mrs. Foulkes, I'm trying to tell you, since I must. There's a bomb—"

"Bomb! Oh! You're trying to kill us all. You—"

With that, she flung herself upon him. The phrase "tooth and nail" suddenly assumed a fresh and vivid meaning for Lieutenant Marshall. He felt blood coursing from the gouge in his cheek as he vainly tried to pinion her wrists to her sides. The long spike heels of her shoes dug viciously into his shanks, and she poured out words that seemed scarcely apposite in so punctilious a critic of conventual etiquette.

At last he secured a firm and clenching grip on her wrists and managed to wrap his long leg around her threshing ankles. "Now, madam," he panted, "will you be good?"

Her next move left him speechless. She looked up, murmured, "You're *so* strong," and kissed him with full and parted lips.

It was, of course, at this moment that the Emergency Squad arrived.

✳

The Squad seemed more interested in this tableau than in the bomb. With a deceptive appearance of ease and carelessness two of the men transferred the ticking package to a metal container full of lubricating oil. Sergeant Borigian said, "There's an undeveloped lot next door; we'll take 'er apart there." With the same routined indifference the two men lifted the container and carried away the oil and the ticking. And all this time their eyes seemed never to leave the red-faced Lieutenant, the buxom and gasping woman, and the unconscious man on the floor.

When the men had gone, Sergeant Borigian grinned and observed, "Looks like you've done a little taking apart yourself, Lieutenant."

Marshall started to speak, but Veronica Foulkes cut across him with, "My husband! Aren't you going to do anything about him?"

"Looks like he's done plenty," the Sergeant ventured.

Hilary groaned. In an instant Veronica was beside him, stroking his forehead and murmuring phrases that might have been better suited to Pitti Sing. Slowly Hilary opened his eyes and seemed astounded to behold himself and the room still in one piece.

"It ticked . . ." he faltered. "Where is it?"

"There," Veronica murmured. "He won't hurt ums again. There's a real policeman here now. With a uniform."

"Lieutenant," said Sergeant Borigian, "what worries me is I can't decide whether to report your conduct to headquarters or to your wife."

Hilary sat up, "Where did you come from, Ron? But that doesn't matter. Where's the bomb, Lieutenant? Where's the bomb?"

"Mr. Foulkes," said Marshall, "this is Sergeant Borigian of the Emergency Squad. His men are looking after the bomb. Everything's under control, and you're perfectly safe."

Veronica gazed from one man to the other. "What is happening here?"

Hilary wavered onto his feet. "There, my dear, there. I'll explain later. And you will find out who, Lieutenant?"

"I've got damned little to go on, Mr. Foulkes, as you very well know, and I'll have to have another session with you tomorrow. But right now what I've got to do is check up on the delivery of this parcel." He hesitated and glanced at Veronica. "One thing . . ."

"You may speak freely before my wife, Lieutenant. It will be hopeless now to try to keep things from her. Hopeless."

"Do you want us to put a guard on your apartment? It can easily be arranged."

Hilary shook his head fuzzily. "I think not. You see, Lieutenant, I want to know who this is. If we frighten him away with a guard, we may never manage to learn his identity."

"Think it over. I'd sooner not know who tried to murder you than prove positively who succeeded. I'll give you a ring in the morning. Coming, Sergeant?"

As they waited for the elevator, Sergeant Borigian suggested, "Want to watch the investigation? From a distance of course; we don't want no amateurs from Homicide cluttering things up."

"No thanks. I've got to check this delivery while the trail's warm. Let the clerk sleep on it and he'll forget everything. I'll phone into Headquarters for your report in about—will an hour be all right?"

"For a preliminary, sure." The heavy-set Sergeant fell broodingly silent. Then he burst out, "Look, Lieutenant. My job's to keep bombs from going off and find out what they're made of. It's nothing to me who sent 'em to who or why. But when I walk in and find a detective Lieutenant . . . Will you tell me what the hell's going on up there?"

"Brother," said Marshall feelingly, "I wish you'd tell me."

5.

Tracing an order is a job that Marshall hates. It always means much brandishing of credentials and the assumption of the heavy policeman role. Executives seem to fear that every inquirer is the sinister agent of some foreign power, or worse yet, of a competitor.

After a great deal of this official brow-beating, Marshall had prevailed upon the central office of the Angelus Parcel Delivery Service to divulge that the package whose number he gave had been sent from the Hollywood branch, and upon the manager of the Hollywood branch to admit that Q73X4 meant our Miss Jones.

Our Miss Jones would have been markedly pretty if she had not been made up on the chance that a casting director might sometime want to send a parcel. "Sure," she said cheerfully, "I remember the guy sent that package." She checked back in her records. "That was at ten thirty-five this morning, only he said we shouldn't make delivery till three this afternoon. I remember him swell."

"You must take quite a few orders in a day," Marshall ventured cautiously. "Was there anything to make you remember this man especially?"

"Sure. First of all I thought it was kind of screwy marking a package RUSH and then leaving instructions not to deliver it for four and a half hours. And then I noticed the name it was going to. Hilary Saint John Foulkes."

". . . all the rooms . . ." thought Marshall. "And why should you notice that name in particular?"

"On account of last night me and my boyfriend were looking at a magazine and there was an ad for men's talcum powder with a lot of signatures-like—you know, endorsements—and they were all big shots only I didn't know who was this one so I said to my boyfriend, I said 'Who's this Hilary?' and he said 'That's the son of Fowler Foulkes' and I said 'But who is he?' and he said 'Just that, far's I know' and I said 'So just because you're somebody's son you get dough for endorsing stuff?' and he said 'Somebody's son? But he's the son of Fowler Foulkes!' and I said 'So who's he?' so then we had a fight. So that's how come I noticed the name."

Marshall nodded satisfied. "All right." Witnesses can be like the overhelpful natives who tell the explorer exactly what he wants most to hear, true or not; and such witnesses never survive cross-examination; but this sounded circumstantial and convincing. "Now, Miss Jones, can you describe the person who sent this package?"

"Sure. He was a funny old boy."

"Old?"

"Yeah. He must've been all of fifty if he was a day. He wasn't so very tall, but he was built big, if you know what I mean. He had a big barrel of a chest on him, like a gorilla or something. His nose was big and kind of hooked—Roman, I guess you'd call it. And he had a great big black beard. You wouldn't forget him very easy. Oh yes, and he carried a cane, with a silver head on it."

Our Miss Jones wondered why the detective should first

look so blankly incredulous and then burst out into an admiring guffaw.

He was, Marshall realized, up against a murderer with a peculiarly outrageous gag sense. The girl had just given a perfect description of Dr. Derringer.

6.

"There's nothing like beer when you knock off from a day's work." Matt Duncan popped the top off and handed the foaming bottle to Lieutenant Marshall.

"Don't you want a glass?" Concha suggested.

"If I can't have a stein," said Marshall, "right straight from the bottle is next best. And besides, why make more dishes for you to wash?"

"Thank you, kind sir."

"Aren't you having any?"

"Uh uh. I don't like beer, and I'm not going to be one of these girls who go around pretending they do."

Matt exhaled loudly after a mighty draft. "Hits the spot, that does. Now what are you on the trail of, Terence?"

Lieutenant Marshall looked mournful. "Curse of the profession. Nobody ever suspects you of just a friendly call in passing."

"This is non-professional?"

"Well . . ."

"It is not," said Concha. "I can see that gleam in your eye. I'll bet it's still that floater with the rosary you were asking Sister Ursula about."

"What's that?" Matt asked idly.

"Nothing important. Fellow named Tarbell got bumped off down on Main Street. But that isn't what I—"

Matt wrinkled his brow. "Tarbell . . . I met a Tarbell somewhere recently. It's not a common name. Jonathan Tarbell . . ."

Marshall leaned forward. "So. Maybe this is a professional call
after all. Where? When?"

"Damn, I can't remember. It was just casual . . . I know. It was
at Austin Carter's."

"You remember," Concha put in. "The man I was telling you
about with the Mañana Literary Society."

Marshall nodded. "Friend of Carter's then, this Tarbell?"

"No, I think he'd come with somebody."

"Who?"

"I can't remember. Nobody I know well. Runcible maybe, or
Chantrelle."

"So." Marshall nodded slowly to himself. "Matt, I'm going to
ask you for a favor, and I'm not going to explain any of my reasons. You'll have to take me on trust."

A buzzer buzzed. Concha said, "Phone. I'll take it," and vanished.

"O.K.," Matt conceded. "Tentatively granted. What goes?"

"I want you to take me out to Carter's for the next meeting of
the Mañana Literary Society. Don't introduce me as Lieutenant;
I'll be just another tomorrower."

"I ask you no questions and you tell me no lies, is that it?"

"That's about the size of it."

"Well for one thing, Terence, you've got a wrong idea of the
M.L.S. It isn't a matter of regular meetings. It's just when some
of the boys happen to get together, usually at Carter's. And for
another, I don't know as I like furnishing the sheep's clothing for
a wolf like you in our quiet flock."

Marshall set down his beer. "Matt, if I talked I could make you
see how important this might be. There's a damned good chance

it could solve one murder and forestall another. And if you insist, I'll talk. But I don't want to. Not yet."

Matt started to speak, then sat glaring into his beer. "Friendship's one thing," he said at last, "and police duty's another. I don't know as I'm willing to—"

It was just then that Concha returned. "The phone's for you, Lieutenant, and it's Sister Ursula of all people. Oh and look, while I think of it: we're going out to Carter's tonight, and he always likes to meet people. Why don't you and Leona come along? You'll like fantasy writers. They're nuts."

Matt shrugged resignedly. "You can't win."

Marshall was smiling to himself as he answered the phone. "Yes, Sister?"

"Leona told me you weren't home yet, so I thought I'd try here. It might be important."

"Yes?"

"That rosary, you know. Sister Perpetua says it's a very famous piece of carving which was thought to be lost. She says it was done by Domenico Saltimbanco, which is apparently a most eminent name from the way she pronounces it, and was carved to order for the first Mrs. Fowler Foulkes."

Marshall expressed himself, and then hastily apologized. "Don't apologize, Lieutenant. It is surprising, isn't it, when we were speaking of Hilary Foulkes only this afternoon? But this isn't Hilary's mother; I think he was born of the second marriage. The first Mrs. Foulkes was a most prominent laywoman, you know."

"I don't know how I can thank you, Sister."

"If you really wanted to thank me . . . But no. I won't even ask it. I do try to be good, you know. Goodbye, Lieutenant."

7.

The sign said:

!!! DANGER !!!

NITROSYNCRETIC LABORATORY

! KEEP OUT !

Marshall paused and stared. "So," he observed. "And what the hell is a nitrosyncretic laboratory?"

Matt Duncan smiled. "Nice gag, isn't it? You see, the way this house is situated on a hill, people come to this door before the proper main door. This is Austin's workroom, and he used to have a hell of a time with *Liberty* salesmen. Poundings on the door are distracting-like when you're working on the collapse of an interstellar empire. But since he put up that sign, salesmen take one look, shudder, and get the hell out."

Leona laughed. "I'll have to try something like that for when the children take naps."

"The children . . ." Concha repeated. "It must be nice to say that so casually."

"Do I really sound casual? I know I try to, but I still go sort of warm all over."

Marshall coughed. "The children are home and asleep and there's a competent girl in charge of them. For the moment they're hers, and we're just people. Come on, darling. Let's see the science fiction menagerie."

Bernice Carter met them at the proper door. "Austin's holding forth," she said softly. "We'll postpone introductions till he's done."

"These people," Matt told her, "are Marshalls. They just want to listen."

"They'll have the chance," said Bernice.

The menagerie was meager this evening. In the large living-room were only five men. The tall thin one established in the heavy chair under the reading lamp Marshall rightly took for his host. Of the others, one was somewhat plump and somewhat short—rather like a poor man's edition of Hilary without that almost unconscious assumption of self-importance which only being born heir to the Foulkes fortune could give. One was a stocky individual with a goatee (and no mustache) and a serious air. One was an open-faced youth who might well be a college sophomore. The fourth was a small sharp-faced man whose little eyes conveyed an odd mixture of boredom and complete absorption.

"And that," Austin Carter was saying, "is just the trouble with his stuff. It's too damned galactic. Science fiction can be interesting only so long as you preserve the human frame of reference. Of course the reader should think, 'Golly, this is wonderful! Space ships and blasters and stuff!' But he should also think, 'After all, maybe that's just the way I'd feel if I rode on a space ship.' If your concepts become too grandiose, you've left the reader a thousand parsecs behind."

"Still," the sharp-faced man protested, "his stuff sells. And his fans yowl for more."

"I'm laying a bet they won't much longer. You can distend a reader's mind with new concepts only so far. Eventually he says 'Phooey!' and goes back to the more homely commonplaces of Joe here, or me, who modestly consider the destruction of a solar system or maybe just a planet as colossal enough, without annihilating galaxies left and right."

The sophomore opened his mouth, considered, and said hesitantly, "Stapledon."

"Olaf Stapledon's a special case. For one thing, he's a great writer, which most of us haven't much hope of being. For another, he's not hitting the magazine market. But most of all, he's got the amazing faculty of leading you on so gradually that you're willing to accept his vasty concepts as familiar."

"And that," said the goatee, "is one of the greatest services that science fiction can render to science. In which respect Stapledon is surely the most notable talent to enter the field since Fowler Foulkes."

Austin Carter frowned at the name of the Master. The sharp-faced man snorted. Bernice took advantage of the silence to become hostess.

"These people seem to be listening raptly, but they might as well know who they're listening to. Or whom, just in case they're that kind of people. Matt, I think you know everybody, and probably you do too, Concha. And these, Matt informs me, are Marshalls. My husband, Austin Carter, Mr. Runcible," (the plumpish one) "Mr. Phyn," (the sharp-faced one) "Mr. Chantrelle," (the goatee) "and Joe Henderson."

Marshall and Leona duly gave and received greetings.

"They're novices," Matt explained. "Don't expect them to show due reverence for a great name. And I don't mean you, Austin."

"So?" Marshall glanced inquiringly at the poor man's Hilary. Runcible, if not a great name, was at least a delightfully freakish one.

Runcible shook his head and waved an indefinite gesture of disclaimer. Austin Carter laughed. "No. Runcible so far is just a name signed to letters to the editor. Though you might mark it down for future reference; some first-rate men have come up from the fan ranks. But the name that struck Matt dumb with awe when he first heard it was Joe Henderson."

The sophomore shuffled and hung his head. "I write a little."

"By which," Bernice Carter translated, "he means that he's the oldest name in science fiction that's still big-time. When he can find the time between hacking out Captain Comet, he can still turn out stuff that puts young upstarts like Austin and me right in our places. He's been leading the field for fifteen years, and he still looks nineteen and if only I had a goose handy I could offer a very pretty demonstration of Joe not saying boo to it."

Joe Henderson's grin spread over his face as slowly as that of the Cheshire Cat and far more warmly. "Get along with you, Berni," he drawled.

Carter slapped him on the back. "The modesty of true genius," he announced. "Which makes me just as glad that I've never laid claim to either quality. But as I was saying to Joe when you folks came in—"

"One more minute of being hostess," Bernice interrupted. "Then you can go on." She collected wraps, took orders for drinks, and vanished.

"Anybody else coming?" Matt asked. "I'd like these poor innocents to see the M.L.S. in full swing."

"Anson Macdonald and Lyle Monroe may be around, and possibly Tony Boucher. Tell me, Matt, what'd you think of that last opus of Tony's?"

"Nuts. He wrote it with his eyes shut and one hand tied behind him. Same old stuff. Mutiny on a space ship, the uncharted asteroid loaded with uranium ore, and Martians trying to steal it on a time warp. Hell, it's routine."

Marshall blinked. "It's a little hard for an innocent, as Matt rightly calls me, to take that all in one gulp. I can't quite think of space ships and uranium and Martians as being drably commonplace."

"You get to think that way," said Austin Carter. "Supposing in real life you broke down a locked door and found a corpse bleeding from twenty wounds with no possible weapon any place. You'd maybe think it a trifle peculiar. But the mystery fan would say—"

Leona, being a mystery fan, picked up her cue. "Just another locked room."

"Exactly. So to us it's 'just another space ship' or 'just another time warp' or—"

"And what," Marshall asked, "is a time warp?"

"Mostly," Carter confessed, "a handy device. The term refers of course to the theory of the curvature of the Space-Time continuum. A warp in that framework could produce most curious results—possibly send you off, not on ordinary time travel, but completely out of this continuum."

"I like 'ordinary time travel,'" said Leona. "So prosaic."

"You can have fun with a time warp," Joe Henderson contributed.

Concha laughed. "The first time I came across one was in a story of yours, Joe. There was a reference to a character in an earlier episode who had gone off on a time warp and never been seen again. I thought it was a new kind of binge."

"Time warps," Carter went on, "are handy. They're part of the patter, like subspace, which don't ask me to explain. They let you do the damnedest things and make them sound scientific. As indeed they quite possibly are. Ask Chantrelle here; he's from Caltech."

"To my mind, Mr. Marshall," the goatee observed somewhat ponderously, "the free imagination of these writers is of more scientific value to the progress of mankind than ninety per cent of the theses written for the doctorate."

"And this imagination is absolutely free? You must get away with murder."

Carter shook his head. "Not any longer. Or at least not in the better markets. Good science fiction requires more self-consistency, more plausibility than any conceivable realism. Your world of the future can't exist in any high-fantastic vacuum. It's got to be real and detailed and inhabited by real people. With all due apologies to Captain Comet, Joe, the days of the pure gadget story and the interplanetary horse opera are over."

Marshall gratefully accepted beer from his hostess. "I'm not sure I follow those terms."

Carter looked about the group. "With two new victims, I'm afraid I'm about to repeat my famous lecture on science fiction. Runcible won't mind because there's nothing a fan loves like listening, and Phyn here is always hopeful I may say something worth stealing. To the others I apologize, but here goes:

"Science fiction is essentially a magazine field. Outside of Fowler Foulkes and H. G. Wells, practically no contemporary imaginative writer has been commercially successful in book form. So its development has to be studied in the mags. And these, way back in the early days, were possibly, to the non-fan outsider, not so good. They had, to be sure, scope and imagination, an originality and a vigor that few other pulps could equal; and neither quality had ever been markedly prized in the slick field.

"But they also had a sort of cold inhumanity. The science was the thing, and the hell with the people involved. On the one hand you had what I call the interplanetary horse operas, which were sometimes pretty weak even on their science. These were pure Westerns translated into cosmic terms. Instead of fighting off bands of hostile red-skins, you fought off bands of hostile Martians, and as you pulled out your trusty blaster, they regularly bit the stardust.

"The gadget stories were more interesting. They frequently made honest attempts at forecasting scientific developments. Atomic power, stratosphere exploration, the rocket flight that so absorbs Chantrelle, all the features that may revolutionize the second half of this century as thoroughly as radio and the airplane have transformed this half—all these became familiar, workable things.

"But the writers stopped there. Interest lay in the gadget itself. And science fiction was headed for a blind alley until the realization came that even science fiction must remain fiction, and fiction is basically about people, not subatomic blasters nor time warps.

"So there's a new school now, and I suppose Don Stuart, the editor of *Surprising,* is as responsible as anybody. Don's idea was this, and it was revolutionary: Grant your gadgets, and start your story from there.

"In other words, assume certain advances in civilization, then work out convincingly just how those would affect the lives of ordinary individuals like you and me.

"For instance, in one story of Rene Lafayette's there is a noble amount of whisky-drinking, and the name of the whisky is Old Space Ranger. And that one phrase paints an entire picture of a civilization in which interplanetary travel is the merest commonplace. No amount of gadgetary description could make the fact of space ships so simply convincing.

"In other words, to sum it all up in a phrase of Don's: 'I want a story that would be published in a magazine of the twenty-fifth century.'"

8.

After this lecture, the conversation grew general. Matt and the

Carters talked shop, the thin-faced Phyn interjected an occasional word of wry commercialism, and Mr. Chantrelle spoke of the coming test run of his latest rocket car.

Marshall sat back and drank his beer. It was indeed a strange new world, and a fascinating one. But he could not give it his whole attention. The policeman's mind kept reverting to duty, and in the midst of phrases about klystrons and space orbits and the positronic brain tracks of Asimov's robots he tried to sum up these people in connection with the attempts on Hilary Foulkes' life.

They didn't fit. Not at all well. Despite the high-flown fantasy of their conversation, they were as quietly ordinary people as he ever encountered. Or were they? Were not their very ordinary traits the possible marks of murder?

Motives he could not know yet; but it seemed not too unlikely that anyone in this field might at some time have had a run-in with Hilary. And granting motive, how could these individuals react?

Bernice Carter was coolly efficient as a hostess and as a conversationalist. Might that efficiency extend to the calm performance of a necessary elimination?

Austin Carter was, in a far more intelligent way, as self-sufficient and self-important as Hilary. Might two such dominances conflict fatally?

Phyn (apparently an agent specializing in this field of fiction) was shrewd and acquisitive. Might he not find personal gain a sufficient motive for any action?

Joe Henderson was inarticulate and repressed. Might repressions gathered too long burst forth lethally?

Chantrelle . . .

But this was random guesswork, unworthy of a detective lieutenant even when off duty. Marshall waited for the next passing of an angel and said, "I met somebody the other day might interest people in your field. Hilary Foulkes—the great Fowler's son."

"Oh," said Austin Carter. "Hilary." His voice was absolutely expressionless.

"You know him?"

"I know his brother-in-law, D. Vance Wimpole. There, sir, is one of the damnedest and most fabulous figures in the whole pulp field, and he tackles most of it. Fair on science fiction and excellent on fantasy. But what I mean by fabulous: One night in New York Don Stuart and I were seeing him off to Chicago. He got talking and outlined a fantasy short ad lib from hook to tag. Don liked it, but said, 'The trouble is, now you'll never write it. You never do write what you've talked out first.' And Vance said, 'Oh, won't I?'

"He left by train for Chicago around eight. The next morning the story was on Don's desk, air-mail special delivery from Chi. I won't say it was a masterpiece, but it was publishable as it stood and it drew good fan mail."

Joe Henderson nodded. "That's Vance for you."

"Where is he now?" Bernice asked.

"I had a letter from him yesterday," Chantrelle said. "Postmarked from Victoria. He's on his way back from Alaska and should be here in a week or so. I'm postponing the test run until he arrives."

"Sure of that?" the agent demanded. "I thought—"

"Yes?"

"Nothing."

"I'd like to meet this prodigy," said Marshall. "But about—"

"Oh," Carter picked up his story, "Vance is something. He uses an especially geared electric typewriter because he composes faster than any ordinary machine can go. He works only six months out of the year and spends the other six hunting anything from polar bears to blondes. He—"

Marshall reluctantly listened to all the unbelievable saga of D. Vance Wimpole. The subject of Hilary had been deftly killed, but not before he had caught a sharp glitter in the little eyes of Phyn and an expression of relief on the face of Bernice Carter as her husband maneuvered away.

Around eleven Leona interrupted a fascinating discussion (on whether you could construct a robot werewolf) to say, "This is fun, but we've got a girl staying with the children and she has to go home sometime."

The Carters' sorrow sounded most sincere. "You too, Matt?" Austin added.

"Afraid so. I want to get some work done in the morning."

"Just a minute then. I want to show you those pictures of the Denvention. I keep forgetting."

As Carter went downstairs to the Nitrosyncretic Laboratory, Marshall asked, "I'm still innocent. What's a Denvention?"

Bernice explained. "The science fiction fans are highly organized, and they have Annual World Conventions. The last one was in Denver, so the fans, ever incorrigible neologists, called it the Denvention. The next one's here in Los Angeles, and I'm afraid it's called the Pacificon."

There followed ten minutes of looking at pictures of people of whom Marshall knew nothing. Carter, he gathered, was an enthusiastic camera fiend with every known photographic gadget and even an adjunct to the Nitro Lab in which he did his own developing and printing. The pictures were good, particularly the nude which had wandered in by mistake. It reminded him of Leona in her unreformed days. He said as much, and the men thereafter accorded her a certain respect which they had not displayed to the mother of two wonderful children.

"And what," he asked at last, "is this weird display?"

"That? They had a costume party on the last night. Come as Your Favorite S-F Character. Berni wanted to go as Dale Arden, but I'm afraid it was an overambitious project."

"And who's this lad with the beard and the stick?"

"That's Austin," said Bernice. "I took this picture."

"So. And what did you finally go as?"

"The Wicked Queen of Ixion in Joe's *Cosmic Legion* stories. It was fun."

9.

"It was fun," Leona echoed as they went down the stairs. "I think I'll lay off mysteries for a while and try this strange stuff. It sounds appetizing. How about you?" After a silence, she repeated: "How about you?"

"Uh? Oh. Sorry dear." Lieutenant Marshall was wondering if he should tell Hilary Foulkes how shrewd a guess he had suddenly made as to the identity of his so far fumbling murderer.

THE THIRD DAY:
Saturday, November 1, 1941

A PHOTOGRAPH, and the knowledge that one of the individuals depicted had himself developed the picture.

It was little enough to go on, Marshall reflected as he sat at his desk and went over the latest routine reports on Jonathan Tarbell, which told him precisely nothing.

And what tied the two cases together? A phone number and a rosary.

Any of his colleagues would hoot at him, or at best smile derisively. But Marshall could not help believing that the two cases were one, and that his prime duty at the moment was not so much to crack the murder of the floater Tarbell as to prevent the murder of Hilary Foulkes.

"Let him get himself murdered," Leona had protested sleepily after they were in bed last night. "Then it'll be a big case and there'll be headlines about Heir to Foulkes Estate and you can solve it and be famous. And who cares if Hilary lives or dies?"

Then Marshall had tried to explain the basic sanctity and importance of human life, any life (which was a curious concept to expound in the 1940's), and the significance of the preventive over the punitive in a policeman's duties until Leona said that having debated at Oxford was swell only at this hour it might wake the children. So he slept, but in his dreams he kept pursuing and trying to frustrate a barrel-chested, black-bearded man who was seeking to garotte with a rosary that oddly named fan who resembled Hilary.

There was something about a rocket too, and an old volume of *Who's What,* though he couldn't remember in the morning where they fitted in. (A complete record of this dream would have been of the greatest interest to Austin Carter or Hugo Chantrelle, both of whom were disciples of J. W. Dunne.)

The dream reminded him. He set aside the Tarbell reports, took up the phone, dialed an inter-office number, and gave instructions for a thorough canvassing of all theatrical costumers to trace the rental of a large black spade beard of the Derringer model. Probably unnecessary, but worth a try.

He hesitated, phone in hand. Then he nodded resolutely to himself, got an outside line, and dialed Hilary Foulkes' unlisted number.

Veronica Foulkes' "Hello" was rich with indefinite emotional overtones. Marshall could imagine her investing a grocery order, if she over stooped to so plebeian a task, with the quality of a Borgia laying in the month's supply of acqua tofana.

"May I speak to Mr. Foulkes?"

"Who is this please?"

"The fiend with the pipe," said Marshall perversely, and wondered if she would hang up.

She didn't. In a moment Hilary's smooth deep voice was asking, "Yes? Yes?"

"Marshall speaking, Mr. Foulkes."

"Oh. Hold on a minute. I'll take this on the extension in my study. Hold on."

Marshall held on and wondered why Hilary always repeated everything. It was like a stammer or a tic, and probably a psychoanalyst could have fun with it.

"Yes," Hilary resumed after a few seconds. "Didn't want to disturb my wife, Lieutenant. She's been terribly nervous since that bomb episode. Terribly. And what did you find out about that? What sort of bomb was it?"

"Very common type. No creative imagination. Anyone with underworld connections could pick one up easily."

"Underworld connections? But Lieutenant . . . You can't mean I'm being threatened by a gang?"

"Don't jump to conclusions, Mr. Foulkes. The damnedest people can have some underworld connections. Especially with the political setup in this town. I'll lay odds that even a stranger in town like you, if he had as much as you have, could get hold of such a machine after a little nosing about and palm-greasing. Our only hope of tracing it is through a stool, and that's not too likely."

"Oh," said Hilary sadly.

"But why I called: Have you thought of any more—shall I say, candidates?"

"No, Lieutenant. Heavens no. Excepting that as I said—"

"Yes. The various people you may have offended as executor of the estate. So tell me: Have you ever offended one Austin Carter?"

"Carter? Carter? Let me see . . . Oh yes. That was the man who wanted to quote all sorts of things from my father's works and wouldn't pay for them. I was firm about it; so then he cut out the quotations rather than pay me anything."

"Was that all?"

"Yes, Lieutenant. Yes, excepting . . . Well," Hilary chuckled, "I confess I may have played some small part in causing Metropolis

Pictures to decide against Mr. Carter's last novel. I naturally felt that a man who has displayed such shocking irreverence toward my father hardly belonged in the same studio that has done such fine work in producing Dr. Derringer films. Naturally."

"Naturally," Marshall echoed, admiring the ingenuous ingenuity with which Hilary presented his case.

"But Lieutenant—"

"Yes?"

"Do you mean to imply that you . . . that you have any evidence against this Mr. Carter?"

Marshall hesitated. "Will you be home this afternoon?"

"Yes."

"Good. I'll be out to see you. I want to ask you a few more questions and give you some idea of what evidence I have. Then we can see if you wish to prefer charges."

"My!" Hilary gasped. "This is such prompt work, Lieutenant. So very prompt. I never expected . . ."

There was a long silence. Marshall said "Yes?" twice. There was no answer. He said "Mr. Foulkes!" loudly, and he heard a groan and a sort of thudding crash. Then there was only silence on the line.

He jiggled the phone cradle fruitlessly, then hung up and dialed again. He got the busy signal; the Foulkes' receiver was still off.

Marshall got an inter-office number, gave certain instructions, hung up, and reached for his hat.

Then, on an afterthought, he dialed the number found on Jonathan Tarbell.

2.

There was no excitement in front of the apartment hotel. No crowds, no patrol car.

"Stable doors, maybe," Marshall said to Sergeant Ragland. "But you stay here in front of the entrance. There shouldn't be much mid-morning traffic. Get the names of everybody that comes out and his reason for being here." His first stop was at the manager's apartment.

Her greeting was reserved. "Yes, I did go up to the Foulkeses'. But Mrs. Foulkes herself answered the door and assured me that her husband was working in his study as usual. I couldn't very well force my way in, could I? And since you didn't choose to tell me what was the matter . . ."

"All right," Marshall said. "Thanks."

"I hope you realize," she went on, "that this apartment house is not accustomed to having the police—"

"Sorry. But we go where we're needed. Thank you."

He rode up in the elevator half-relieved. If Veronica Foulkes, in the same apartment, was not aware that anything was wrong . . . He paused in his thoughts. Unless, of course, Mrs. Foulkes herself . . .

The maid Alice answered the bell at the Foulkes apartment.

"I'd like to speak to Mr. Foulkes."

"He's in his study, sir, and I'm afraid he won't want to be disturbed."

"It's most important. I—"

"I remember, sir. You're the police. But even for the police I don't like to interrupt Mr. Foulkes. He's very particular, sir."

"What is it, Alice?" Veronica Foulkes, in a negligee too impressively sumptuous to be seductive, came up behind the maid. Her eyes gleamed as she saw the visitor. "You again!"

"Sorry, Mrs. Foulkes. But it's highly important that I speak with your husband at once."

She seemed to repress a whole anthology of remarks as she glanced at the servant. "You were talking to him on the phone not half an hour ago."

"Have you seen him since then?"

"No. He's still in his study."

"Then I'm afraid I must ask you to let me in. Or," Marshall added as she hesitated, "must I use official persuasion?"

Veronica made a gesture of resignation. "Very well. Come in."

She crossed the living-room and knocked on the door of the study. She repeated the knock twice, then opened the door.

As Marshall followed her into the living-room, a gentle voice said, "Good morning, Lieutenant."

Marshall looked about and started. He was so amazed to behold Sister Ursula in this apartment that he had still found no words of greeting when Veronica Foulkes' sharp scream shrilled through the room.

"He's dead!" Veronica gasped. There seemed to be terror and genuine sorrow in her voice. She stood rooted in the doorway, unable to make her body follow her gaze to what lay on the floor.

Marshall pushed past her and bent over Hilary Foulkes. There was almost no blood; but only the ornate metal handle of the weapon was visible between the plumply fleshed shoulder-blades. The knife itself was buried. The telephone lay sprawled on the floor as inert and voiceless as its owner.

"You!" Veronica went on intensely. "Until I met you, nothing ever happened. Life was all right then. And what do you do? First you insult me, then you beat poor Hilary into unconsciousness, then you attack me, and now . . ."

Marshall rose. Some of the tension had faded from his face. "I'm sorry to be anticlimactic, Mrs. Foulkes, but your husband is still alive. And medical aid is more important right now than disrupting your version of the facts." He went past her again into the living-room and turned to Sister Ursula. Sister Felicitas, he noticed, was there too, and as usual, asleep.

"Sister," he said sincerely, "I don't know how in the name of your favorite saint you got here, but I've never been gladder to see anyone. I'm going to ask you to be useful. If I were a sheriff I'd swear you in as deputy. Watch these women and don't let anyone, for any reason, enter that study till the doctor comes."

Sister Ursula nodded and said "Certainly." The maid goggled, and the cousin whom Marshall had met before hesitated in the hall doorway, looking questioningly at Veronica.

"My husband's dying!" Mrs. Foulkes exclaimed. "And you forbid me to—"

"I'm afraid I do."

"I'd like to see you stop me!"

She saw. As she started toward Hilary's body, Marshall's hand clamped down on her wrist and a quick jerk brought her across the room and deposited her on the sofa beside the nuns. "And stay there!" he said tersely.

Marshall used the manager's phone downstairs. To use the Foulkes phone would mean replacing the fallen apparatus, and he wanted an exact photograph of that. While the dowager-like manager dithered about murmuring prayers that the name of the house could be kept out of the papers, he requested an ambulance, a doctor, a fingerprint man, and a photographer, and thanked his stars for the foresight which had made sure before he left headquarters that such a request could be instantly filled.

Sergeant Ragland stood in the lobby, still guarding the door. "There wasn't anybody tried to get out," he said.

"Sorry, Rags. Come on upstairs. May be something for you there."

"D.O.A., Lieutenant?" Ragland brightened.

"Not quite. Keep your fingers crossed."

The Lieutenant stationed his disappointed Sergeant at the door leading into the study and confronted the assembled witnesses. Five of them, and all women. He groaned a little, but the thought of the astute Sister Ursula on the scene of the crime consoled him.

"All right," he began. "At ten thirty-five I telephoned Mr. Foulkes. You, Mrs. Foulkes, answered the call and brought him to this phone here. He wanted to talk privately and went off to the extension phone in the study. I take it he shut the door after him?"

Veronica nodded.

"All right. Go on from there."

"Then the manager rang the bell and wanted to see my husband, heavens knows why. I told her he was working."

"My doing, I'm afraid. I thought that if anything had happened she might get needed help to him before I could get here. And then?"

"Then," said Veronica Foulkes with deadly restraint, "you came."

"But that's a half hour later, and what happened from then on I know myself. What I want to find out now is the in-between."

Sister Ursula spoke up. "But Mrs. Foulkes is quite correct. So far as we in this room knew, nothing happened—that is, nothing concerning Mr. Foulkes—between the time he took your call and your own arrival here."

"You were here all that time, Sister?"

"Here in this room, with Mrs. Foulkes and Sister Felicitas."

He turned to the maid. "And where were you?"

"In the kitchen, sir, baking. That's why I didn't answer the phone when you called. I'd just finished my work when you rang the doorbell, sir."

"And you, Miss—?"

"Green," said the cousin. "And may I hope you forget other things as easily as my name?"

Marshall blushed and felt Sister Ursula's curious eyes upon him.

"You . . . you did send for a doctor?" the girl went on eagerly.

"Of course, Miss Green. And there's nothing we can do for your cousin meanwhile. Any amateur attempt to shift him or to remove the knife might be exceedingly dangerous."

"But he—?" Her voice shook a little.

"I don't think there's any danger. And the best way you can help him is by helping me to prevent another such attack." His voice was surprisingly gentle. It was pleasantly unusual to find somebody who seemed really to give a damn about Hilary. "So if you'll tell me where you were from ten thirty-five until my arrival here?"

"In my room, typing some letters that Cousin Hilary had dictated."

"So." Marshall frowned. "I'm not very certain of the ground-plan of this apartment."

"I know." The girl half laughed, and Marshall reddened again. "But it's simple enough, at least as far as you're concerned now. East of this living-room—on that side, that is—there's only Hilary's study and a bath opening off it. To the west there's the rest of the apartment: two bedrooms and the kitchen and dinette and the maid's room."

Marshall digested the description. "So. Then anyone—say either you or Alice—coming from the rest of the apartment to the study would have to come through this room?"

"Yes. Or of course we could go out into the hall and around. The study has its own separate entrance."

Marshall nodded. "All right. Now, Sister, what time did you get here?"

"A little after ten, Lieutenant."

"You were here in this room when Mr. Foulkes took my call?"

"Yes. He was in the dinette finishing breakfast. He came in here (I must say he looked rather surprised to see Sister Felicitas and me) and went on into the study."

"And you stayed here . . . ?"

"All the rest of the time until you arrived. And if I may anticipate your next question: No one went through this door to the study after Mr. Foulkes."

"Neither in nor out?"

"Neither."

"And Mrs. Foulkes was with you all that time?"

"This is too much!" Veronica exploded. "Not only must you ask my guests and my dependents all the questions that you should rightfully ask me, but now you go as far as to imply—"

"Please, Mrs. Foulkes," Sister Ursula interposed gently. "The Lieutenant has only been performing his routine duties. I hope," she added, with what might, from any one else, almost have been a wink.

"Thank you, Sister. And Mrs. Foulkes was with you?"

"Yes."

"Did you hear any noise from the study?"

"I confess that I didn't. Did you, Mrs. Foulkes?"

"No." Veronica was careful to speak to the nun rather than to the officer.

"But then she and I were deeply engrossed in conversation, and Sister Felicitas, as you know, is rather deaf. I think it would have had to be a serious struggle to make itself heard."

"So. Then it's clear that Mr. Foulkes' assailant came in through the hall door to the study and struck him down silently without any scuffle. All right. I think that's all I need to ask you at the moment. Please remain here, however, until after I've talked with the doctor, who should be here any minute." He rose, made a slight bow, and went into the study.

Hilary sprawled there undignifiedly in his shirt sleeves. (Today's shirt was a delicate mauve.) The splendid red-and-gold dressing gown was draped over a chair across the room. He was still unconscious. A good thing, that. Movement before the arrival of doctor and ambulance would simply entail needless pain and danger. Marshall contemplated the hilt and its angle, and calculated that the worst damage possible would be slight. He hoped.

He fumbled in his pocket, drew out a piece of chalk, bent down, and outlined the position of the body, worrying a little about the effect of chalk marks on a Persian rug. Leona, he was sure, would raise hell.

"Lieutenant!"

He stared up. "Sister! How did you get in here? Ragland!"

The Sergeant looked abashed. "She come in right after you, Lieutenant. I thought she was with you."

"All right. Well, Sister, since you're here—?"

Sister Ursula stood by the hall door. "Look at this."

Marshall looked. Not only was the button pressed which indicated that the door was locked. You could easily enough lock it behind you that way. But the night chain was on.

He said nothing. Holding the knob gently in a handkerchief, he turned it to release the lock and opened the door. With the chain on, it opened about an inch. Not conceivably far enough for a hand to reach in and hocus it.

Obstinate annoyance settled on his face. "Somebody put the latch on afterwards."

"Who? When? Remember, Lieutenant, that no one but Mr. Foulkes went into this room before your arrival. After that, Mrs. Foulkes went only as far as the threshold. When she tried to go farther, you jerked her back. While you were gone, I obeyed your instructions and saw that no one came in here. Since then, Sergeant Ragland has been at the door."

"So?"

"So . . . Please don't let my presence restrain you, Lieutenant. Express yourself as freely as you please. But I'm afraid you're confronted again with what Leona calls a locked room problem."

3.

The doctor rose from his examination. "Nasty," he observed. "But I'll pull him through all right. O.K., boys!" He gestured to the ambulance attendants with the stretcher.

"Can't you wait till the photographer gets here?" Marshall protested.

"Sorry, my boy." He was younger than Marshall, but the phrase seemed part of his professional equipment. "Which would you sooner do: photograph a corpse or interview a healthy victim? Get along with it there."

"Hold on. We'll need his prints at least if we're to learn anything from this room. If this desk yields a stamping pad . . ." It did, and Marshall busied himself with Hilary's limp hands. "When can I talk to him?" he asked as he worked.

"Do I know? This afternoon possibly. Come around late and see. May have to put him under opiates though. Near thing, that. From where it went in, you'd expect it to have struck the heart. But the blow was directed toward the right. Odd."

Marshall set aside the printed paper. "You can load him now. You'll be careful of the hilt when you remove the knife?"

"Prints? I know my business, my boy, and if the murderer knew his it won't matter anyway. See you tonight."

"Just a minute," Sister Ursula interposed.

"Yes, Sister?"

"Could that wound possibly have been self-inflicted?"

The doctor gave a superior snort. "Look." He grabbed the Lieutenant, whirled him around, and jabbed a long finger at a point between the spine and the left clavicle. "Try stabbing yourself there. Just try it."

"I'm afraid my habit is rather hampering." Sister Ursula tried. "But it does seem as though if I had no sleeves I might reach there."

"Reach there, certainly." The doctor demonstrated. "Strain on the shoulder muscles, but you can reach. Possibly even strike. But you reach from below. So even if you struck with enough force to penetrate, which I doubt, the blow would be directed upwards. This wound points down."

"You couldn't reach there the other way?" Marshall asked. "From above?"

"Physical impossibility," the doctor snapped dogmatically.

The stretcher-bearers had passed into the next room. Veron-

ica Foulkes was making inarticulate little moans as her unconscious husband passed by.

"Then he positively was attacked," said Marshall.

The doctor snorted again and stalked out wordlessly, in a sort
of Groucho Marx crouch.

"So." Marshall whistled. "Thanks for specifying that point, Sister. I'd taken it for granted—always a bad thing to do. But now we
know for certain, and where does it get us?" He walked over and
opened the door of the bathroom. There was one small window.
A midget might conceivably have squeezed through it, but even
a midget must have disarranged the neat row of shaving things
arranged on its sill. (They did not include, Marshall noticed, the
talc which Hilary St. J. Foulkes had nationally endorsed.)

He pushed the shower curtain all the way back. The stall was
empty.

He returned to the study. One of the large windows was open.
Both had screens which were hooked on the inside. He unlatched
one screen and leaned out. The wall here was absolutely blank
save for windows. No cornices, nothing but window sills a good
fifteen feet away in any direction. Three stories below was a bare
cement area.

He turned around. "The problem" he stated, "isn't getting
in. There's nothing to show that the assailant mightn't have been
waiting in here, possibly hidden in the bathroom, when Hilary
came to answer my call. But as for getting out . . . I can give you
three possible descriptions, Sister, of this would-be murderer."

"Yes, Lieutenant?"

"All right. A, he is the Invisible Man in person and walked
right past you out there. B, he has suction pads on his feet like a
gecko, and hung on to the wall out there while he worked some
sort of string-trick on the screens, then clambered to the ground

or to the roof, still by suction. C, he has a pseudopodal finger that he inserted through the one-inch crack in the door to maneuver the chain into locking position. There you are; take your pick."

"I like the first one best," said Sister Ursula seriously. "The Invisible Man."

"And why?"

"Remember, Lieutenant, that that is the title, not only of a novel by Wells, but also of a short story by Chesterton. As a Catholic, I naturally prefer the latter."

Lieutenant Marshall shrugged resignedly. But before he could pursue this cryptic hint, the photographer and the fingerprint expert had arrived. The next twenty minutes were crowded.

When the experts were through, Marshall's patience was near an end and he knew no more than he had to start with. The prints in the room were almost exclusively Hilary's or the maid's, with here and there a random and plausible specimen of Miss Green's or of Mrs. Foulkes' (and securing the specimen prints of the latter had been one of the major nightmares in the expert's life). The hall door had only Hilary's prints on both inner and outer knobs, and no trace of gloved smudges. The telephone also had only his.

Marshall himself lay in the chalked outline for a photograph of the crime. That is, he lay in it as well as his six foot two could fit into the outline of Hilary's five foot nine. Then he experimented with falls from various positions, and concluded that Hilary must (as had indeed seemed obvious all along) have been struck down while he was seated at the desk telephoning. Sister Ursula checked that in the next room, with voices talking, the sounds even of Marshall's heavier body were audible but not strikingly noticeable. You heard them only if you were listening for them.

At last the Lieutenant again confronted the women in the

living-room. "I've done all I can here now," he said, "and there's nothing further I need to ask you until I've talked with Mr. Foulkes. You'll be doing the police a favor if you don't pester the hospital with attempts to see him until I notify you that he's receiving. In the meantime, you can all be trying to remember any events of this morning or earlier that might throw light on the matter, and especially any individuals you think likely to have made such an attempt. Of course, Mr. Foulkes may, and we trust he will, be able to tell us his assailant's identity without further ado. But we must be ready in case he can't. Sister, may I drive you home?"

"Certainly, Lieutenant. And you have room for Sister Felicitas too?"

He had forgotten the other nun completely. One always did.

4.

Sister Ursula occupied the front seat of the sedan with the Lieutenant. Sergeant Ragland climbed in back with Sister Felicitas and felt embarrassed by the combination of back seats and nuns until he decided that he might as well take a little snooze too.

"All right," said Marshall at last. "Now tell me why you were there."

Sister Ursula hesitated the least trifle. "You remember what I told you about Sister Patientia and her brailling *Beneath the Abyss?*"

"Yes."

"Well, she did want that work to get into the hands of the blind readers, and Mr. Foulkes' refusal made a terrible legal obstacle. She thought that if she appealed to him personally he might perhaps relent. But she is quite unused to dealing with the public; she lives almost as though she were in a cloistered order.

And since I'm the one that Reverend Mother always uses for what you might call public relations work . . ."

"Was this Sister Patientia's own idea?"

"Well . . . I may have suggested to her that the personal approach often helps . . ."

"And how did you find out where Hilary lives?"

"I called the society gossip editor of the *Times.*"

"So. And all because I was working on a murder case that somehow involved a rosary of the first Mrs. Foulkes."

"Lieutenant!" Sister Ursula frowned, but there was a smile half-hidden in her voice. "How can you accuse me of such a thing? You . . . you aren't angry with me, are you?"

"Angry?" Marshall grinned. "Sister, when I came to see you yesterday, my chief fear was that the Tarbell affair was too dull to tempt you. Things have changed now. If there ever was a case that demanded your peculiar perspicacity, this is it. And you don't have to worry about temptations any more. You're right in the middle of this. And you're going to hear all I know about it." So he told her, from Jonathan Tarbell through the attempts on Hilary's life on to his evening with the science fiction writers.

She nodded as he finished. "And you're suspicious of this Austin Carter?"

"Who could help being? He has a first-rate revenge motive, if Hilary queered a film sale for him. His photographic lab must contain some cyanide preparation, such as was used in the chocolates attempt, and he owns a Dr. Derringer disguise, which figured in the bomb episode."

"And does he," Sister Ursula asked gently, "have feet like a gecko or a pseudopodal finger?"

"Does anybody? Until we can crack the method of this attempt, the best thing to do is to ignore it and concentrate on the others. We saw once before, or rather you saw how an absolutely impossible situation can have a perfectly simple solution. And now tell me what happened when you went calling on Sister Patientia's behalf. Did you see Hilary?"

"He was just getting up when we arrived. I said we'd wait. And then imagine how amazed I was when our hostess came in to entertain us!"

Marshall chuckled. "Not nearly so amazed as she when she found me straddling her husband's body with a bomb ticking beside me. But what did she want with you that day at the convent anyway?"

"I think she wanted what every person wants at some time: peace and quiet, solace and solitude. Oh, I know she's a foolish, flamboyant, melodramatic woman, and quite possibly none too bright. But that's all the more reason why I think she was sincere. Her whole behavior is pointless, aimless. She has no foundation, nothing fixed to cling to. And she came there seeking something solid."

"She has a marriage. That's solid enough for Leona and me."

"She isn't Leona. And you aren't Hilary. In fact, Mrs. Foulkes seemed to have some romantic notion of breaking up that marriage and becoming a nun. 'Abandoning the carnal wedding bed for the spiritual,' she called it, which I assured her was hardly a correct interpretation of the Church's attitude toward marriage."

"So. And do you think there's any danger of her doing that?"

"Only under the most unusual circumstances, say a very long desertion or the hopeless insanity of a husband, would there be even the remotest chance of a convent's accepting a married woman."

"Nothing but virgins?"

"Spinsters at least. And widows, of course."

Marshall jerked his head up. "Widows! There's a sweet thought. Do you suppose— Hell, this is nuts, but when religion goes fanatic no motivation is impossible. Do you suppose she could be so wrapped up in her Bride-of-Christ idea that she might make herself a widow?"

Sister Ursula smiled. "Beautiful, Lieutenant. I congratulate you on as admirably perverse a motive for murder as I have ever heard. But I'm afraid it couldn't apply here. Mrs. Foulkes is a self-indulgent emotionalist rather than a fanatic. I can't imagine her having the intense, the (if I may use the word in all seriousness) damnable wrong-headedness to pursue such a course. And besides, I think I cured her of her desire to join our order."

"How?"

"Simply by showing her what we do. You know why we're called the Sisters of Martha of Bethany. Our founder, Blessed Mother La Roche, was willing to admit that Mary had chosen the better part only because after all Our Lord said so; but she thought there was much to be said for Martha, who did all the housework while her sister was devotedly spiritual. So ours is an order that does the dirty work.

"Some of us nurse, some work with the blind, many of us simply do menial housework for poor invalid mothers. We salvage clothes, we help to establish hostels for youth and what you call floaters . . . Oh, we keep ourselves busy, Lieutenant. We glorify God by doing even unto the least of these all the good that we can. And I'm afraid Mrs. Foulkes' vision of being a nun was composed solely of song and incense and beautiful white garments."

Marshall grinned. "I guess that'll hold her. And what did you talk about this morning?"

"Mostly more of the same. Though she didn't quite out and say it, what she wanted to know was if there were any religious orders in which one could be ecstatically holy by doing nothing whatsoever."

"And did this religious tête-à-tête happen to verge upon, say, rosaries?"

"Oddly enough, yes. But I don't think I learned anything. She brought the matter up herself. She said that she had read a pious memoir of her father-in-law's first wife which mentioned that unusual devotion of the Stations, and she wondered if it was such a rosary that she had seen in my hand. I said it was, and she wanted to know where it came from; but I managed to evade the question. I asked if perhaps her husband had such a rosary as a family relic, but she did a little evading herself and left us with the score tied."

"Love all. Nice Christian result. And goose-eggs seem to be what this case runs to . . ."

"It was nice of you to drive us home," Sister Ursula said after the car had stopped at the convent and she had waked Sister Felicitas. "And your next step?"

"To find out where Austin Carter was at ten-thirty this morning."

"Good luck. And," she added, "watch out for that pseudopod."

5.

There was a sound of rapid typing behind the door of the Nitrosyncretic Laboratory. Marshall knocked.

Over the typing came a casual, "Go to hell!"

Marshall opened the door.

Half the room was filled with mysterious apparatus which he took to be for the developing and printing of pictures. The rest of the room contained a couch, a desk, and bookcases, filled chiefly with pulps. On one wall hung a vivid picture of a space ship being engulfed by what was presumably a space octopus. On the far wall, too distant to read distinctly, was a hand-drawn chronological chart.

Austin Carter typed three lines without looking up. Then he jerked the paper from his machine, laid it on a pile of manuscript, and said, "If I had any conscience, Marshall, I should firmly tell you to go to hell and stay there. But I've reached a good stopping place and I could stand a moment's rest and some beer. Join me?"

"Thanks." Marshall sat on the couch. "The room's a let-down after that admirable sign."

Carter went to a small refrigerator, such as usually serves for infant formula, withdrew two cans of beer, punctured them, and handed one to his guest. "Your health, sir!"

He was tall, this Carter, even a little taller than the Lieutenant, and of one same even slenderness from shoulders to hips. He held himself rather stiffly and moved with precision. Marshall groped for what the man reminded him of, and finally decided that it was Phileas Fogg, who went around the world in eighty days.

"I had an interesting time last night," he said. "Afraid Matt has seduced me into a new field of pleasure."

"Good. Always glad to make converts. Have you read any of Matt's stuff?"

"Not yet."

"He's a comer. Bit weak on the science side, but first-rate on fantasy."

Marshall glanced at the typewriter. "What did I break in in the midst of?"

"That? I think maybe that's going to be fun. Wheels-of-If sort of thing, you know."

"I'm afraid I don't know. Remember I'm an innocent."

"Well, it's— You know a little about modern time theory? J. W. Dunne, or maybe Priestley's popularizations of his work? But we needn't go into the details of that. To put it simply, let's say that every alternate implies its own future. In other words, whenever anything either could happen or not happen, it both does and does not happen, and two different world-lines go on from there."

Marshall thought a moment. "You mean that, say at this point in history, there will be one world if Hitler goes on unchecked or another if he is defeated?"

"Not exactly. That's old and obvious. What I mean is that there will be one world in which he goes on unchecked *and* another in which he is defeated. Each world exists as completely as the other. And so in the past. We are in a world in which the American revolution was a success. There is a world in which it was a failure.

"Now for instance in this story: I'm writing about a world in which Upton Sinclair won the EPIC campaign here in California, but Landon beat Roosevelt in '36. As a result California drifts more to the left and the nation to the extreme right until there is civil war, ending in the establishment on the west coast of the first English-speaking socialist republic. From there on . . . but I'm not too sure yet myself of all the details. You'd better wait and read it."

Marshall whistled. "You boys think of the goddamnedest things."

"Oh, the concept's not original with me. Just this application. I think Stanley Weinbaum was the first to play with it seriously in his *Worlds of If* in the old *Amazing*. Then there's de Camp's brilliant *Wheels of If*, and a Broadway turkey called *If Booth Had Missed*, and an excellent short story of Stephen Vincent Benét's about if Napoleon had been born twenty years earlier. And of course there's *If, or History Rewritten*, by Belloc and Chesterton and Guedalla and a dozen others—noble book!—or on a less cosmic plane, just the *if's* of a human life, there's the Dunsany play *If* or Priestley's beautiful intellectual thriller, *Dangerous Corner.*" He reeled off this comprehensive bibliography as casually as he drank his beer.

"I'll try some of those," said Marshall.

"The best thing in that book of collected *If* essays is one called *If Lee Had Lost at Gettysburg.* You read that title and do a double take and say, 'But he *did* lose.' Then as you read on, you realize that the essay is written as by a professor living in the world in which Gettysburg was a great Southern victory, speculating on the possibilities of an *if*-world in which it was a defeat (that is, of course, our world) and thereby revealing the nature of his own. Dazzling job, and you know who wrote it? Winston Churchill, no less. There's a certain satisfaction in claiming him as a brother fantasy writer."

"I'll watch out for this story of yours," Marshall said, and meant it. "What's its name?"

"*EPIC.* Don Stuart likes one word titles, and that has a good double meaning in this case. Only it won't be under my name; it'll be by Robert Hadley."

"Why?"

"Because all the Austin Carter stories have to fit that chart over there. They're all interdependent—running characters and a consistent scheme of the future. That is, the events of story A are part of the background to story N happening a thousand years later. Sort of a millennial and galactic *comédie humaine,* and hard as hell to keep track of without that chart. And even with it. So whatever's outside the series is by Robert Hadley—that is, in a one-cent market or better. I don't like to hurt the commercial value of those names, so whenever I sell a reject for under a cent it's by Clyde Summers."

Marshall found himself fascinated, almost against his will. Austin Carter was possibly a trifle too fond of hearing himself talk, but he talked well. Another man's shop talk, if the man is intelligent, is the most interesting listening to be found; and this particular brand of shop talk was exceptionally so.

Nevertheless, the Lieutenant was there on duty. "What are your working hours?" he asked.

"I get up around eight-thirty as a rule, and I'm down here pounding by nine-thirty. Grab lunch whenever I feel like knocking off, and then if it's going good work on till three or four. Some men, I know, work best at night; but I like daytimes unless I'm rushing against a deadline."

"You've been working all day on this?"

"Yes, except for a sandwich a little while ago, and doing pretty nicely. It flows today."

"And alone, of course?" Carter looked at him oddly, and Marshall shifted to, "I mean, I wonder if you have many intruders like me?"

"No, and frankly I'd add 'Thank God' if you hadn't happened to hit me just at a moment when I was glad to knock off. Like another beer?"

"Thanks, I think I will. Tell me, Carter. You have a nice speculative mind. Do you ever apply it to other problems than science and fantasy?"

Austin Carter handed over the beer. "You mean like murder?"

"Why do you ask that?"

"I remembered your wife was a fan. Thought maybe she'd been springing some problem on you."

"As a matter of fact, that's just the case. She's trying her hand at a whodunit herself, and she's written herself into a locked room that she can't get out of. I thought maybe you'd like to play."

Carter nodded. "Go ahead. I'll try anything. Kick an idea around enough and sometimes you get places."

"All right: You've got a man with a knife plunged into his back at such an angle that the doctor swears the wound can't possibly be self-inflicted. He's in the study of his apartment, a room that has three doors. One of these leads to a dead end in a bathroom. One has three absolutely reliable witnesses in front of it who swear that no one has used it. The third is chained from the inside, and opens only an inch so that no hand could conceivably have reached in to fasten that chain. The window screens are latched on the inside, and the wall outside the windows, which are three stories from the ground, is absolutely sheer. She was trying a locked room to end all locked rooms, and I'm afraid she's over-reached herself."

Marshall was watching his host carefully throughout this recital, but he failed to detect the slightest flicker of guilty knowledge. Instead a growing grin of amusement spread over Carter's lean face. He took a long swig of beer and announced, "Simplicity itself, my dear Watson."

"That's nice," Marshall observed dryly. "So how did the murderer get out?"

"Well, I can think of three possible methods: A, he never got out because he never was there. The dagger was conveyed through space and plunged into the victim's heart by teleportation. See Charles Fort and don't laugh too hastily. If stones can fall from the ceiling in a closed room, if people can burn to death on unburnt beds, teleporting a dagger should be simple. Not that I'm certain of the angle of the direction on a teleported stab; but aside from that, do you like it?"

"Go on."

"B, the murderer dissembled his component atoms on one

side of the wall, filtered through by osmosis, and reassembled them on the other side. Not that I think much of that one. I'm inclined to believe the conscious or subconscious rearrangement of the corporeal atoms accounts for the change of a werewolf and for the vampire's ability to pass through locked doors; but I doubt if any normal, non-supernatural being has mastered the power."

Marshall entered into the spirit of the thing. "Is there any guarantee that the murderer is normal and non-super-natural?"

"In a whodunit, yes. Rules of the game. In life, of course, you couldn't be so sure, could you? But C, and far more likely, the murderer simply entered and left through the fourth dimension of space. Remember that to a dweller in two-dimensional space, the problem of how to enter a square bounded on all four sides is a fantastic and insoluble one. To us, there's nothing to it; we simply enter through the third dimension. For instance—"

His deft fingers arranged four matches in a square on the desk. "Our friend Ignatius Q. Flatman" (who was a paper clip) "wants to get in there. He tries each wall of the square, *Im*-possible. But I can simply lift up Ignatius . . . so . . . and put him plumb square in the middle of his impossible situation. Just so your murderer could leave the locked room by means of another dimension perpendicular to all three of those we know. Or maybe prettier yet: maybe Something lifted him up out of that room, just as I now lift up Ignatius, and maybe Something will eventually, in Its whimsical mood, drop him . . . so . . . right into your lap."

Marshall picked up Ignatius Q. Flatman and began twisting him cruelly. "That's all?"

"Did I say three? Well, here's a fourth, and this I like best. D, the murderer entered the room by perfectly ordinary methods and left it equally ordinarily, probably by the living-room door."

"But the evidence states—"

"I know. Only you see, the murderer did this at— What time did the murder occur?"

"Between ten-thirty and eleven."

"Then the murderer left around say nine o'clock."

"*Before* the murder?"

"Of course. He committed the murder, set the dials of his trusty time machine back an hour or so, and left the room. He could lock every conceivable exit from the inside and then calmly go back and leave by one of those exits *before* he had locked it. And better yet, to the Impossible Situation he could add the Perfect Alibi. He could then call on the detective in charge of the case and be visiting with him at the exact hour when the murder was being committed."

"I'm groggy," said Marshall.

"You see why we can't have detective stories in science fiction? It's the one impossible form for Don's hypothetical magazine of the twenty-fifth century. So many maneuverings are logically possible that you could never conceivably exclude the guilt of anyone. So you understand now how childishly simple your locked room is to a science fictioneer?"

"I understand." Marshall sounded a little grim.

"And now, Lieutenant, maybe you'll be so kind as to tell me if you have any idea who killed Hilary?"

Marshall was drinking beer when this grenade was so lightly tossed at him. His spluttering did not do his suit any good, and it was the one that had just come back from the cleaners. Now he was on his feet, and towering over the seated Carter.

"Unless," he said slowly, "you can offer me some convincing explanation of that remark, you're going to take a little trip downtown."

"I believe I am supposed at this point to light a cigarette nonchalantly? Very well, I hereby do so." The flame of the match was steady in his hand. "Of course I knew who you were, Lieutenant. No, Matt didn't betray you; but I remembered your name faintly from accounts of the Rheem business and the Harrigan case, and I knew that Concha Duncan was a Harrigan. So when you, a homicide detective presumably on duty, come here and listen obligingly to my ravings until you get a chance to ask where I was this morning, I begin to have my suspicions. Then you propound in detail a 'hypothetical' murder case supposedly being written by your wife. That was too much, Lieutenant. My own wife writes, I know, and very well indeed thank you; but I doubt if she'd do much with two children to look after. No, you miscast your wife so grievously that I became sure I was being Grilled for my Guilty Knowledge of a true murder."

"And why Hilary?" Marshall insisted quietly.

"Then it was? You don't mind if I emit a small *Yippee!*, do you?"

"You admit that you'd be glad to see him dead?"

"Of course. That's why I guessed that your visit concerned him. You'd mentioned him last night, and he was the only person I could think of that I might possibly have a motive for murdering."

For a moment the two men contemplated each other in silence. Then Austin Carter said, "Another beer?"

Marshall relaxed. "No, thanks."

"I've heard sinister rumors that the police won't accept the hospitality of murderers."

"That's the British for you. We're not so ritualistic. But I've got to go talk with Hilary."

Carter raised an eyebrow. "Lieutenant! Spiritualism yet?"

Marshall smiled. "No. You see, Carter, the attack failed. Hilary Foulkes is still very much alive."

Carter was startled and displeased. "Oh well," he said after a pause. "Half a loaf . . ."

"Of course."

"And I'm not under arrest?"

"We'll see what Hilary has to say. Thanks for the beer." Marshall paused in the doorway. "By the bye, confidential-like, which of those methods *did* you use?"

"The time machine, of course. Care for a demonstration?"

"Some other time. Soon."

The typing was resumed almost as soon as Marshall had shut the door behind him.

6.

Marshall mounted the impressive steps leading to the Cedars of Lebanon Hospital. At the Emergency Hospital they had told him, "He was well enough to move all right, and he insisted he wanted to recover in comfort." And the Cedars, which is *the* hospital in Hollywood, was of course far more fitting for a Foulkes scion than the Emergency.

"I'd like to see Mr. Foulkes," he said at the desk.

"Are you from the press?"

"Lord, no. I'm from the police."

"Oh. Just a moment. I'll see if he can see you."

Marshall frowned. "He's all right, isn't he?"

"Yes, but—"

A young man with buck teeth said, "What room's Hilary Foulkes?"

"Are you from the press?" the girl repeated.

"Sure thing, baby?" The youth waved a card.

"Go right on up. Third floor. The floor desk will direct you."

Marshall gasped. "Look!" he expostulated. "You keep the police waiting while you send that pup—"

"I'm sorry, sir. Mr. Foulkes left orders to admit only the press. If you'll wait a—"

But Marshall was already in the elevator. He didn't bother to be polite at the third floor desk. He showed his badge and said "Foulkes?" in a derby-hat voice.

There were five men in Hilary's room, all with pencils and pads. There was a pneumatic nurse deftly arranging flowers. And there was Hilary, propped up in bed, leaning forward to ease the wound in his back but looking otherwise as good as new. "D-e-r," he was saying, "r-i-n, g-e-r. Oh, Lieutenant, glad to see you. Very glad. Can you imagine it? Some of these youths haven't read the Dr. Derringer stories."

"A corrupt generation," Marshall observed. "As soon as the limelight begins to tire your eyes, Mr. Foulkes, there are a few matters I'd like to take up with you."

"Lieutenant," one of the reporters echoed. "Say! You wouldn't be from Homicide, would you?"

"It's an honorary commission from the Swiss navy," said Marshall, and watched the nurse abstractedly while Hilary made certain that every significant detail of his father's career went into the reporters' notebooks. Two books, presumably rushed from home for the occasion, stood by the bedside: *Life and Dr. Derringer: An Autobiography* by Fowler Foulkes, and *Foulkes the Man* by Darrell Wimpole. But Hilary never found the need to refer to them. He knew his subject as thoroughly as an actor in *Tobacco Road* must have known his lines toward the end of the run, or perhaps more appropriately, as thoroughly as a priest knows the words of the daily sacrifice of the Mass. The ritual words had their ritual gesture too. Instead of the gnawing of a turnip or the sign of the Cross, this was the pulling of a lobe. And with this echoing tug at the ear, Hilary seemed to recapture a little of the domineering dignity so characteristic of his father's publicity photographs.

"By the time," Marshall said when the last of the pressmen had left, "that all that goes out over the A. P. and the U. P., it ought to sell a few thousand more Foulkes items."

"You mean . . . ?" Hilary laughed. "Why, Lieutenant, I do believe you think me guilty of playing this up simply to stimulate the influx of royalties. Heavens, I am shocked at such an idea. Shocked. It's simply that I owe so much to my father. Everything, you might say."

"You might."

"So naturally I feel that it is incumbent upon me to keep his memory green. I could hardly pass up the one pleasant aspect of this most astonishing occurrence."

"You're cool, Mr. Foulkes, aren't you?"

"I'm alive," said Hilary simply. "Alive. And that in itself is such a sheer and beautiful relief that I don't care to contemplate how close to death I was."

Marshall turned to the nurse. "Could you go have a beer or something? I'm afraid this conference is confidential official business."

The nurse looked from the badge to the Lieutenant's face. "I like Dick Tracy's jaw better," she said, but she left.

Hilary leaned farther forward. "Tell me, Lieutenant, have you arrested him?"

Marshall nearly sighed with relief. "Then you did see who it was. And I suppose the press learned it before I did. Well, come on. There'll be a warrant out for him in nothing flat."

"Oh no, Lieutenant. You misunderstand me. I thought that by now *you'd* know."

Marshall swore. "I not only don't know Who, but I haven't the remotest idea of How. But start in at the beginning; maybe your story will give me some sort of a lead."

"I was talking to you," Hilary said slowly. "You remember. You were asking me about Austin Carter—" He broke off sharply. "Did he do it? Austin Carter, I mean?"

"Sure," said Marshall sourly. "He confessed. He did it with his little gadget."

"I don't understand."

"Do I? But go ahead. We'll catch up on Mr. Carter later."

"Very well. I was talking to you, as I say, when suddenly I heard a light footfall behind me. I started to turn, but before I could do so I felt a terrible pain between my shoulder-blades. A terrible pain. It was accompanied by a blow so strong that it knocked me forward against the desk. I tried to rise, but I lost my balance and fell to the floor. And that is the last that I remember until I was in the Emergency Hospital."

"You saw nothing, and you heard only a 'light footfall?'"

"Correct, Lieutenant."

"Could you gage anything by that footfall? Male or female? Large or small?"

"I'm afraid not. I didn't have time to listen carefully."

"It surprised you?"

"Very much."

"Then wouldn't that perhaps indicate male and heavy? If the sound could possibly have meant the not abnormal presence of your wife or the maid, you mightn't have been so startled."

Hilary beamed. "Beautiful, Lieutenant, beautiful. I am convinced that you will have apprehended this villain in no time. No time at all."

"Now tell me: When you went into the study, was the night chain fastened on the hall door?"

"I don't know. I'm sure I don't know. It usually is."

"And were the windows open or closed?"

"Closed."

"All of them?"

"I open one window when I go in to settle down for my morning's work on the estate accounts. But this morning I had come directly from the breakfast table to the phone."

Marshall grunted. "Gecko," he said.

Hilary peered at him curiously. "Yes, Lieutenant?"

"Hell, I might as well tell you. Even if a window was God knows why opened, nobody could get in or out through those windows."

"No. Of course not."

"Your wife and two visiting nuns were watching the door to the living-room. No one came out between the phone call and when I found you. And the night chain was on the hall door."

"My . . . !" said Hilary in an awed voice. "My . . . !"

"In short, if it weren't for the medical evidence on your wound, I'd suspect you of staging the whole thing for the sake of that press conference you just had—all purely to keep your father's memory green, of course."

"Lieutenant! Then this . . . Why, it's a locked room! Heavens, I am fortunate!"

"Fortunate?"

"Because it's you on the case. That Harrigan business was a locked room too, and look how neatly you disposed of that. *So* neatly. Why, you're the ideal man for this. And it's the ideal case for you."

"That's nice."

"And there must be some way of telling who was in there and attacked me. Fingerprints?" he suggested with the layman's blind confidence.

"Only yours and the maid's. Even yours alone on the dagger, with superimposed smudges, some of which were doubtless made in extracting it from you. Which while we're at it . . ." He reached into his breast pocket and produced a murderously beautiful piece of Persian metal work. "Do you know this?"

"Why, of course! That's my paper cutter. It was my father's. The Zemindar of Kota Guti presented it to him after reading *The Purple Light.* So many people think that was my father's best book, although he himself always preferred *The Missions in Twilight.* What do you think, Lieutenant?"

"I'll take up esthetics with you later, Mr. Foulkes. God knows there's nothing I like better than talking about Dr. Derringer; but right now I want to know if this back-stabbing paper cutter was on your desk this morning?"

"Frankly, Lieutenant, I don't know. Frankly. I was hurrying to answer the phone. I didn't notice my desk."

"It's unlikely that the murderer reached over your shoulder to snatch up the weapon. It was probably taken earlier, which would indicate . . . Was it there yesterday?"

"Yesterday? Yes. Yes, I'm sure. I used it to open my mail."

"At what time?"

"About three."

"Then at some time between three yesterday and ten-thirty this morning, this knife was stolen. Or even if the murderer somehow snaffled it right from under your nose, its use still implies familiarity with your study." Marshall ran his thumb along the blade. "See how short that is? That's what you probably owe your life to. The same wound with a longer blade could have been fatal."

"But Lieutenant . . ." Hilary's round face was puzzled.

"Yes?"

"There isn't anyone familiar with my study. Oh, of course Ron and Jenny and Alice. But all these others that we've spoken of, the people whom I may have offended as executor—that's all been by mail."

"So. And your brother-in-law?"

"Vance? But he's I don't know where and anyway . . ."

Marshall rose. "Just the same, I'd like to have a complete list of all your potential business enemies."

"I think Jenny could give you that more easily than I could. Miss Green, that is. She sometimes acts as my secretary, you know. She understands all about files and things."

"I'll speak to her. And I want you to know, for your own comfort, Mr. Foulkes, that there's going to be a police guard in the corridor of this hospital until you leave and another at your home thereafter. And I'd advise you not to see any newspapermen except in groups, and even then not without checking their credentials. I would advise you not to see them at all, but one impossible problem is enough to tackle at a time."

"Thank you, Lieutenant. Thank you. And you'll let me know when you catch my murderer, won't you?"

That last request was so touchingly childish that it set Marshall off on a new train of thought. Perhaps that was the key to Hilary: his infinite childishness. Like a child he avidly hoarded his treasures, like a child he marveled adoringly at the perfection of his wonderful father, like a child . . . Marshall thought of the ripe-fleshed Veronica Foulkes. What would it be like to be married to a child?

A telephone booth reminded him of a distasteful but necessary piece of routine work. He stepped in, dropped his nickel, and dialed the Duncans' number. They lived in the apartment house across the street, but he preferred the impersonality of a phone for this purpose.

He was glad that Concha answered. "Terence Marshall speaking," he said, "and don't tell Matt. Is he in earshot?"

"He went out for a walk. But what is this, Lieutenant? I suppose I ought to feel flattered when a handsome officer asks me to keep secrets from my husband, but I'm just plain puzzled."

"Only this: Where was Matt this morning?"

"Working, of course."

"You were in the apartment too?"

"I was ironing and mending. All but when I went out to shop."

"How long were you gone?"

"A half hour or more. Maybe almost an hour."

"And this was when?"

"Between ten and eleven. But Lieutenant, you sound like an alibi. I mean, like trying to check one. Are you—?"

"Please, Concha. You'll understand soon enough what this is all about. And you'll see why I insist you don't say a word to Matt about this. For the sake of routine, I had to check up on him; but there's no use worrying him."

"And he's in the clear?" Concha's voice was breathless.

"He's in the clear," Marshall lied, and hung up.

7.

The newspapers did well by the event. Even in the midst of wars and rumors of wars, the mysterious stabbing of a celebrity is always welcome, and Hilary had gladly provided further details of bombs and poisoned chocolates. The story was enriched by a brief biography of Fowler Foulkes and a condensed bibliography of his best known works; and all in all neither Hilary nor his publishers had the slightest cause for complaint.

Bernice Carter was reading the evening paper when her husband emerged from the Nitrosyncretic Laboratory. "Fate, milord, is just," she observed.

"Hilary?" Austin Carter asked casually.

"Uh huh. Somebody tried to carve him up under highly unlikely circumstances. That'll teach him to frustrate film sales. Here's the paper; you can— But hold on a minute!"

Carter struck a match on the stone fireplace and lit a cigarette. "Yes?"

"How did you know I meant Hilary?"

"People," he sighed, "keep asking me how I know things. Haven't they any faith in E.S.P.? Don't they realize my latent potentialities as a telepath?"

"But how did you know?"

"My trusting helpmate . . . That Lieutenant Marshall dropped in this afternoon and, as I believe the proper phrase goes, grilled me. Oh, very unobtrusively, you understand."

"And what did you do?"

"What should I do? I confessed, of course. Worked out a magnificent scheme for committing murder with a time machine. I think it'll make a good novelet for Don."

Bernice smiled. "Scavenger! Here I try to frame my imaginings out of whole cloth, but you simply grab everything that happens and twist it into science fiction. Thank God at least for Don's strict standards of censorship. They're all that prevents my most intimate secrets from being broadcast to every newsstand at a cent a word."

"A cent and a half, I think," Austin Carter said judiciously. "They'd surely rate a bonus."

"But, sweet . . ." Bernice's cool voice was for once a trifle perturbed.

"Yes, madam?"

"If the Lieutenant thought you were worth grilling . . . You haven't—you aren't tied up with this in any way, are you? You didn't . . . do anything to Hilary?"

"No, madam." His voice was level and convincing.

Bernice smiled again. "Then why the hell didn't you?"

8.

Veronica Foulkes threw down the paper. Her teacup rattled ominously as she stirred it. "Not a word about me! Why, Hilary might not even have a wife for all that . . . that rag says."

"Come now, Veronica," Jenny Green protested. "How can you worry about a trifle like that when Hilary's lying there in that hospital—"

"—in perfect ease and comfort with a beautiful nurse and reporters simply flocking around him. No, Jenny, I haven't much sympathy to waste on Hilary. Heaven knows how he got into this trouble, but I think he's come out of it very luckily. Hilary doesn't know what nerves are, any more than you do."

"But is he out of it? If they've made all these attempts, they aren't going to stop now, are they?"

Veronica set down the cup she was lifting. "My God, Jenny! That's true. They might come back and . . . Oh but no. That dreadful Lieutenant has given him a police guard and it's coming home with him and we're perfectly safe. So do relax, dear. Can't you see how I need soothing? A woman with my nerves can stand only so much."

Jenny Green left a fresh cup untouched and rose. "I see. You know, Ron, I can stand only so much too."

"You can stand . . . ! Oh but my dear! And what concern is it of yours, I'd like to know? Oh, I know Hilary is your cousin, and very fortunate you've been having such a lovely home here with us, and that's all the more reason you should show a little consideration for me. How many wives, I ask you, would let their husbands bring relatives into their own house to live with them?"

"Come off it, Veronica." Jenny Green was not quite smiling. "If you hadn't tolerated me in your lovely home, Hilary would have had to have a typist. And how many wives would let their husband et cetera as above?"

Veronica laughed. "Now that, my dear Jenny, is simply non-sense. Do you think for a moment that I could be *jealous* of Hilary? Do you think I don't know . . ." She stopped herself. "All I can say is, if any woman could ever lure Hilary into being unfaithful to me, she'd be welcome to what she got. And what do you think that means to a woman of my—"

"Veronica." Jenny's voice was cold. "Sometimes I think it would be better for everyone, and certainly for Hilary, if you would simply stop talking and go ahead and take either a lover or the veil. But I'm afraid the trouble is you'd want to do both."

"How dare . . . !" Veronica's ordinarily throaty voice grew speechlessly shrill. "If Hilary ever— Where are you going?"

"To my room. I need to do some typing for Hilary."

Veronica Foulkes, left alone, bit her lips, stamped her foot, and squeezed from her eyes the start of a spate of tears. Then abruptly she reconsidered, wiped her eyes, and examined her face in a compact mirror. It was possible that reporters might call.

9.

The green-furred, six-legged corpse of the blasted thryx slung across his brawny shoulders, Captain Comet made his laborious way over the endless Martian desert. For two days he had seen no sign of life, save for the thryx, whose murderous attack he had foiled at the last minute by the decompo-rays of his blaster.

Now even the blaster was no longer of use. It needed recharging, and that must wait until he found the space ship again. His emergency sythetic rations were dwindling too. Gah-Djet, the mechanical brain, was in the hands of the xurghil smugglers. Adam Fink was a clanking prisoner in the power of the mad priests of Ctarbuj. And the Princess Zurilla . . .

Captain Comet shook his weary head to clear it of these dismal thoughts. The bright orange blood of the thryx dripped down his shoulders as he mounted yet another of the endless dunes of rosy Martian sand. Might the space ship lie beyond this one? His radio-sensitive indicator gave clear evidence of a source of atomic power somewhere nearby.

He topped the dune. And there, spread out before in the shadow of evening, gleamed . . .

Was it a typical Martio-mirage? Or was it . . . his heart stopped . . . was it the fabulously Lost City of Xanatopsis?

Joe Henderson jerked the paper from the typewriter. "Now I wonder," he said quietly in answer to his own question. Then he looked at the couch. "Still counting ping-pennies?"

M. Halstead Phyn granted a negative. "Reading the paper."
He was silent for a minute, then let out a loud *Kee-rist!* "But in
spades!" he added feelingly.

"What is it?"

"Look at this. Just look at this, will you?"

Joe Henderson read the article. "My!" was all he said.

The agent was aflame. "But look, Joe. It's perfect. See, it says
here this is only the latest of a series of attempts. All right, so if
anybody's working on a series he's not going to stop with this in-
stallment. He's going to carry right on, and the tag's going to put
the quietus on Hilary."

"But why should you be so hepped up about it?"

"Why? Remember the deal with *Galactic* about the reprints?
So now Hilary gets polished off, and who'll be the executor of the
estate? I don't know for sure, you understand, but it's odds on that
it'll be Vance Wimpole. All right, so Vance is executor. We can talk
to him. He's in the business. And after publicity like this, a Dr. Derringer reprint series'll clean up. We won't be able to turn 'em out
fast enough. They'll melt away from the stands, but melt! It's perfect. Joey boy, if you ever prayed, do some tall praying for me now!"

"I don't know," Joe Henderson drawled. "I don't know as I
could pray for a man's death. Not even," he added after mature
reflection, "for Hilary's."

"It's dog eat dog in this racket, Joe. The hell with a conscience."

"Besides," Henderson added practically, "how can you be so
sure Vance'll kick through?"

"I'm sure enough. Oh, I'm sure all right." A new and even
brighter light began to glint in Phyn's little eyes. "You know what,
Joe? Vance never uses an agent, does he? Always sells direct?"

"Far's I know."

"I think . . . Yes, I think I'm going to handle all D. Vance Wimpole's sales after this. He doesn't know it yet; but he's going to be glad to do it. Glad." Phyn relaxed on the couch, grinning to himself.

10.

Concha Duncan set the steak on the table at once proudly and ruefully. "I'll have to learn to be a better cook, Matt. I can broil a good steak, but . . ."

Matt whetted the carving knife, with a gleam in his eyes betokening an already whetted appetite. "Steak's all right by me. Show me the man that doesn't welcome it."

"I know. But you keep saying I ought to shop within the budget and I keep getting good advice from Leona on what to do with cheap cuts and they go all wrong so I get some more steak, and look what it does to the budget If you'd only let me . . ."

Matt cut through crisp brown into succulent red and watched rich warm juice flow onto the platter. "Now, darling. We won't go into that again. We are living on my income. Such, God help us, as it is."

"All right." Concha seated herself and began to serve the peas and the mashed potatoes. "I think they're good this time for once. No lumps. Maybe I'll reach up to Leona's standards yet."

"Leona," Matt stated, "is probably the most admirable wife man ever had. And I wouldn't swap you for her, not even with Terry and Ursula and the Lieutenant's salary thrown in."

Concha blew a kiss across the table and said, "Sweet."

"And the potatoes are wonderful."

"The man said they were an extra good shipment. Oh, when I was out shopping I ran into Doris Clyde. You wouldn't know her, but she was at school with me. Awfully nice girl. And first thing

I thought when I saw her was, 'Maybe here's a girl for Joe.' Only it turns out she's married. He's a draftsman out at Douglas and doing ever so well."

"Everybody we meet outside of the M.L.S. is either in aircraft or in social service. They're the two great professions of the day. And the draft coming up for tomorrow. I bet you could get some symbolism out of that if you worked on it . . . But why is it you women are always trying to find a girl for Joe? Bernice is just as bad. Why not leave the poor boy alone?"

"Because he's . . . I don't know . . . he's so kind of sweet and helpless. You go all over motherly and you think the poor lamb needs a Good Woman."

"He wouldn't want a Good Woman if he had her. I think what Joe really wants is an honest-to-god bitch unhung, like his villainesses. Good women bore him terribly—or at any rate, that's his story."

"But the . . . the other sort'd be so bad for him. He's so kind and gentle."

"Then leave well enough alone. I'm glad your girl friend was married. Any other exciting adventures while marketing?"

"No . . . Matt . . . ?"

"Yes?"

"Were you home all the time I was gone?"

"Sure. Why? Expecting a delivery or something?"

"No, it's just . . . Oh, I just wondered." They ate in silence for a moment. "Matt . . . do you think you really ought to talk that way you did the other night at the Marshalls? I mean about . . . you know."

"About murdering Hilary?" Matt asked cheerfully. "Darling, was that shiver what is technically known as a wince? I've always wondered what one looked like."

Concha laughed. "Don't be silly. A wince is what you pull buckets out of wells with."

"Oh. I thought it was something you made jelly out of."

"Or of course," Concha suggested, "it could be what you start a bedtime story with. Wince upon a time . . ."

Matt looked into her eyes. "All right. Bright gay nonsense dialog. Swell. Only something's worrying you. What's wrong about Hilary?"

"I . . . I heard it on the radio while I was working in the kitchen this afternoon. Matt: Somebody did try to kill Hilary."

Her husband stared at her. "Well shut my big mouth!" he said softly.

11.

In the lounge car of the Lark, Pullman train from San Francisco to Los Angeles, a tall thin man with a pale face and flaming hair sat contentedly with two highballs and a blonde.

". . . and just as I fired," he was saying, "the jaguar sprang between us. The force of the rifle bullet was so great that it carried him right on into the gaping jaws of the lion, so violently that the lion choked to death. Thereby saving me one bullet."

"I don't believe it," said the blonde.

D. Vance Wimpole smiled to himself. "I'll try another one. This evening I read in the paper, much to my astonishment, that a murderous attack had been made on my brother-in-law. He was stabbed almost to death in a room that was locked or watched at every entrance. No one could have got in or out, and there in the middle of the room lay my brother-in-law with a dagger in his back. Do you believe that?"

"No," said the blonde.

"I don't blame you." Wimpole twirled his drink meditatively. "I don't blame you at all. That's why I'm going to Los Angeles, you know. If anybody's really set on murdering my brother-in-law, I wouldn't think of missing the fun for worlds. But meanwhile—"

"Hn?" said the blonde.

"Meanwhile the night is young and first we're going to have another drink and then there's no telling what may develop."

"I believe that," said the blonde.

12.

Sister Ursula had learned nothing fresh from the newspaper accounts, but the facts of Hilary's locked room continued to plague and distract her as she aided Sister Rose in arranging the altar for tomorrow's Mass.

Tomorrow would be November second, All Souls' Day, the day that the church consecrates especially to the memory of the dead. Hilary would recover from this wound; that seemed certain. But murderers are a notoriously persistent breed. By another All Souls' Day, would there be his departed soul to pray for? And perhaps another, a soul that had departed this body in a small chamber filled with gas?

And there was the floater Tarbell, so nebulous a character, whose soul had already gone to the private judgment. *Animula vagula nebula,* Sister Ursula thought wryly, and then shifted to more appropriate church Latin: *Requiescat in pace.*

And is not that, she mused, a fitting prayer for the living too? Let them rest in peace. Those who suffer and struggle and strive to kill, let them rest in peace. Let us rest in peace.

INTERLUDE:
Sunday, November 2 to Thursday, November 6, 1941

URSULA MARSHALL, happily full of formula, kicked her chubby legs. It was a friendly and joyful gesture, but it did not help the process of changing her diaper.

Her four-year-old brother looked on wide-eyed. "That looks like fun maybe, daddy. Is it?"

Lieutenant Marshal said, "What do you think?"

Terry gave the problem due attention. "Maybe yes," he announced. "Can I do it sometime, daddy?"

Marshall's large hands moved with surprising deftness. "By the time you can reach on top of a bathinet, I hope your sister won't be needing it"

"Then could I have another sister maybe?"

"We'll see about that. Perhaps we ought to get you practised up for when you have one of your own. And when you do, Terry, remember these words of fatherly advice: The more you help your wife with being a mother, the more time and energy she'll have for being a wife."

"What's energy?"

"Breakfast!" Leona called from the kitchen, thereby sparing her husband the grievous semantic problem of defining a term with no visible referend.

"You see, Terry?" he elucidated as they sat to table. "Because I got up and gave Ursula her early bottle, your mother had time" (he omitted the confusing new word) "to whip me up a buckwheat batter."

"I want a buckwheat batter," Terry announced inevitably.

"There dear," said Leona soothingly. "You've got your nice mush."

"Leona." Marshall firmly overrode Terry's outspoken comments on the nice mush. "Did you get anywhere sleeping on it?"

"Nowhere at all. That does usually work with mystery novels. I read them up to where the detective says, 'All the clews are now in your hands, my dear Whozit,' and then I go to sleep and in the morning I know the answer. But this didn't work out. Maybe it's because all the clews aren't in our hands."

"That's just it. There aren't any clews but a rosary and a photograph. Everything's so god—"

Leona glanced sideways at their son. "Terence!"

"So terribly nebulous. And a corpse is a—a darn sight more cooperative than a living victim who sits calmly back swiddling his press notices and murmurs gently, 'All right. Now you tell me who did it.'"

To most children a corpse at the breakfast table would be unbearably exciting. But Terry was too young yet to realize how romantically thrilling his father's profession would seem to others. Murder and corpses were just funny things that his parents talked about a lot. He now barely heard the word and went right on with his mush, which he had remembered that he liked.

"What I keep coming back to," Leona reflected, "is Sister Ursula's reference to the Invisible Man. She doesn't say things at random. So I reread that Chesterton story last night."

"Does it help?"

"It's the same moral as so many of his, of course: the easy danger of overlooking the obvious. The Invisible Man is the postman. All the witnesses swear that no one came near the house, and of course they never think of the man who comes and goes all the time. But who's your Invisible Man here? You checked on the maid?"

"Naturally."

"And—I know this sounds funny, but still . . . and Sister Felicitas?"

Marshall laughed. "I see what you mean. She is the Invisible Woman right enough."

"I knew you'd laugh at me. But remember the Holmes dictum: Eliminate the impossible . . ."

"Dr. Derringer put it another way in one of his scientific researches: 'Eliminate the impossible. Then if nothing remains, some part of the "impossible" was possible.' I think that might be more helpful here. But to please you, darling, I'll check on the good Sister. Her motive, I suppose, was to avenge the insult to Sister Patientia in the Braille work?"

"How many times, Terence, have I heard you say, 'Juries convict on evidence, not on motives?'"

"All right. But I doubt if Sister Felicitas could stay awake long enough for a murder . . . And what are the chances on some more b-u-c-k—"

"Buckwheat batter!" Terry crowed.

2.

Jenny Green received Marshall with a friendly, "Good morning, Lieutenant."

"And to you, Miss Green."

"Veronica's at the hospital," she explained.

Marshall repressed a sigh of relief. "It's chiefly you I wanted to see anyway. You and that room."

"Me? How can I help you? But I'd be so glad if I could."

"You were Mr. Foulkes' secretary, weren't you?"

The girl shuddered. "Please don't say *were*, Lieutenant. You make it sound as though—as though whoever it was had succeeded."

"Sorry. Professional habit, I guess. This living corpse situation is a trifle irregular. You are, then?"

"Yes."

"Then might I ask you to go through your files and make me a list of everyone Mr. Foulkes ever had any serious financial or literary disputes with?"

She half-smiled. "I'm afraid that will take a while."

"I'm not surprised. But meanwhile I'll see if I can prise some secret out of that devilish study."

There's a time-honored dictum, Marshall thought as he stared at the unresponsive walls, that the more complex a situation has been made, the easier it is to solve. The simply conceived crime is the brain-twister. Which is doubtless true enough. Most complexities unravel instantly once you get hold of the right end of the thread. But when there are no threads . . .

Now there has to be a reason for any locked room situation. Criminals do not create locked rooms out of sheer devilment. The simplest reason is to make the death look like suicide; but if that were the case here, Hilary would have been stabbed in the front or the side. That was out. So was a framed accident. The reason might be to give the criminal an alibi. It had been in that Harrigan case. But of possible suspects so far, the only ones with alibis at all had such impeccable ones that they could not be questioned for an instant. Perhaps in Miss Green's list . . .

Or there is one kind of locked room without a reason. That is the accidental one, never planned by the criminal. Some little thing might have gone wrong by chance to produce this effect of apparent impossibility.

. . . *and if nothing remains, some part of the "impossible" was possible* . . .

Marshall clucked irritably, left the study, and followed the sound of typing. He found Jenny Green methodically hunting through files and copying down names with a line or two to identify the cause of trouble in each case. She looked up and asked, "Yes, Lieutenant?"

"Did you, Miss Green, ever grab a stick by the wrong end and then find the end wasn't there?"

"Am I supposed to answer?"

"Rhetorical. It's what I've been doing. I'm grabbing at the factual clews and I don't know enough about the people. Maybe you can help me?"

Jenny waved a hand at the typewriter. "But I don't know anything about those people. To me they're just names to type at the heads of letters."

"I don't mean those people necessarily. I mean Mr. Foulkes, his wife, his brother-in-law—you."

"Lieutenant, surely you—"

"I don't suspect anybody yet. I don't unsuspect anybody either. But the whole thing focuses around Hilary Foulkes, and I've got to know this—this Foulkes focus. The Foulkes-lore, if you'll forgive me."

"I'll try. I mean, try to tell you; I don't think I can forgive you. But sit down. And you can light your pipe if you want."

The only furniture beside the chair at the typing table consisted of a bed and a low boudoir chair covered with flowered chintz. Marshall chose the latter and did not feel so out of place as one might have expected; it was almost identical with the chair in which he gave Ursula her bottles.

"I've gathered," Jenny Green began slowly, "how people feel about Cousin Hilary. Sometimes I can even understand it a little. But he's been so different with me that I . . . Well, it isn't only that I owe a lot to him. My mother was some sort of forty-second cousin of Fowler Foulkes. My father was killed in the last war, before I was born. Mother went back to grandfather and I was born at the vicarage. Mother wasn't ever really well after that, and when grandfather died . . . Oh, I'm not going to tell you the whole story, but before Hilary came to England and decided to track down his transatlantic relatives, there were days when we didn't eat. So I feel gratitude all right, but more than that too. Hilary is . . . well, he's nice to me. Quite aside from being good to me, if you understand."

"I think I do."

"But to make you see him . . . You'll have to go back. You'll have to see Fowler Foulkes. Yes, and Darrell Wimpole too. I never knew them, but from their books, and from hearing their children talk— You must read those books, Lieutenant Foulkes' autobiography and the Wimpole memoir. They might help."

"I shall. But if meanwhile you—"

"Fowler Foulkes . . . well, he was a lot like Dr. Derringer except for his appearance. He looked very much like Hilary; but I suppose you remember pictures of him?"

"Yes."

"But he acted as though he did have a barrel chest and a black spade beard and a silver-headed cane. He boomed and he dominated and he crushed people with his trenchant wit. It wasn't a pose. He was the real thing; a major personality. And Darrell Wimpole—"

"That's Mrs. Foulkes' father?"

"Yes. He was . . . he was the same sort of thing gone wrong. He was a major personality that didn't come off. He'd started with a freak success in some strange mathematical theory that sounded brilliant and was later disproved. He wrote a little and kept being on the verge of success. He was great at dominating salons until anyone of interest appeared. Then when he met Foulkes, he changed entirely and became just a Boswellian satellite. Do you understand it? Because he couldn't succeed in being what he wanted, he could write about its perfection in Foulkes, because he was simply a Foulkes manque. Does it make sense?"

"I think so. And the children of these men?"

"It's as though there were only so much vital energy, so much perfection; and father and son had to split it between them. Hilary's father, you see, achieved himself completely."

"So Hilary lives simply on his father's energy and is nothing in himself?"

"I wasn't going to put it so cruelly, Lieutenant; but that's much what I meant."

"And Wimpole's son? What is his name . . . Vance?"

"Vance . . ." Jenny Green leaned back and clasped her hands around her knees. Her eyes blurred away from their usual alertness. "Now Vance—"

At that point the doorbell rang. "And Alice is still out marketing." She jumped to her feet. "We'll finish this later, Lieutenant."

Marshall looked at the sheet in the typewriter. Scads of names, many unfamiliar. Webb Marlowe, Cleve Cartmill . . . Austin Carter, but he knew that already . . . Matt too, of course.

Marshall listened and heard Miss Green's tentative "Yes?" as she greeted, obviously, a complete stranger. Then there was a voice, a voice he knew slightly, saying, "I'd like to speak to Mr. Foulkes' business manager."

"I'm afraid Mr. Foulkes is his own business manager."

And God knows that's true enough, thought Marshall, trying to place the not quite unfamiliar voice. Then it identified itself.

"My name is Phyn. M. Halstead Phyn."

There was a smile in the girl's voice. "Oh yes. I remember typing letters to you. In fact, I was just about to refer to that file."

So the little agent, too, had had his troubles with Hilary. Hardly surprising. But perhaps worth looking into.

Marshall stepped out into the living-room. There were two men at the door. The second was that deceptively young and callow-seeming individual who was, Matt had informed him, unexcelled at either hack or creative fantasy. Henderson, that was the name.

Phyn registered surprise. "Mr. Marshall!" he exclaimed.

"I'm afraid we met under false pretenses, Phyn. The handle is Lieutenant. Homicide. Miss Green, is it all right with you if I ask these gentlemen to step in?"

"Certainly, Lieutenant. I'll finish that list for you."

"Thank you. Please come in, gentlemen."

Phyn sidled in uneasily. Henderson seemed lankily unperturbed by the Lieutenant's status, but somewhat awed by the apartment.

"I want," Marshall explained, "to ask you boys a few questions. First let's get the name straight. What beside Phyn?"

"M. Halstead. And it's P-h-y-n."

"The M. stands for?"

Phyn hesitated, and Henderson laconically supplied, "Michael."

Marshall grinned. "And I'll bet the Phyn used to be F-i-n-n. Can't blame you for changing it. Mickey Finn isn't a good name for a man in a position of trust like an agent."

"Does anybody," Phyn asked ruefully, "trust an agent?"

"That I can't say. But I'm willing to try. Now tell me just why you should choose this bright morning to visit the scene of the crime?"

Phyn wisely chose not to answer the implication. "I don't know how much you understand about the literary business, Lieutenant—"

"The pulp racket," said Joe Henderson.

"A little, Phyn. And by the time this case is over, I expect to be an authority. But what should I understand to account for your call?"

"You do at least know the standing of the Dr. Derringer opi? Of course. Well, you see—"

It was then that Veronica Foulkes threw open the hall door and caroled joyously, "Look who's here!" When she saw the Lieutenant, her voice fell and she repeated, in a markedly different tone, "Just *look* who's here . . . !"

But her reaction hardly mattered. The pale and wiry man behind her took over and dominated the scene. Jenny Green had abandoned her typing and come at Veronica's call. Now she ran eagerly into the thin man's arms and said "Vance," very simply and happily. And D. Vance Wimpole was kissing her and greeting Phyn and Henderson and getting introduced to Marshall and demanding unlimited rounds of drinks all at once.

The next half hour was something nightmarish for Marshall. He wanted to talk with this brother-in-law for at least two reasons: first, because he might have information, being in the trade, of Hilary's business relations with science fictionists, and being in the family, of Hilary's relations with his wife and cousin (Miss Green's family narrative, though clear and suggestive, could always bear checking against another source); and second, because Marshall was markedly interested in just where the hell Wimpole himself had been for the past several weeks.

But there was no opportunity for coherent questioning. Wimpole had welcomed Marshall eagerly enough (". . . delighted to meet the man who's going to unlock Hilary's locked room . . . rotten taste in a murderer to go out of his way to be difficult, isn't it?"), but then he was off on the narrative of his travels or trading shop talk with the agent and the other writer, whose presence here at the Foulkes apartment he seemed to accept with infinite casualness.

And sandwiched in between narrative and shop talk were fraternal kisses for Veronica, affianced kisses for Jenny, and a meticulous attention to the replenishing of glasses which suggested that Wimpole was host here rather than guest.

One unasked question he did in a way answer.

". . . and I'm having the polar bear mounted. Make a wonderful rug for you, Ron. Or should I save it till Jenny and I set up housekeeping? Which by the way, Joe. Beautiful idea hit me. What happens if you mount a werewolf skin as a rug? Does it keep changing so you every so often look down and find you're treading on human parchment? Don't think I'll use it. Too busy. You can have it if you want."

Veronica shuddered. "Grisly!"

"Isn't it? Almost as bad, good mother, as lock a room and

in it stab my brother. -In-law, of course, but that wouldn't rime. Which by the way, Lieutenant, where do I stand on the suspect list?"

"High," said Marshall. In the presence of Vance Wimpole, anyone tended to become as laconic as Joe Henderson.

"I thought so. They say you're a shrewd man. It wouldn't be hard to see what a pretty motive I have. Financially, I mean. You can disregard the incest angle. So here. This is what they left me of my ticket and Pullman stub. Proves I was in San Francisco yesterday. Just thought you might like to know. Keep them if you wish. Press them with your dance programs. And did I write you, Ron, about that amazing sect of christianized voodoo I found in Santo Domingo?"

Marshall slipped the stubs back in their envelope and tucked them into his wallet. He'd have them checked, of course; but he had a fairly precise estimation of their worth without that. He only half listened to the narrative, colorfully incredible as it was, while he surveyed the other listeners.

They were themselves not too attentive to the words; but with one exception they were raptly fixed on the speaker. Jenny Green looked devotedly glad at this reunion, which was to be expected. What was less expected was that Wimpole's sister gazed upon him quite as devotedly, quite as—hell, you might almost say amorously as his fiancée. Phyn's interest was harder to analyze; he regarded D. Vance Wimpole almost as he might an un-anticipatedly favorable contract, and seemed to be studying him, forming in his shrewd mind the proper approach to extract the last drop of profit. But why? Was this purely some angle of the agency business, or did it somehow tie in with the Foulkes situation?

The one exception was Joe Henderson. Marshall had not

seen him notice a woman before, not as a woman, that is. Miss Green, Mrs. Carter, Concha, even Leona he had hardly more than glanced at. But now his stare adhered fixedly to Veronica Foulkes.

Marshall would have liked to stay. There were possibilities that might develop here with another round or two. But the presence of a police official would simply act as whatever was the opposite of a catalyst and damn it he was beginning to think in the quasi-scientific jargon of these boys. And besides, there was plenty of routine, both Foulkes and Tarbell, waiting for him at headquarters.

At the point in Wimpole's narrative where the christianized voodoo sect had developed a schism on the question of whether it was valid to baptize zombies, Marshall rose.

"I've some other matters to check up on," he said regretfully. "But I want to see you later, Mr. Wimpole. Where are you staying?"

"Here, naturally." It was Veronica Foulkes who answered.

"I'll sleep in the study," Wimpole explained. "Let you know, Lieutenant, if anything says, 'Now we're locked in for the night.'"

"I'll phone you, then. And when is your husband expected home from the hospital, Mrs. Foulkes?"

"Tomorrow or next day. They say he's recovering wonderfully."

"Grand!" Wimpole cried. "We'll have a recovery party. And it fits magnificently. Chantrelle—you know my mad friend over at Caltech—"

"You have mad friends any place," Jenny murmured.

"I know. Won't you have fun being hostess to them? But Chantrelle has his model rocket car all ready for a demonstration. He's been holding it up till I got here. How's about it? We'll make it Hilary's Saved-from-the-Jaws-of-Death party. You'll come, of course, Joe, and Phyn. I'll ask some of the other fantasy boys, the Carters and the Bouchers and who's that bright new protégé of Austin's? Matt Duncan. I know," he added maliciously, "they'll love to celebrate Hilary's good health. And by all means you, Lieutenant." He beamed all over his pale face, and drained his glass. "If only we could make the party complete! Invite the murderer. But maybe that can be arranged."

As indeed it was.

3.

Sister Ursula had keep the Foulkes case from her mind during the day's services and her All Souls' Day visit to the cemetery in Long Beach and the grave of her father, that Stalwart Iowan Captain of Police. But now, as she read the office of Compline before retiring, it recurred to plague her.

Oddly enough it was the *Qui habitat* that set her off, the ninetieth psalm.* This noble hymn of confidence in the Lord seemed to accord so curiously with Hilary Foulkes' trust, apparently so well deserved, in something that protected him. *Scapulis suis obumbrabit tibi* . . .

> With His pinions will He shelter thee, and under His wings thou shalt be secure.
>
> Like a shield His truth shall guard thee; thou shalt not fear the terrors of night,
>
> Nor the arrow that flies by day, nor the plague that prowleth in the dark, nor the noonday attack of the demon . . .

---

* The numbering is of course that of the Douay version. In the King James, this psalm is the ninety-first.

It had been almost noon, the attack, hadn't it? And was this as reasonable an explanation as any?

> A thousand shall fall at thy side and ten thousand at thy right hand, yet no evil shall come nigh thee . . .
>
> He has given His angels charge over thee . . .

A favorite line of the Devil's this, Sister Ursula smiled to herself. He quoted it to Christ on the pinnacle of the temple, and was answered by a brilliantly twisted quotation which put him in his place as a scriptural authority. But was it chance that the Tempter chose this line? Was there not something dangerous in a certain kind of confidence?

There was something here, something in this confused melange of reflections on psalms and angels and devils and Hilary and religion . . . Sister Ursula paused and tried to put her finger on it, but it slipped away mockingly. At last she turned back to her breviary and went on to the *Nunc dimittis.*

4.

Lieutenant Marshall was checking over the reports on the rentals and sales of beards. They were not helpful. No beard of the Dr. Derringer type had been out on rental at the time of the bomb episode, and of the eight sales in the past year, only one was to a private individual, Bernice Carter. The rest had been to amateur theatrical groups.

The damnable thing was that this did not even narrow it down to the Carters. The bomb-sender might have owned such a beard for years. He might have bought or rented it out of town. He might conceivably have improvised it himself.

There had been equally little luck on the cyanide. The poison register would be a great and valuable institution if there were any reasonable certainty that the individuals signing did not simply make up their names and purposes in the spirit of free improvisation. If you have a suspect, with a good case proved against him otherwise, you may be able to trap him on a falsified entry with the aid of a handwriting expert (whom the defense will, of course, match with one quite as eminent); but as a source of much-needed leads, the system is hopeless.

Marshall had checked over one or two registers himself, in moody restlessness, and had grown weary of the number of people in Los Angeles who were troubled with rats and wanted arsenic. He liked, however, the arsenic entry which was signed *George Spelvin* and read, not *Rats*, but *Mice*. He wondered what actor with a cruel gag sense had decided to dispose of his superfluous girls, and rather hoped that such a piquant case might fall to his lot in time. But there was no trace anywhere of any of the names so far involved with Hilary Foulkes, save of course the Carter cyanide. (This too had been bought by Bernice, who seemed effectively to shelter her husband from such distracting crudities as shopping.)

Marshall was growling into his own non-existent beard when the phone rang. "Borigian speaking," he heard when he picked up the receiver. "Think I've got a lead for you on that bomb of yours. Can you come to the jail now?"

"Be right over," Marshall promised. Any kind of fresh lead sounded good. He needed to clear his head.

"I got thinking it over," Borigian explained in welcome, "and it seemed to me like there was something familiar about the screwy way whoever made that bomb attached the fuses. Then last night

I was drinking beer down at the Lucky Spot and that boogy-woo-gy-playing dinge they've got was going good and all of a sudden it hits me. Louie Schalk. Remember the Austerlitz case?"

Marshall nodded.

"That bomb was Louie's work, though a smart mouth-piece got him off. And it had the same fuse-fastenings. So I decided to have a talk with Mr. Schalk."

"How'd you get him to talk?"

"He's been branching out lately, Louie has. He's a good chemist, and there's pretty strong evidence he's been making counterfeiting inks. So we pulled him in and talked about how we'd turn him over to the Feds unless he came clean."

"And he came clean?"

Borigian frowned. "I don't know. You talk to him, Lieutenant."

A half hour later Marshall had learned little beyond an interesting study in how an addiction to cheap wine can turn a promising' chemist into a sordid criminal. Louie Schalk was little and thin and white-haired. His pale blue eyes showed hardly any remaining trace of intelligence, but his hands were the deft skilled hands of a good artisan.

"Honest, Lieutenant," he repeated for the seventh time, "that's all I know."

"The letter contained nothing but a hundred dollar bill and the instructions?"

"That's all."

"Repeat them again."

"I should put the unset bomb and directions for setting it in a parcel locker in the P.E. station at Sixth and Main. Then I should mail the key to General Delivery. I'd get another hundred after. And I did too."

"No signature to the letter?"

"No."

"Anything you remember about the typing?"

"Should I? A typewriter's a typewriter, ain't it?"

Marshall shrugged hopelessly. "And you went ahead just on that?"

"Why shouldn't I? Most people want bombs, they don't want you should know who they are, do they?"

"You get orders like that often?"

Schalk's thin lips tightened. "You're booking me on this one charge."

"All right. I'll take it that means Yes, but you've got your constitutional rights. So. And how do people find out about your . . . profession?"

Schalk was silent. "Hell, Lieutenant," Sergeant Borigian broke in, "everybody knows about Louie."

"Yes, but not in the circles I'm concerned with. Well, one more try. Tell me, Schalk: What was the name at General Delivery?"

Borigian grunted disapproval. "Don't think he'd give his real name, do you?"

"No. But the phony a man chooses can be just as indicative as his true name. What was it, Schalk?"

Louie Schalk frowned, trying to remember. "Got it," he said at last. "It was Dr. Garth Derringer."

While Marshall expressed himself, his eyes rested on the card on which Schalk had been booked. Suddenly his self-expression ceased, and his face took on a look almost of pleasure. One lead. One thing that fitted:

Residence: ELITE HOTEL

In the Elite Hotel, Jonathan Tarbell had died.

5.

The Princess Zurilla shrank back against the gem-encrusted wall, her golden tresses gleaming brighter than the gems. Changul, High Priest of Xanatopsis, drew yet nearer and extended a lean hand, all seven of its bony fingers avidly twitching.

"From this hidden space port," his harsh voice droned on exultantly, "our ships used to blast off for Atlantis, in those glorious days when Terra was but a fragment of our colonial empire. We have not lost our cunning through the millennia, as Terra will learn to its disaster."

The fleshless hand clutched the smooth arm of the Princess. Zurilla's firm warm flesh trembled. "And you shall behold all this with me, my dear. You shall reign with me . . ." He broke off and crackled a command in Xanatoptic to the three-armed Rigelian servant who stood in attendance.

"No!" Princess Zurilla implored him. "Let me go! Let me return to my own people!"

"To your lover, you mean," the High Priest snarled. "To that too clever Captain Comet who will yet learn that he has met his match in me. No, you shall not go! You shall be mine down through the eons of the triumph of Xanatopsis!"

An agonized scream burst from Zurilla's throat. "Is there no escape?" she moaned. "Will no one save me?" The slavering lips of the mad High Priest neared hers—and then the Princess Zurilla beheld a strange thing. The third arm of the Rigelian servant fell to the ground.

Another arm twitched the horn from his forehead . . .

"Captain Comet!" she cried joyously, and knew no more.

✳

"That's what I call timing," Joe Henderson observed, "when people knock on the door just when I reach a tag line."

M. Halstead Phyn said "I'll answer it," and jumped up from the couch eagerly. He opened the door, saw the visitors, and grinned like a cat given the freedom of a fish cannery.

"We're on our way to bring Hilary home," Vance Wimpole announced as he and his sister entered the room. "Thought we'd stop off and remind you about Chantrelle's rocket party. It's this Friday."

"Fine," said Joe Henderson.

"You're the damnedest one, Joe. I've never seen you miss a party yet and I think you love them; but you never say a word and you drink maybe two beers."

"I have my fun," Joe said.

"I guess you must. How goes the Cosmic Captain?"

"All right."

Phyn broke the ensuing silence. "Have you got a minute to spare, Wimpole? Because if you have . . ."

"Yes. I've been wanting to talk further about that business you mentioned. Got another room here?"

"We could go in the kitchen."

"O.K. Ron, you mind entertaining Joe?"

Veronica Foulkes had not said a word since they came in. Her brother's presence seemed to subdue her. But now that he had vanished with Phyn, she came alive again. She crossed her legs (she knew they were good) and leaned forward (she knew they were good too).

"Don't you think Vance is stimulating, Mr. Henderson? He makes life so much more vivid, so much more real."

"He's a good joe," said Joe.

"He has so much fun and yet he does so much work too. I like a man who *does* something, who really *is* somebody and not . . . not just a filial ghost. A man like Vance who makes all his money from writings that he really writes himself. . . . You write too, don't you, Mr. Henderson?"

"Some." Joe Henderson seemed even more tongue-tied than usual, and he was having trouble keeping his eyes polite.

"Writers are so understanding. They know about people. They understand how a woman like me ticks. You do understand, I think, don't you?"

"Uh . . ." said Joe Henderson sympathetically.

"I knew you would. You'd see how lonely I am, or was until Vance came. And soon he'll be off again to Lord knows where and I . . . Won't you come and have tea with me some afternoon, Mr. Henderson? Just you and me and Pitti Sing?"

"I'd like to very much, Mrs. Foulkes." There was eagerness behind Joe's stiffly formal phrase.

"Mrs. Foulkes! But you must call me— No, everybody calls me Ron. You . . . you shall call me Nikki . . . Joe."

"Nikki," said Joe Henderson. His voice sounded as though it were changing.

Then the room was full of D. Vance Wimpole. He glanced at Joe's manuscript, smiled and nodded, downed the drink he was still carrying, shook hands with Phyn, clapped his fellow author on the back, took his sister's arm affectionately, and steered her out the door, all the while recounting an anecdote concerning the habits of the Galapagos turtle, which was equally improbable and improper.

When quiet had returned, Phyn thrust his hand out at Henderson. "Congratulate me, Joey. From this time forth M. Halstead

Phyn collects ten per cent of every D. Vance Wimpole check, including the Scandinavian and plus five pseudonyms."

The startling statement had to be repeated before Henderson took it in. When he did, he whistled. "That's good going. How did you do it? Do you know where the body's hidden?"

"Something like that," said Phyn smugly.

6.

"Cousin Hilary's taking his nap," said Jenny Green. "I know he's anxious to see you, Lieutenant, but the doctor was very strict about a properly sensible convalescence."

"Commendable. And Mrs. Foulkes?"

"She and Vance went out together."

Poor kid, Marshall thought. Your fiancé goes gallivanting with his sister while you stay home to tend to Hilary's correspondence. But a man like Vance Wimpole must have the irresistible appeal of color after the vicarage and poverty . . . "Well," he said aloud, "that's all to the good, Miss Green. You and I can resume that conversation we were having the other day. Unless you're too busy?"

"I should be catching up on—but then, I suppose this is really doing Hilary's work too, isn't it? Very well, Lieutenant. Come in and make yourself comfortable."

The latter injunction Marshall found it impossible to obey in that room; but he lit his pipe and settled down to listening.

"Let's see . . . How much had I told you when those pulp people interrupted us? That Mr. Henderson is an odd one, isn't he? But he seems . . . I don't know, rather sweet."

Marshall laughed. "It's hard for a man to see that adjective applied to another man, but you may be right. Well, you were telling me about Wimpole and Foulkes and how they affected their children."

"Oh, yes. One thing I don't think I'd mentioned about Mr. Wimpole: He was an atheist. I don't mean just the ordinary kind of atheist that so many people are or think they are. He was a crusading atheist, who took it for a religion. He was always quoting Tom Paine and Bob Ingersoll, though there was, I gather, more of Ingersoll than Paine in him. And that worked on his children, though in different ways. It gave Vance his independence, that fine rational self-reliance that he has. He found what he needed inside himself. But Ron didn't. She's the sort of person who needs something, because she—please don't think this is catty, but because she isn't anything in herself. So she gropes and fumbles and reacts to a situation the way she thinks someone might react only she isn't really anyone. Or is that clear at all?"

"I think it is, a little. Say that we all, even if we can't accept a capitalized God, still need a lower case god of some sort. Mr. Foulkes found it in his father and Mr. Wimpole in himself, but Mrs. Foulkes is still hunting. Or has she—isn't it true to some extent she finds it in her brother?"

Jenny Green hesitated. "Yes . . . A little, perhaps. But Vance is . . . He's a hard god to worship. He doesn't stay put on the altar. You never know quite where you are. He can give you excitement but not peace. He's a god for a maenad but not for a nun, if you follow."

"And Mr. Foulkes?"

"What about him?"

"For his wife's lower case god."

Jenny frowned. "I don't think Ron understands Cousin Hilary. I don't think they understand each other."

"Tell me, while we're at this: It seems an odd marital pairing. How . . . ?"

"I think Cousin Hilary married Ron because she was her father's daughter. I gather she was more like Darrell Wimpole when she was younger. His atheism was enough for her then, and she felt or seemed to feel much as he did about Fowler Foulkes . . . I think Hilary wanted—well, should we say a high priestess for his religion?"

"And she failed him?"

"You can get tired of anything, Lieutenant. Now Ron says all she needs for hell is a world where all the books are by Fowler Foulkes and all the films are about Dr. Derringer."

Marshall puffed slowly at his pipe. That perverse use of Dr. Derringer as the murderous bomb sender . . . would not that appeal to just such a resentment? To use the symbol to destroy the reality . . .

"I've been talking more than I should," said Jenny Green. "More than I ever do, in fact. But you can see how important this is to me? If any word I say can prevent some devil from killing Cousin Hilary . . . Have I said anything helpful?"

"I'm damned," said Marshall, "if I know."

7.

"That Miss Green," Marshall said, "thinks you're sweet."

Joe Henderson was sitting cross-legged on a cushion before the stone fireplace. "Miss Green?" He looked up innocently.

"Hilary's cousin-secretary."

"Oh. I was over there today, Lieutenant. I went to . . . well, Mrs. Foulkes asked me to have tea and I . . . Your policeman almost didn't let me in."

"That's as it should be."

"But am I a suspect?"

Austin Carter laughed. "Put Joe up on the top of your list, Lieutenant."

Marshall looked puzzled. "Why? We've just been over all the Hilary-complications of the Mañana Literary Society (and thanks, Carter, for your cooperation), but it seems to me Henderson is about the only one to emerge with a clean bill of health."

"Ah, but you see, Lieutenant, we agreed, did we not, that the locked room attempt was made with a time machine? And Joe is our greatest authority on gadgets like that. See *Time Tunnel* in the current *Surprising*."

Marshall smiled. "That is suspicious. And motive?"

"Mrs. Foulkes. You should have seen Joe just after that tea party."

Joe Henderson, though seated, seemed to give the effect of shuffling his feet embarrassedly.

"But he didn't meet Mrs. Foulkes until after the attack."

"Lieutenant! How prosaically literal you can be! If the whole business was hocused by a time machine, why shouldn't the motivation arise after the fact? All the more ingenious a crime—alibi yourself by going back to when you had no reason to kill."

"I'm afraid, Henderson, Carter has bared your dread secret. Better confess."

Joe Henderson shook his head. "I'm not that smart."

"But seriously, Lieutenant," Austin Carter went on, "you ought to read *Time Tunnel*. That's Joe being nonhack, and it's a beautiful job. One of the swellest novelets to hit science fiction in years."

"You really think so?" Joe Henderson, Carter's professional senior by ten years, looked as beamishly pleased as an amateur actor who has just received a kind word from the Lunts.

"Indeed I do. Henderson is still the Old Master when he wants to be. And that Storm Darroway . . . dear God, what a wench! If I could meet a woman like that, a thousand interplanetary civilizations could smash and much I'd care!"

"The heroine of *Time Tunnel?*" Marshall asked.

"Of course not. You don't know your Henderson, Lieutenant. The villainess. The heroine is duller than dishwater. You see, one of the Henderson trademarks is the Two Women. They're the same two that run through all of Rider Haggard too. One represents Virtue and is blonde and beautiful and good and dull. The other represents Vice and is black and beautiful and evil and marvelous. It's always puzzled me why Joe can write only wicked women."

"Could I play at amateur psychoanalyst? Perhaps he has a secret conviction that women are evil and can therefore write only an evil woman convincingly."

Carter nodded. "Pretty. What do you say to that, Joe?"

Joe Henderson hesitated. "I don't know," he drawled at last. "I guess it's just a subconscious belief that the human female has spider blood."

8.

"Yes," said the clerk at the Elite Hotel, "it'd be easy enough for anybody hereabouts to pick up who Louie Schalk was. Of course he was acquitted on the Austerlitz business, but we all knew what his racket was."

"And do you think," Marshall asked, "that Tarbell knew?"

"I can't say. He didn't talk much to people. But he could have easily."

Marshall nodded. This fitted all right. Whoever had known Tarbell, visited him here, and killed him, could have learned where to order a bomb.

"Oh, and Lieutenant."

"Yes?"

"You told me to tell you if anybody was asking for Tarbell."

"So?"

"Well, there was somebody. Not exactly asking for him; but asking about him."

"Good man. Who?"

"It was one of those nuns that come around here on social work sometimes. We've got a poor lunger up on the fourth, and she was fixing up to get him sent away. So we got to talking about the murder and she asked questions about this man used to visit Tarbell occasionally, and she showed me a picture and said did that look like him, and damned if it didn't."

Marshall's eyes popped. He was not surprised that Sister Ursula's proud curiosity had led her to investigate the Elite; but where on earth could she have secured a picture of any of the suspects? "You were so vague in your description," he objected. "What was it like?"

"I'd almost forgotten," the clerk apologized. "So many people come and go. But when I saw the picture, it all came back to me. She left it with me to show you. It's around here somewhere . . . Oh, here it is."

He handed it over. It was a page torn from a movie fan magazine, a striking still of that admirable actor Norval Prichard in his great role of Dr. Derringer.

9.

"So there are all the latest pieces of the jigsaw," said Marshall as he whisked a brush over the coat of his best suit. "And tonight you'll meet the people."

Leona executed some complicated maneuvers before the dressing table. "With your next bonus you're going to have to buy me a full length mirror. Does my slip show?"

"Just a little."

"It's nice of Mr. Chantrelle to ask us to his party. And I am curious to see this Hilary of yours. I never get a chance to meet the victims in your cases while they're still warm."

"I don't know that warm's the word for Hilary."

"A rocket party . . . That should be fun. And a rocket could be symbolic for clearing up a case. A loud noise and a spreading light. . ."

"Beauty falls from the air," Marshall said, and added questioningly another quotation: "Beauty is truth? Well, we'll see."

Leona was listening to shouts and murmurs off. "Oh my . . . A howl. I'll bet it's a burp left over from that last bottle. Will you check, dear, while I . . ."

Lieutenant Marshall picked up his screaming daughter, put her against his shoulder, and patted her resolutely with no result. He sat down on the low chintz-covered chair, held her on his knee, and shook her gently. The internal rattle was deafening.

Ursula stared questioningly in her father's face and parted her lips as though to emit the desired burp. Then her gaze switched. There had been no extraneous sound to distract her. Nothing had moved. But something in the corner of the room demanded her attention.

She stared fixedly at the thing and followed its slow and hesitant movements. Her father shook her again. "Don't pay any attention to that, darling," he said. "Make with the burp. Be a good girl."

Just as Leona entered the room, the baby relaxed her attention and burped splendidly. "She saw a Thing," Marshall said. "I don't know how the child authorities account for that phenomenon, but it always gives me the creeps when she becomes so damned absorbed in something that isn't there."

"Maybe it's our Invisible Man," Leona suggested.

"Gives me gooseflesh," he insisted. "I'll bet some of our fantasy boys could work it into a very pretty omen."

"Of what?"

"Of what? That, my darling, is what we're going to this party to find out. Come on."

THE NINTH DAY:
Friday, November 7, 1941

HUGO CHANTRELLE told the story of his rocket party so often to the police that he came to know it by heart, came even to believe that he had in fact felt a sensation of dread premonition from the start of the evening. This sensation he accounted for with manifold references to Extra Sensory Perception, the Serial Universe, the common reaction of I-have-been-here-before, and the free movement of the mind in dreams along either direction of the time stream. It was an impressive explanation, even though the premonition was strictly after the fact, and emphatically a characteristic one.

For Hugo Chantrelle was an eccentric scientist. In working hours at the California Institute of Technology he was an uninspired routine laboratory man; but on his own time he devoted himself to those peripheral aspects of science which the scientific purist damns as mumbo-jumbo, those new alchemies and astrologies out of which the race may in time construct unsurmised wonders of chemistry and astronomy.

The rocketry of Pendray, the time-dreams of Dunne, the extra sensory perception of Rhine, the sea serpents of Gould, all these held his interests far more than any research conducted by the

Institute. He was inevitably a member of the Fortean Society of America, and had his own file of unbelievable incidents eventually to be published as a supplement to the works of Charles Fort. It must be added in his favor that his scientific training automatically preserved him from the errors of the Master. His file was carefully authenticated, and often embellished with first-hand reports. And this was one reason why he had so gladly acceded to D. Vance Wimpole's notion of turning the rocket launching into a party for Hilary.

For locked rooms fit into the Fort pattern, if pattern it can be called, and Hugo Chantrelle looked forward to meeting Hilary much as he might to an encounter with a survivor of the *Mary Celeste* or with Benjamin Bathurst, the British diplomat who once walked around a team of horses and was never seen again.

So expectancy was Chantrelle's dominant emotion that night, expectancy of the meeting with Hilary and the success of the demonstration of his model rocket. The premonition of disaster came later, in his account to Sergeant Kello of the Pasadena police.

Too great expectancy must always involve anticlimax, which is possibly only a pedantic way of rephrasing the idea of the song *I'm building up to an awful let-down*. Chantrelle's let-down was double: He never had a chance to talk with Hilary alone, and nobody seemed to give much of a damn about his beautiful rocket. It was turning into just another party, and the host began to regret that Wimpole had talked him into serving liquor, a disturbing element which ordinarily never entered his life.

There were some of his own friends present, of course: several faculty members from the Institute, where he seemed to get on better with representatives of the departments of English and mathematics than with his own colleagues. There were some of the fantasy writers whom he cultivated: Anson MacDonald and

Austin Carter and that promising newcomer Matt Duncan and Anthony Boucher and their several wives and Joe Henderson inevitably wifeless.

Ordinarily these might have been tractable guests, who listened with absorbed interest and occasionally contributed stimulating ideas of their own. Chantrelle was wont to maintain that the company of fantasy writers is invaluable to a scientist; they are the prophets of the future even as Verne and Foulkes were the prophets of today. Only occasionally did he admit to himself that he enjoyed their company because they received his heterodox views on the borderlands of science far more courteously than did his laboratory associates.

But even they were not receptive tonight. There were too many others. There was Hilary Foulkes, who had invested his entrance with wife and cousin with the air of a potentate leading a cortege, and who had thenceforth held court, in the chair most nearly approaching his own body in comfortable plumpness, dispensing anecdotes of his Immortal Father and of his own providential escape from death.

There was Veronica Foulkes, who had prowled about commencing a tête-à-tête with each available unattached male. Yes, even with Chantrelle, though women interested him as little as did liquor, and the nebulous stupidity of her egocentric mysticism had disgusted him; for his mind, though eccentric, was stringently logical.

There was the agent Phyn. He was unobtrusive enough save for his fruitless endeavors to wangle a private conference with Hilary Foulkes and for an oddly dominant, whip-hand quality in his attitude toward Vance Wimpole; but Hugo Chantrelle disliked the presence, even the existence of agents. They reminded him that writers (even, or perhaps especially, writers of science fantasy) are commercial workers, when he preferred to think of them as free souls, as soaringly independent as, thanks to the canny marriage of his grandmother, was he himself.

There were two people whom he faintly remembered meeting once at the Carters, but whom he could not successfully place. The man named Marshall seemed not to fit in anywhere. Five minutes' conversation showed him up as neither scientist nor science-fictionist; and his suit, though good enough and well pressed, certainly proved that he did not belong to the circles in which the Foulkes moved. And yet he seemed in some curious way closely attached to the Foulkeses; his alert eyes hardly ever left Hilary, even for his own attractive wife.

Then there was the odd little man named Truncheon or Runtle or something equally unlikely. A fan, Chantrelle decided; Austin Carter was apt to have such satellites. He felt sorry for the lonely little man at one point, and went over to him to enlighten him with some details about the by now almost forgotten rocket. But Vance Wimpole came up at the same time, and Trundle's eyes lit up with the true fan's glow in the presence of An Author.

Wimpole, of course, was everywhere. He tended bar, he told stories, he introduced to each other with the most intimate charm people whom he had himself met five minutes earlier, he heckled Hilary's levee, he plagued his sister, he made casual love to the cousin, who seemed to be his fiancée—in short, he had by now turned a serious gathering of odd-minded men of scientific interests into the start of a first-rate brawl.

If Hugo Chantrelle's Extra Sensory Perception (or his awareness of past phases of seriotemporal existence; he had not definitely decided which) had been as keen as he liked later to suppose, he might indeed have had premonitions.

He might have had a premonition when young Duncan was introduced to the comfortably enthroned Hilary Foulkes.

"Ah yes," Hilary murmured. "Duncan. Duncan. Oh yes, the daring young man with the audacity to write new Dr. Derringer stories. Most daring of you, Duncan. Delighted to meet you. Delighted. You know, I feel that I've been most generous to you. I really should have refused permission for your series. Duty to my father's memory and all that, you know. But I'm not such an ogre as some people make me out. After all, you pulp writers have to live, don't you?"

Duncan's pretty, Spanish-looking little wife had drawn him away, though not before he had uttered an ugly and threatening phrase. The scowl on his face was blacker than her hair.

He might have had a premonition when Veronica Foulkes, after having had no more success with several of the guests than she had had with her host, disappeared into the garden for some time with Joe Henderson.

She does rather resemble one of Joe's villainesses physically, Chantrelle had thought; but, their minds are always astutely evil. Hers is merely commonplace and silly.

He was rather surprised to notice that Henderson returned with lipstick smudged on his face, so badly that the cousin caught hold of him and drew him aside for repairs before he met Hilary's eyes.

He might have had a premonition when Wimpole eventually, being (as Chantrelle's Scots grandfather would have said) under drink taken, gradually ceased making casual love to his fiancée and began to bestow tentative but certainly not casual advances upon others.

He had an enviable field to choose from. Carter and Marshall and Boucher and Duncan were all men blessed beyond the average with attractive wives. And of them all it was the long-legged Leona Marshall, whose red hair blended so notably with Vance's own, who seemed most to attract him.

Chantrelle missed the climax of this development; but its nature was not hard to deduce from Wimpole's nose-bleed and the quiet, earnest, and somewhat apologetic conversation of the Marshalls in a corner.

He might most appositely of all have had a premonition when he went down to the shed to check up on preparations for the rocket test; for he was going to hold that test come hell or high water. Some few of his guests, he was sure, were still interested; and the others could . . . Well, after all, consider the shape of a rocket.

There were three figures standing by the workshed. They were on the edge of the pool of light cast by the shed's window, and they gave in the dark night a curious effect of optical illusion. The central figure was a woman. The others were men; or rather, and this was what was perturbing, they were the same man. It was as though the woman were being escorted by a man and his *Doppel-ganger.*

There is a pleasure in being deceived by our eyes. Perhaps it provides us with the consolatory thought that our senses are not perfect and that therefore things need not be quite so terrible as they seem. Chantrelle watched this double apparition with the same uneasy satisfaction that he had once felt when he stared too long at a waterfall and the very earth and rocks began to move as though serenaded by Orpheus his lute.

Then at the same time Chantrelle's assistant Gribble opened the door of the shed and the tall and sturdy Marshall stepped from somewhere out of the shadows. In the light the three figures were simply Hilary Foulkes, abandoning his throne at last for a breath of air, his cousin Miss was it Green?, and that Frangible individual.

"All ready any time you say, boss," Gribble announced.

And the extra-sensitive and serial-living Hugo Chantrelle had still not felt a premonition.

2.

Gribble turned a switch, and bright lights picked out the course which the rocket was to follow. This was a carefully constructed trench four feet deep and extending some hundred yards down the arroyo, making a slight arc twice in its meanderings and ending in a spring-backed shock cushion of raw cotton.

Leona Marshall let out a loud sigh of disappointment. "The rocket just goes along there? But that's no fun. I thought rockets went up in the air *boom!*"

"And maybe off to Mars," Concha added. "Or leastways to the moon."

"Hush," Matt advised. "Austin's going to make a speech; I think that'll clear up your confusions."

The party was gathered on either side of the trench in front of the workshed. They had split more or less involuntarily into two groups: those who were in some way connected with Hilary Foulkes and those who led carefree and innocent lives.

On the western lip of the trench were the Bouchers and the MacDonalds and the several Caltech men. On the eastern lip were the Marshalls and the Duncans, Henderson and Phyn, D. Vance Wimpole, and the Foulkes-Green family. Hugo Chantrelle was in the pit of the workshed beside the rocket, and the Carters stood in the doorway of the shed facing both groups of auditors.

"Let there be silence," said Austin Carter. "I will have hush."

And the mumblings of the party slowly died down, leaving nothing but the voice of Vance Wimpole saying ". . . marry the chief's daughter. Of course she was attractive enough, in a lard-laden sort of . . ." He sensed the silence, and let the phrase trail off.

"Thank you," Carter smiled. "Ladies and gentlemen . . . scientists, writers, housewives, and detectives . . . Hugo has asked me to say a few dedicatory words on rockets. You don't expect me to resist that, do you?"*

The murderer shifted restlessly. There were other matters more pressing than rockets. The murderer began to regret ever having come to this party.

"Most people," Carter went on, "know that a rocket is fun to shoot off on the Fourth. A few know that it's useful for signal flares. And for a very few, our host and me among them, the rocket is something to which to pin our hopes for the human future.

"Its origin goes back into legend, and almost inevitably Chinese legend at that. It was first used in warfare, chiefly as a creator of panic, as at the battle of Pienking. The rocket became known in Europe late in the fourteenth century. By 1405 von Eichstadt was writing of its military value, and by 1420 Joanes de Fontana was constructing fantastically shaped rockets and drafting plans for a never-constructed rocket car. To Fontana belongs the honor of first realizing that the rocket was not an end, but a means."

A means . . . The murderer frowned down at the rocket in the pit. Could this creation of the eccentric Mr. Chantrelle conceivably be a means of necessary elimination?

"For the next four centuries, the development of the rocket

---

* For much of the following material, Mr. Carter asks me to acknowledge his indebtedness to P. E. Cleator's *Rockets Through Space: The Dawn of Interplanetary Travel,* New York, Simon, 1936. (The British edition, London, Allen, 1936, has even more fascinating pictures.)

was at a standstill, until Sir William Congreve had the genial notion of encasing the gunpowder, not in paper, but in iron. The success of this device set inventors everywhere to fretting over rockets as a motive power of flight.

"But the modern history of rocketry begins with Konstantin Eduardovich Ziolkovsky, who in 1903 made the first scientific application of the rocket principle to the problems of space travel.

"Man has always aspired to reach the stars. But when he finally sprouted wings, he knew that they would be futile as those of Icarus in interplanetary space. Wings must beat against air. So must propellers. In the vacuum of space they would be helpless. But the force of an explosion is as strong a motive power in a vacuum as in air."

Force . . . Force exerted, not in a vacuum, but against a . . . Yes . . . Yes.

"It's a popular misconception that this force requires air for the exhaust gasses to push against. This is arrant nonsense. See Newton's third law of motion. A gun, for instance, fired in a vacuum, has the same recoil as in the air. And a rocket fired in space would, by the reaction from the explosion, propel a space ship, which nothing else known to us could do.

"This Ziolkovsky concept of rockets in space gave the necessary impetus at last to serious rocket research. I don't need to do more than mention the first great names in the field: Goddard, Oberth, Esnault-Pelterie; or refer to the the more important societies: the pioneer *Verein fur Raumschiffahrt,* the British Interplanetary Society, the American Rocket Society, to remind you of the vast amount of practical work which has been going on especially in the past twenty years."

The murderer gazed from the rocket to the plump victim and back again to the rocket. The plans were ripening nicely.

"Among these workers is Hugo Chantrelle. If the name of Chantrelle does not ring down with the ages with those of G. Edward Pendray and Willy Ley, it will be because our heterodox host, even within this heterodox pursuit of rocketry, has followed his own doubly heterodox path. For what absorbs him is not the rocket ship, but the rocket car.

"For both theoretical and technical reasons, the rocket car has been neglected by the societies. But Chantrelle has persevered, because he believes in its value as an icebreaker. Man rejects anything too new and startling. He would have rejected the miracle of radio if it had not snuck up on him gradually through the telegraph and the simple signaling of wireless telegraphy. He may reject the miracle of space travel unless he is first accustomed to the rocket as a means of terrestrial transport. Thus Chantrelle's first goal in rocket tubes connecting major cities, through which freight and mail may be sent even more rapidly and far more cheaply than by air. He envisions a network of such tubes, spidering all over the continent."

But has he, the murderer thought, envisioned the notably practical use to which this tube is about to be put?

"One main problem is the difficulty of steering these pilotless transports in tubes which can rarely be built in a straight line. To solve this, Chantrelle has contrived a robot governor based on the principle of the reflection of sound-waves, and this is what we are to see tried out tonight. You will notice that the walls of this trench curve twice. The rocket should, in theory, keep itself always a certain distance from each wall and thereby negotiate the curves readily. The rocket used for this test is a slow one. There has been no attempt to attain maximum exhaust velocity. It will move at only about fifty miles an hour. The final commercial rockets for the tubes will, of course, move at between two and three hundred miles per hour."

But fifty, the murderer thought, should do beautifully for this occasion. The murderer's eyes glistened, and a pink tongue licked dry lips. A certain pleasure can be derived from sheer necessity.

Austin Carter's normally assured voice grew a trifle hesitant. "There's just one point about rockets I'd like to venture on my own before we start the demonstration. I don't know if Hugo agrees with me on this; he probably hasn't even bothered himself about it. But it's this: That the rocket carries in its zooming path the hopes of all men of good will. By leaving this planet, man may become worthy of his dominion over it, and attain dominion over himself. The realization that there is something beyond this earth, if only in a purely physical sense, may unite this earth, may change men from a horde of wretchedly warring clans to a noble union of mankind.

"I may be deluded in my hopes. The discovery of new worlds may be as futile as the discovery of the New World. It may mean only further imperial wars of conquest, new chapters in the cruel exploitation of subject native races. But it may mean new unity, new vigor, new humanity, and the realization at last of all that is best in mankind. I hope so anyway," he ended, quietly and anti-climactically.

The murderer has heard little of this idealistic peroration. The murderer's eyes were fixed with a smiling glint upon Marshall. That detective, the murderer mused; this will give him to think.

3.

Hugo Chantrelle had added a few words of his own, chiefly technical details which only his colleagues seemed to follow. He had spoken affectionately of his long months of work on the *Aspera IX*. All his model rockets, he explained, were named *Aspera*, for *per aspera*, eventually, *itur ad astra*, and he deplored the tendency of the facetious to refer to them as *Aspidistra*.

The group at the shed end of the trench crowded forward close to the lip and peered into the pit beneath the shed. The *Aspera IX* was some five feet long and a trifle under a foot in diameter. The gleam of light on her dull copper gave her the quality of a living thing forcibly holding itself back from motion. Chantrelle and Carter and the assistant Gribble conferred in the pit in voices too low to be heard. Then Chantrelle held up his hand.

There was silence. Gribble bent over the rocket. There was a flare of exhaust and a loud explosion. All eyes turned, tennis-wise, to watch the rocket shoot past. But those eyes saw something else.

They saw a plump figure topple over the lip of the trench into the immediate path of the *Aspera IX*. The ears heard a crunch of bone and flesh, and sharp ringing screams.

The *Aspera IX* righted herself from the shock. She adjusted herself admirably to the curves in the trench and plunged undamaged into the cotton bales at the end. But no one heeded her epochal performance.

"Hilary!" Veronica Foulkes was screaming. *"Hilary!"* And Jenny Green was saying the same word softly and intensely.

"So they got him," Marshall swore with feeling. "Got him at last and right under my very exceedingly goddamned eyes . . ."

"Heavens!" a voice murmured. "Heavens!" The voice was shocked and trembling with terror and relief, but there was no mistaking its deep round tones.

Marshall whirled and stared at Hilary Foulkes. He followed

Hilary's gaze down to the bleeding mass in the trench. "Then who . . . ?" he demanded loudly.

No one answered him.

4.

From then on it was Lieutenant Marshall's party.

It was Marshall who ordered Chantrelle and Carter to let no one climb down into the trench. It was Marshall who sent Gribble to the house to phone the Pasadena police. It was Marshall who delegated his wife, aided by Concha Duncan, to minister to the women present and prevent hysterics. It was Marshall who himself descended into the trench, identified the plump pulp as that of the fan Runcible, made certain that it was dead (as though anyone beholding that impact could have had any doubt), and covered it with a tarpaulin (which is after all the same word as *pall*) from the shed.

Now it was Marshall who addressed the group gathered in Chantrelle's vast living-room. "The police," he began, "will be here in five or ten minutes."

"But Lieutenant," Hilary protested, "I thought you *were* the police."

"I am in Los Angeles. Here in Pasadena, I'm just another civilian. But a civilian with specialized knowledge and experience, and that I'm putting at your disposal now. We're going to spend those minutes before the Pasadena boys arrive in trying to get this business straight."

He looked about the group. They were sober enough now, in either meaning of the word. Nothing less like a triumphant rocket-launching party could be imagined. Social gaiety and scientific fervor were both obliterated by the sudden emergence of death.

But it was an impersonal sort of sobriety. As was, indeed, natural enough. No one here had known Runcible more than casually. He was an extra, a hanger-on, a spear-toter. His death had been terrible to see, but it had stirred only physical response; there was no mourning, no personal sorrow at his passing. And with Hilary and his cousin, perhaps even with his wife, the emotion of relief so effectively drowned out any casual regret for Runcible's death that they looked almost jubilant.

It was one of the Caltech men who spoke up. "But why is there any need for the police? It was a most tragic accident, and there will doubtless be a highly unpleasant inquest; but the police . . ."

"Accident, hell," Marshall snorted. "Maybe some of you read the papers; but most of you must know that there has recently been a series of attempts on the life of Mr. Foulkes here. You also know, from your own observation, that Mr. Foulkes and the dead man were much of a build. In fact, both Mrs. Foulkes and I, seeing that body hurtle into the trench, thought at once that it was her husband. So. I think the conclusion's obvious."

"That poor man!" Hilary sighed, his sorrow serving as an inadequate mask for his relief. "To think that he laid down his life for mine!"

"Involuntarily, no doubt; but what Mr. Foulkes says is nonetheless true. The bright lights were focused on the trench. We on the edge were in half-darkness. And the curiously inefficient murderer who has previously made five unsuccessful attempts on Mr. Foulkes' life tonight made his sixth and most spectacularly unsuccessful."

There was another sigh of relief, this time from Hugo Chantrelle, who followed it with a fervent "Thank God."

"And why, sir?" Marshall demanded.

"Because, Lieutenant, if this is murder, there can be no public furor about the dangers of rocket experimentation. After Valier's sad death in 1930, there were shortsighted but rabid demands throughout Germany for the legal prohibition of all further work on rockets. But in this case . . . You can see why I thank God for your murderer."

"So. All right: Now did anyone see clearly what happened? I know that all of us (save one) had our attention firmly fixed on the *Aspera IX*. The murderer knew his principles of stage conjuring. I'm not expecting anybody to produce a diagram of just where each person was; but did anyone see any sudden movement that might have been the fatal shove?" Marshall paused, mentally biting his tongue for such a banal utterance as that last phrase.

There was silence.

"All right I know how you might feel. You say to yourself, 'After all, I'm not too sure of what I saw, and I'm not going to send a man to the gas chamber on my guess.' But remember that this is a clumsy murderer, an ineffectual, frustrated murderer. He'll strike again when he gets the chance. And we've got to see that he never gets it. So come on. Tell anything that might help."

Matt Duncan rose, hesitantly, as one might to recite an unprepared lesson. He shoved his tousled black hair away from his brow, and the freakish white streak in it seemed to emphasize the bitter torsion of his features. "O.K., Terence," he said.

"So. Yes, Matt? You saw who shoved Runcible?"

Matt gulped audibly. "Saw, hell! I shoved him."

Concha's reaction was more a squeak than a scream. She put out one small hand as though to halt her husband's confession. Hilary was on his feet and booming something about Justice and At Last.

Marshall cut him short. "You shoved him, Matt?" he said gently.

"I couldn't help it. I was standing behind him. I'm a head taller than he is . . . was . . . so he didn't obstruct me. Then just as the rocket went off, I got a hell of a sharp jab in the back. I started to fall forward, so I put out my hands. You know how you do . . . I hit what's-his-name. I saw him stagger and then go forward and over and straight into . . ."

No one had noticed Leona slip away from the group, but now she stood beside Matt with a tumbler half full of whisky. "This'll help," she said.

He took it at a gulp and his body was unshaken. "Thanks," he nodded. "There. I've done it now. I've confessed. According to the notions of my wife's church, it ought to be clear sailing from here on in. But I still . . ."

"Lieutenant," Hilary demanded, "arrest this man! A sharp jab in the back, indeed! He's afraid someone else saw him, and he's trying to beat them to it. Arrest him, I say!"

"In the first place," said Marshall slowly, "I can't arrest anybody outside the city limits of Los Angles; and despite all gags as to their extent, we're outside them now.

"In the second place, I believe him. Go on, Matt. Can you tell us anything more about this jab?"

Matt's voice was unsure and wavering. "I can't, Terence. I didn't look around because all I could see was Whoozis falling and falling and then . . ." He shuddered and covered his face with his hands.

"Pull yourself together," said Marshall, feeling as futile as the phrase.

Matt lowered his hands. "Sure. Pull myself together. With these hands, no doubt. These hands that killed a man . . ."

A harsh dry voice spoke from the doorway. "Hot stuff!" it said.

"A confession already!" Its uniformed owner grinned, then called over his shoulder, "Come on in, boys. We've got it all cleaned up."

The officer strode into the middle of the room. "Kello's the name, folks. Sergeant Kello. K, e, l, l, O-O-O-O-O, like they sing on the radio. And it looks like we're going to have a short and easy time of it, don't it? All right, big boy," he addressed Matt, "what's your name and who'd you kill?"

"I'm afraid, Sergeant," Marshall interposed, "you're plunging in too fast. It isn't a question of handcuffs yet."

"Hell, brother, a confession's a confession, ain't it? And who're you anyway to tell me where I get off?"

Marshall showed his badge. "Marshall, Lieutenant, Homicide."

Sergeant Kello's round red face narrowed unpleasantly. "Marshall, huh? Quite the big shot in L.A., ain't you? Well, brother, this is Pasadena. Keep your nose clean."

5.

"Hell of a mess, ain't he, doc? Anyways there can't be much doubt about cause of death. Die right away?"

"Instantly."

"Never knew what hit him, huh? Serves the poor bastard right for playing around with rockets. The whole kit and caboodle of 'em's screwy if you ask me. Rockets . . . You identify this man, Mr. Carter?"

"As best I can from what's left of him. At any rate, that's the suit Runcible was wearing, you found his draft card in it, and he's the only member of the party not accounted for. His dentist can probably identify him more positively than I could."

"Don't teach your grandmother to suck eggs, Carter. Look at it this way: Would I try to tell you how to write a story?"

"Probably."

"Let's see: Runcible . . . First name, William? Address . . ."

"So this list, Mr. Chantrelle, is the people who were on the same side of the trench as Runcible, and these were on the other side?"

"Yes. My assistant Gribble, Mr. Carter and his wife, and I were in the pit."

"So, it's just these ten who could've . . . But hell, what are we wasting time for? We know who did it."

"You ever have any trouble with this Duncan, Mr. Foulkes?"

"Trouble? I don't know that you'd call it trouble. But perhaps . . . One never knows how these pulp writers will react to the most ordinary business proposition. One never knows. We did have a . . . I suppose you might call it a financial disagreement. I referred to it casually this evening and Duncan burst forth into wild threats and gave me a look as though he . . . why, as though he wanted to murder me. And by Jove, he did!"

"Threats, huh? What kind of threats, Mr. Phyn?"

"You understand I wouldn't ordinarily talk like this about a friend, Sergeant, but under the circumstances . . ."

"Sure. Never does no harm to stand in good with the law. Shoot, brother."

"Before this evening, I mean. I think before he'd ever met Mr. Foulkes."

"What sort of threats?"

"Well, not threats exactly. Maybe just a lot of loose talk. But I do know that Duncan was all shot to hell when he learned about this financial finagling of Foulkes', and one night at Carter's when we were talking about the Perfect Crime he said he had at least the Perfect Victim. It sounded as though he meant it. He meant something anyway."

"You saw this push, Mr. Boucher?"

"I'm afraid so. Something bit me and I happened to jerk up my head just as the rocket started. I noticed Duncan because that odd white streak in his hair took the light. And it did look as though he himself was being shoved too."

"You saw him shoved?"

"I can't quite say that. He's tall, and whoever was behind him must have been shorter; I couldn't see anyone. But Duncan's body lurched forward as though—"

"You'd swear in court that you saw him shoved and that he didn't do the shoving himself?"

"I couldn't swear to that, no. But it's my firm impression that—"

"That's enough, Boucher."

"O.K., Marshall. We're smart in Pasadena too, but if somebody else does the spadework it's oke by us. You've been investigating these other attacks on Foulkes?"

"Yes."

"Duncan included among your suspects? Come on, brother. Talk. If you won't, I can go over your head and get an order from your chief for you to cooperate or else. Did you investigate Duncan?"

"Yes. Inevitable routine. He was one of the many business enemies that Hilary Foulkes had a habit of making."

"Find anything to tie him up with the attacks?"

"Nothing."

"But did you find anything that cleared him? It was possible for him to make every one of the other attacks on Foulkes, wasn't it?"

"It wasn't possible for anybody to make the last one."

"Yeah. I read about that. You boys just didn't go over the room careful enough. But Duncan hasn't got any alibis?"

"None."

"That's all I wanted to know, brother."

Sergeant Kello looked at his wristwatch. "We've been here an hour, boys. That's what I call making time. Sixty-minute Kello, that's me. And I didn't need that much. The more I talk to these dopes the surer I am of what I knew right the minute I came in that door. 'Somebody shoved me, officer . . .' Nuts! He knew somebody must've spotted him from across the trench, so he tried a fast one to clear himself. They can't get away with it, not with Kello on the job."

Hugo Chantrelle peered into the study which Kello was using. "I beg your pardon, Lieutenant—"

"Sergeant right now, brother. But you wait till the papers get hold of this. Pasadena Sergeant Frustrates Attacks on Celebrity after L.A. Police Star Fails. Lieutenant Kello . . . Sounds kind of good, don't it?"

"Yes indeed, Sergeant. But what I wanted to ask: My guests are getting exceedingly worried and tired. I simply can't put them all up for the night. And Mrs. Marshall and Mrs. Boucher are fretting about their children, who are in the charge of high school girls who apparently expect to go home long before this hour. And Mr. Wimpole—"

"Tell 'em they can go home now," said the future Lieutenant Kello expansively. "Tell 'em they can all go home. All but one." He jangled a pair of handcuffs playfully.

6.

Leona Marshall clicked on the light of her living room, crossed to the couch, and shook the shoulder of the sleeping high school girl. The girl sat up, rubbed her eyes, and said, "Oh. Have a nice party?"

Leona didn't try to answer that one. She just said, "I'm sorry we're so late, Doris. Here's your money, with the extra for the hours after midnight. Mr. Marshall's out in the car. He'll take you home."

"Sit down, Concha," she added when the girl had left, "I just want to take a look at the children to make doubly sure. Be right back."

Concha sat. It was easy to obey simple commands. This must be the way zombies feel, a sort of relief at just having to obey, after all the living problems of trying to shape life because now there isn't any life to shape any more. She sat and stared blankly in front of her until Leona returned.

Leona stood looking at her for a moment, then laid a gentle hand on her shoulder. "I prescribed whisky for Matt," she said quietly, "but I don't think it'd help you. Nothing could at the moment but maybe sleep. Here's some phenobarbital. Take another one later if you still toss, but one ought to do it."

"He didn't, Leona." Concha's voice was little and frightened.

"Of course he didn't. It's just that stupid Sergeant trying to do the job in record time and get a promotion."

"I know. That sounds so safe and simple. But first it's a Sergeant that wants a promotion. Then it could be a prosecutor that's coming up for reelection. Then it could be a jury that wanted to get home. It could all be so simple and commonplace only Matt . . . Matt'd be dead."

"Nonsense. They haven't got any kind of a case. Why, even Sergeant Kello only dared arrest him on a manslaughter charge. He admitted he'd have to have more evidence on the other attempts to prove premeditation before he could make it murder."

"But when they know what they're looking for they can find it even if it isn't there . . . Oh Leona . . ." The girl's sobs were dry and aching.

"There," Leona said soothingly. "You hear a lot about miscarriages of justice, convictions of innocent people. But they're one in a million. That's why you hear so much about them, just because they are so rare. He'll be all right."

Concha tried to choke back her sobs and force a smile. "You're sweet, Leona, trying to whistle in the dark for me. But how much of this do you believe yourself? Oh," she added with a gasp, before Leona could answer. "Hilary!"

"What about him?"

"He thinks Matt did it. And Hilary has money, ever so much money, and he can . . ."

"If it comes to fighting that way, you have money too, haven't you? And I'll tell you what you have to do with it first thing tomorrow. Go to your lawyer and have him get Matt out on bail. Since the present charge is only manslaughter, that'll be easy."

"But it'll be . . . murder as soon as that dreadful Sergeant . . ."

"Well," said Leona, "there's one certain and sure way of seeing to it that Matt is proved innocent. And that is to prove beyond any doubt who did it."

Marshall came in just then. "Applause," he observed. "And

that, I promise you, Concha, is what I'm out to do. Quite aside from the fact that it's the job I'm paid for."

Concha Duncan lifted a damp face. "Have you any ideas, Lieutenant? Any at all?"

Marshall grunted. "I did have one. And it stood in the pit beside Chantrelle. In this case we're strictly limited to the group on our side of the trench. Outside of the four Marshalls and Duncans, that leaves Mrs. Foulkes, the cousin, Vance Wimpole, Henderson, and the agent. And on the bomb," he mused aloud, "it has to be a man. No woman could get away with the Derringer getup, especially feminine women. That leaves us Wimpole, Henderson, and Phyn. See how easy it is, Concha?"

The note of blithe confidence in his voice did not quite ring true.

THE LAST DAY:
Saturday, November 8, 1941

EARLY THE next morning Marshall was at the rooming house on West Adams which had been the abode of William Runcible. Runcible, it seemed obvious, was a sideline; but as a corpse inevitably an important one. They knew nothing about this accident victim, Marshall reflected, not even how he made his living. And the Lieutenant's orderly mind rebelled against such lack of knowledge of the focal individual in a murder case.

The landlady looked paler than a woman of her build had any right to be. She held the morning paper clenched in a hand that shook slightly.

Marshall identified himself, and she gasped, "About Mr. Runcible? I saw it in here," she added hastily, brandishing the paper.

"A terrible thing," said Marshall gravely. "I wanted to ask a few questions about him and see his room."

"I'll be glad to tell you anything I can, officer."

"All right. How long had he been here with you?"

"Almost six months."

"And do you know where he came from?"

"He never said anything about that. He wasn't much of a one for talking about himself."

"Know anything of any family?"

"Not a thing, officer."

"Where did he work?"

"At the Safeway down the street. He was a grocery clerk there."

"A good tenant?"

"He was a nice-spoken young man and he paid his bills and he never made any trouble."

"Thank you." He considered her pale face and still trembling hand. "The news of his death seems to have been quite a shock to you."

"Yes . . . Yes, I guess it was. But it was coming on top of . . . You see, we had a burglary here last night or early this morning I guess I should say. Mrs. Svoboda, she's a waitress in an all-night drive-in and when she came home she found this strange man prowling around in the halls and she screamed and woke me and I saw him leaving but when we called the police of course it was too late and we don't know if he took anything yet, but I was all upset and then this on top of it, why—"

"I can understand," said Marshall soothingly. "Now if I might have that key . . . ?"

Lieutenant Marshall had never gone over so unprofitable a room, unless perhaps it was the cheap cubicle in the Elite Hotel where Jonathan Tarbell had died. You could learn from the room that its owner cared little for clothes and much for science fiction. And that was about all.

No letters save correspondence with other fans (Marshall automatically abstracted a couple of the least impersonal), no private papers, no note or address books. But infinite numbers of pulp paper science fiction magazines and those curious mimeo-graphed fan bulletins that are known by the portmanteau name of fanzines, a complete set of Fowler Foulkes, almost as reverently bound as Hilary's, a goodly lot of Shiel and Stapledon . . .

Nothing personal. Nothing at all. One curious item: a picture hook with no picture hanging from it and a blank space on the wall over the Foulkes collection. But this might be a relic from some earlier tenancy. Nothing . . .

Marshall was about to leave the room in disgust when his sharp eye caught a glint of white in one corner. He went over and investigated. There was a crack in the floorboards just beyond the wastepaper basket. This would be a note hurled at the basket, overshooting its target, and later trodden into the crack.

Marshall unfolded the paper and read:

He (or was it *H.?*) *says maybe. Keep hoping keed.*

J. T.

J. T. . . . No. That would be too much. Too pretty to be true. But now he suddenly remembered that Matt had mentioned meeting a Tarbell at Carter's. Runcible frequented Carter's . . .

Marshall felt in his coat pocket. His luck was in; he still had the morgue photograph of Jonathan Tarbell. He hurried down-stairs to the landlady.

"Yes," she admitted. "He used to come to see Mr. Runcible right often. But he hasn't been around for a week or so. But what's this?"

This was the still of Norval Prichard as Dr. Derringer, which had fluttered out of Marshall's pocket as he took out the Tarbell photo.

"Why goodness me!" she gasped. "That's our burglar!"

2.

In the quiet and sunny patio of the Sisters of Martha of Bethany, Concha Duncan struck a discordant note. She still wore the gay and flaunting scarlet gown which she had put on for the rocket party, and looked even more sorely out of place here than she had on the bus coming out.

But there was nothing gay and flaunting about her voice. "You've got to help us, Sister. You've simply got to. If anything happens to Matt . . . We haven't been married even a year yet, but we've been married all my life. All my life that counts is being married to Matt, and if anything happens to him, I . . . I'll have to die too."

"Life is God's gift, Mary," Sister Ursula said gently. "We can't toss it away at our own whims."

"I don't mean that. I just mean that if I haven't got Matt, I simply *can't* live any more. It'll stop inside me. So you must save him, Sister. You're so wise and good. You can do it."

"Lieutenant Marshall is an admirable man. Since Matt is innocent, and I cannot entertain the slightest doubt that he is, the Lieutenant will surely establish that fact in short order."

"But it's not his case, don't you see? It's that dreadful Sergeant from Pasadena. The Lieutenant can't do a thing; he hasn't any official standing."

"And you think that I, with even less standing, could succeed if he fails? The previous attempts on Mr. Foulkes' life are still in Lieutenant Marshall's domain. If he finds the man who is guilty of those, Sergeant Kello's case can never be made to stand up so long as he insists that Runcible was killed in error for Mr. Foulkes."

"Then you won't do anything?"

"I can't do anything. There's no need for me."

"All right." Concha rose smoothing her skirt. "I know what's the trouble. I've heard you talk to the Lieutenant like this. You're worrying about spiritual pride. You're worrying about the temptation of power over human life. You're worrying about your soul. All right. Save your soul. And pray for my husband's."

She turned to go. Sister Ursula rose and stood terribly still. One hand clutched the crucifix of her rosary, and her lips moved soundlessly. "Mary . . ." she said at last.

Concha was at the arcade leading out of the patio. She turned. "Yes?" she said bitterly.

"Tell me, Mary: How certain is the Lieutenant that Runcible was killed by mistake?"

Concha's face lit up. "Then you will help?"

"If asking questions will help for a start. Come back here and sit down with me on the bench. Now. Is he positive of that mistake?"

"You're a . . ." A laugh and a sob were contending in Concha's throat. "You're . . . I can't say it. I can't say anything."

"Blow your nose," Sister Ursula suggested softly. "Here. And don't try to say it. Just tell me about things."

"Well," (a gulp and a loud snuffle) "well, the Lieutenant's awfully certain on that. You see, the two men did look a lot alike. Hilary's maybe I'd guess ten years older than Runcible, but they're both the fleshy type that looks pretty much the same from twenty-five to fifty. And they both had on similar gray suits that night. Of course Hilary's must have cost about three times as much as Runcible's, but at night . . . The Lieutenant says it was funny when he saw them together with the Green girl; it looked as though she had the same man on each side of her."

Sister Ursula's eyes revealed a slight gleam. "The two of them together? Runcible and Mr. Foulkes? When was this?"

"It was just before the rocket test. The Lieutenant was keeping a close eye on Hilary of course. Hilary'd raised a fuss and said he couldn't go lugging bodyguards around to parties, so the Lieutenant pretended to agree only you see he was the bodyguard. So when Hilary went outside the Lieutenant followed him, and the cousin was with him, and they met this Runcible and talked for a while."

"And when the murder occurred, then, the Lieutenant was watching Mr. Foulkes instead of the rocket?"

"No. He admits he slipped up there pretty badly. Because there was a lot of shifting around so as to get a better view of the pit and he lost sight of Hilary just for a minute. But it wouldn't have made any difference anyway because it wasn't Hilary that got killed, it was Runcible, and we've got to find out who did it and now you will help us, won't you?"

Sister Ursula rose, smoothing down her robes. "Please ask Lieutenant Marshall to come to see me as soon as he can. And in the meantime . . . Where are you to meet Matt when he is released on bail?"

"At the lawyer's office. I couldn't stand going over to Pasadena and seeing where they . . . *keep* him. I want to see him free and try to think he's always going to be that way. And besides I wanted to come out here."

"Why don't you phone your lawyer's office and leave word for Matt to come here to meet you? If you wait downtown, you'll simply worry more; and I'm sure he won't want you to be all frowning and tear-stained when you meet him. Stay here in the good sun, or make a visit to the chapel. Ask our Lord and His blessed Mother to help you. For if I do succeed in freeing your husband, Mary, it will only be through Her intercession and His grace."

Concha nodded. "I will. It helps, prayer does. Even when it doesn't help from outside, it helps inside you."

"And you've helped me, Mary. You've shown me that my fear of pride was in itself a very special kind of pride. The soul saved at the expense of a brother's life can hardly be a cause for great rejoicing in heaven."

"But look. You said 'stay here.' Where are you going?"

Sister Ursula smiled. "The thought just crossed my mind that there was so much attendant confusion, that day when Mr. Foulkes was attacked in my presence, that I never had the opportunity of speaking with him about my real errand, clearing the copyright permission for Sister Patientia's braille work. I think, if Reverend Mother will allow me, that I shall go see him about that now."

3.

Lieutenant Marshall read over again the note that he had taken from Runcible's room. He still didn't understand it. It involved chiefly the law of entropy, the paradoxes of Space-Time, and the theory of wave-mechanics, all couched in a jargon of technical erudition that made Austin Carter's conversation seem infantile. But the last paragraph was more personal, and seemed to imply that this Arthur Waring had known Runcible better than most of his correspondents.

An infant with pink and downy cheeks answered Marshall's ring. "I'd like to speak to Arthur Waring," the Lieutenant announced!

"That's me," the lad replied in a clear soprano.

"You—" Marshall checked himself; to ask if it mightn't be his father could simply antagonize the boy. He could remember his own youth, and how a boy's desire to seem older than his age is as strong as a woman's yearning to seem younger. But still, the precocity of that letter . . . "You're the Arthur Waring who was a friend of William Runcible's?"

The boy's face lit up. "Oh jeepers! Are you the police? I read about it in the paper."

Marshall nodded. "If I could talk to you a few minutes . . . ?"

The boy led the way to a small room. Marshall gasped as he entered. The entire wall was pictures. The same sort of pictures that he had seen in the Nitrosyncretic Lab, originals of illustrations for s-f magazines, but hundreds, seemingly thousands of them.

Waring heard the gasp. "Aren't they swell? That's a Rogers cover over there, and I've got a half dozen Boks and three Finlays. And look over here; that's an original Cartier, and did that take some getting! When I'm illustrating for the mags I'm going to do like Rogers and just rent my originals and then I can be nice to the fans."

"You're an artist yourself?"

"Sort of. Only when you live on the West Coast you can't get a chance to do any commercial illustrating, but when I finish college I'm going back to New York and— Only you wanted to ask me questions, didn't you?"

Marshall, always willing (if sometimes reluctantly so) to spend long minutes buttering up a witness as a good investment, was pleased by this directness. "Yes. It seems hard to get any information at all about Runcible. If you were a friend of his, maybe you can help us."

"Well, I don't know if I was so awfully much of a *friend* of his. Of course we both belonged to the Califuturions (that's a fan club), and sometimes we'd swap mags or mostly he'd borrow mine because I had more. I've got some nice stuff here, officer."

Marshall looked about the room. No books here. Just an infinite number of pulp magazines, all carefully arranged by title and date; apparently almost complete files of a half dozen different publications, and assorted samples of others.

"I've got them all indexed too," Waring went on. "I made a complete index of all the best magazines from their start and I mimeographed it. Would you like to have a copy? Only you wanted me to tell you about Runcible. But what about him?"

"Well for instance: Did he have any family? We ought to notify them if he had, but I couldn't find any hint in his room."

"I don't think he had. He was a lot older'n most of us. He must've been . . . oh, almost thirty. I guess his folks were dead; he never talked about 'em. He never really talked about much of anything excepting science fiction. He was nuts about Fowler Foulkes. He had a big framed autographed picture of him in his room. He used to talk about him like he was God or something." There was a note of scorn in the high young voice.

"You don't like Foulkes?"

"Naw. He's a classic. I'm going to do an article for one of the fan-mags debunking the classics. Who cares about Foulkes or Poe or Verne? They're old stuff, and I'm going to show them up."

"Have you read them?" Marshall asked with quiet amusement.

"Well . . . no. Not much anyway. But all these people that rave about the classics, which maybe they were all right when *they* were young, but have they read what's being published now? You bet your life they haven't."

The point, Marshall was obliged to admit, had turned against him neatly. "So Runcible was all for the classics?"

"Especially Foulkes. He was funny other ways too. He was I guess what you might call a purist. He thought people ought to read books too besides all the mags only how could you have time? And he kept saying what fans ought to support was pro writing instead of fandom."

Apparently William Runcible, so silent in the presence of the Mañana Literary Society, had been voluble enough among the Califuturions. But his tastes and theories were hardly to the point. "What was he like?" Marshall wanted to know.

"That's hard to say now. He talked a lot and he used to write pieces for the fanzines—he wrote one for mine once—"

"You're a publisher?"

"Sure. Here." Waring crossed to a pile of mimeographed sheets and picked up a stapled magazine with a lithographed cover. It was called *Fandemonium*. "Take one. Only about Runcible. Somehow nobody ever got to know him very well. He did have a friend he brought around a couple of times; he seemed pretty close. Maybe you'd better try him, only I don't remember his name."

Resignedly Marshall brought out the picture of Tarbell.

Waring nodded eagerly. "That's the joe. Couldn't he tell you anything?"

"Not a thing," said Marshall truthfully.

"I think they were working on something together. They seemed thick as thieves. Maybe they were collaborating; Bill (that's Runcible) always said he wanted to write some time cause it was in the family. Only when he was doing the arm trick, this man said, 'Maybe that'll help too,' and how could it with writing?"

"The arm trick?"

"That was something Bill used to do at parties. It was a good trick only nobody else could ever do it. It looked awful, like something in a horror story illustrated by Cartier. He'd put his arm all around his neck and reach back to the ear on the same side as the arm if you see what I mean. And then he'd put both arms around his neck and clasp them under his chin. Wait a minute—I've got a picture I drew of it someplace here."

Marshall shuddered involuntarily as he looked at the pen-and-ink sketch. Not that it was so bad as that; it was, in fact, a surprisingly good piece of work. But it depicted a horrible apparition. It looked eerily like a severed head being borne by two unattached arms—John the Baptist displayed by a bodiless Salome. It was somehow more grisly, more dead than the crushed pulp of Runcible's factually dead head had been.

"You can have that too, if you want," Waring added. "Bill Runcible was funny maybe, but he was kind of a good guy. If I can help any, I want to."

"Thanks." Marshall failed to see how the macabre head could help, but it would be an unusually picturesque illustration for a dossier. "Anything else you can think of about Runcible? For instance, did he spend more money than he'd possibly make as a grocery clerk?"

"No. The only thing he spent much on was books. And he used to say he liked his job fine only I don't see why, but then he was expecting to be drafted pretty soon anyways."

"You don't—" Marshall started to say, then stopped and stared at the boy. "Mr. Waring," he said gravely, "you have helped. Immeasurably. And I, sir, am an idiot."

4.

"Look at you!" Veronica Foulkes' throaty voice was scornful. "One thing at least you've spared me all these years. You've never been a drinking man. If you knew all I've gone through with

Vance, and how terribly trying it is for a woman of my . . . And now look at you! Drinking even before lunch!"

Hilary poured himself another glass of straight scotch. "My dear!" he protested. "Surely one who talks as much as you do about her sensitivity must realize that others can be sensitive as well. Last night was a terrible shock for me. A terrible shock. That poor innocuous fan . . . And it might so easily have been me lying in the depths of that trench, crushed and mangled and pulped. So easily . . ." He gulped the glassful hastily and stared at his plump white hand. It still quivered slightly.

Veronica turned to the wall mirror and adjusted her hat. "I do hope," she observed tartly, "that I'll find you conscious when I get home. To think that I should learn at this late date that I married a drunkard!"

"One swallow," said Hilary seriously, "doesn't make a summer. Heavens! That's a pun, isn't it?" He seemed amazed.

"You can spare me your drunken wit."

"I didn't mean to. It just happened. It simply came up like . . . like . . ." A burp appositely ended his quest for a smile. "Like that. But seriously, Veronica, you can't call this a habit. After all, it's not every day that one has just escaped murder."

"It almost seems to be with you."

"Those other attempts . . . I can't explain it, but they didn't seem quite real. Even when I was stabbed. After all, nothing serious actually happened. It wasn't possible to realize fully what I had escaped. Not possible. But this time, when I could see that poor devil and have before my eyes what I should have been . . . I can't explain it, but—"

"*Please!* You might at least wait till I leave before you go on poisoning yourself."

Hilary set aside his freshly poured glass. "And what is this luncheon engagement?"

"I told you last night. But then you never hear a word I say anyway."

"I'm afraid last night I may have been a trifle preoccupied, my dear. Just a trifle."

"It's with that Henderson boy. You know, he's really a darling. I think he understands me. And you could never appreciate what a relief that is after the cold blank wall of indifference that I meet in my own house."

Hilary sighed and reached out for his glass. "Goodbye, my dear."

"You . . . you don't mind?" Veronica asked hopefully.

"Why should I? Why on earth should I?"

She shrugged. "Some husbands might be jealous. A little. A husband that was half a man himself . . . Hilary."

"Yes, my dear."

"You don't like me at all any more, do you?" Her voice was for once simple and direct.

"No, my dear."

"So," said Veronica. "That's that." Her voice rose cheerfully. "Now I simply must fly. I'm late as it is and—"

"Veronica."

"Yes . . . ?"

"Have you ever liked me?"

"I . . . I do have to hurry now, Hilary. I—"

"Have you?"

"I've tried. Honestly I've tried . . ."

"How typical of you, my dear." Hilary's voice was flat. "You always try. You tried music once, remember, and painting. Self-expression. You tried religion. You've tried lovers. Oh yes, I know.

But whatever you try turns out to be too hard and you stop trying. You stop. You always try and you never do. You . . ." Hilary's voice stopped. For a moment he stared in silence at his wife.

"Goodbye . . ." she said hesitantly.

"Always trying and never succeeding," he repeated slowly. "And I am still alive . . ."

Without another word Veronica Foulkes snatched up her bag and left. Hilary laughed once, harshly. Then the room was still.

For five minutes he sat there motionless. Sometimes his eyes fixed speculatively on the study within which he had been so mysteriously wounded. Sometimes they gazed as though focused on a distant and invisible object, such as a rocket trench in Pasadena.

Finally he bestirred himself sufficiently to pour another whisky, and as he did so the doorbell rang. In a moment the maid ushered in two nuns. Hilary set the glass aside and reluctantly rose to his feet.

"Yes?" he asked, wavering almost imperceptibly.

The younger of the two (as best one can judge ages beneath the agelessness of religious habits) said, "We met briefly, Mr. Foulkes, on the day you were so mysteriously attacked. Just a murmured introduction in passing, and I can hardly blame you if later events drove it from your mind. I am Sister Mary Ursula and this is Sister Mary Felicitas, of the Order of Martha of Bethany."

Hilary made a polite acknowledgment and indicated chairs. The small old eyes of Sister Felicitas seemed to close the instant she was seated.

"Indeed I do recall you now, Sister. Indeed. The police lieutenant mentioned you as one of the witnesses who proved the apparent impossibility of . . . of what happened in there."

"May I congratulate you on your escape? You seem to have a singularly efficient guardian angel. And you are further fortunate in having Lieutenant Marshall on the case."

"Indeed I am. A most able officer. Most able."

"I did not refer simply to his ability. I can imagine how many of the police would be sarcastically scornful of such an 'impossible' situation; but since the Lieutenant had such an experience once before, he must be far more receptive."

Hilary smiled. "I had hardly thought that a woman of your order would have such an acquaintance with murder, or with police ways of thinking."

"My father was a policeman, and a good one. And I was planning to be a policewoman myself when my health broke down and I was forced to change my plans."

Hilary was politely sympathetic, but fidgety. He expressed due pleasure at the news that Sister Ursula's health for the past dozen years had been enviable and due appreciation of the fact that she had nonetheless never regretted the change of vocation. He accepted her further congratulations on his happy escape of the night before; but at last he said, with a trace of impatience, "But Sister, I am sure that you did not come here to discuss my fortunate avoidance of the Black Angel."

"No indeed. When I met you before, I had come on business; and I fear I am persistent."

"Business? Business? But go on."

"You have possibly heard a little from your wife concerning the purposes and activities of our order—"

Hilary's manner visibly froze. "If you are soliciting donations, Sister, I think I should explain that the state of the book market in these uncertain times is far too parlous to leave me in a position where I should feel free to contemplate.... Far too parlous," he concluded, leaving the overcomplicated sentence hanging in air.

Sister Ursula smiled. "In a way, I suppose, it is a donation that I am soliciting, but it will cost you nothing, Mr. Foulkes. I merely wish to ask you to reconsider your refusal of copyright to Sister Patientia, who wished to transcribe some of your father's work into Braille."

Hilary looked hurt. "But my dear Sister, I did not refuse her the copyright. By all means I wish the blind to enjoy my father's work. By all means. She may transcribe those stories whenever she wishes. I simply asked for a conventional reprint fee."

"But this is voluntary, non-commercial work. The book will be read first by a few of the blind whom we look after. Then it will go to the State Library and from there circulate to all the blind of California. And no one will pay a cent for it."

"Books circulate freely from public libraries, my dear Sister, but the libraries pay the publishers and thereby indirectly the authors for the books. It is a necessary tribute to the literary profession. I owe it to my father's memory to collect what fees I can. And moreover, a man must live."

Sister Ursula glanced about the chastely expensive room. "Do you find bread alone a satisfactory diet, Mr. Foulkes?"

"I don't understand what you mean by that remark, Sister. I don't understand it. But I must make clear to you" (Hilary leaned forward, tugging impressively at the lobe of his ear) "that under no circumstances, for no matter how worthy a cause, will I countenance the wanton pirating of my father's works."

"I don't suppose it would affect your attitude to point out that every author or publisher that Sister Patientia has previously been in touch with has always given Braille rights free as a matter of course?"

"What an author chooses to do with his own work in a moment of caprice is no concern of mine. But this is not my own work. I hold it in sacred trust for my father, and I must be a good steward."

"There is another parable about a steward," Sister Ursula observed. "Perhaps its motivation is more— But please forgive me. That was an uncharitable thought. Even, perhaps, an inaccurate one. Please do not misunderstand me."

Hilary rose. His legs were perfectly steady now. "Not at all, Sister. Not at all. And I'm sure you'll find some generous patron who will enable you to meet my trifling fee. I would so gladly waive it myself, were it not for my duty to my father."

The hall door had opened and closed as he spoke. Now a thin pale face thrust itself into the room. "Hiya, Hilary! Oh, sorry. Company? Has Ron corrupted you? Are you going in for Spiritual Consolation too?"

Hilary beckoned his brother-in-law into the room. Jenny Green (a very smiling, happy and devoted Jenny Green) followed him. "Sister Ursula, may I present my brother-in-law, Vance Wimpole? And my cousin, Miss Green? Or did you meet her when I . . . ?"

"I did, but am happy to meet her again. And Mr. Wimpole."

"Glad to meet a nun, Sister. Variety. Which by the way," Wimpole jerked a thumb at the other nun, "who's the Seventh Sleeper?"

"My colleague, Sister Felicitas."

"Give me her address. I'll borrow her some time when a Good Girl wants a chaperone."

"Vance!" Jenny Green protested.

Sister Ursula smiled. "You seem very blithe for a household over which Death has been hovering for weeks."

"Why not?" Wimpole demanded. "They've got the guy that did it all, at the insignificant cost of the life of one fan. Of course no writer likes to lose even one fan, but I'm willing to get along without Runcible for Hilary's sake."

"Vance! That's no way to talk."

"You see, Sister? I'm henpecked already. I need a drink. Hilary! It can't have been you hitting that bottle before noon? Or did the good sisters need their schnapps?"

"Don't mind him," Jenny reassured the nun. "He's a boor and he loves it. But would you . . . do you . . . I mean, are you allowed . . . ?"

"I might take a small glass of port if you have it," said Sister Ursula.

The presence of the nuns had apparently restrained Hilary from his unwonted tippling. This avowal of tolerance sent him promptly back to the bottle. Vance Wimpole stared at him amazed.

"What, my dear brother-in-law, is the use of your being snatched from the hand of the assassin if you're going to plunge yourself into a drunkard's grave? Filthy stuff," he added, tucking it away.

"I think I can understand," Sister Ursula ventured. "The terrible relief of knowing that it's over, that you can breathe without wondering if it's your last breath. For I suppose you are sure that this young man who was arrested is the cause of it all?"

"Not a doubt in the world," said Wimpole broadly. "Hell—I beg your pardon, Sister—we've got witnesses saw him do it. He even admits it himself. Somebody pushed him, indeed! What jury's going to believe that?"

"If that is true, I should imagine he would hate you more than ever now, Mr. Foulkes. Now that you've had him arrested and disgraced. If he were let out on bail, if he were free again now . . ."

Hilary's glass dropped from a shaking hand. "Hang it, Sister! You mean that devil would try it again?"

"It seems plausible, doesn't it? When a murderer has killed the wrong man, I should imagine that his passion to kill the right man would increase all the more. It would certainly seem strange if the death of this poor fan, may he rest in peace, should put an end to the attacks upon you."

Hilary picked up the glass and refilled it. He muttered "Thanks," apparently to no one in particular.

"Did you know this man who was killed, Mr. Foulkes? That would make it all the more painful for you."

"No. Never saw him before that night. Never."

"And did you become acquainted with him at all then? One is naturally curious as to what the poor victim was like, even though he is really unrelated to the case."

"What bloody tastes you've got, Sister!" Wimpole remarked.

Hilary answered the question. "No. Didn't see anything of him."

Vance Wimpole's eyes narrowed. "But you and Jenny were alone with him for a while, remember? Which by the way, that's been puzzling me. What went on?"

"Oh that," Hilary shrugged. "I went out for air. People can be most trying when one is something of a celebrity. Most trying. This fan followed us and pestered me with all sorts of questions about my father and his works. That was all, wasn't it, Jenny?"

"Yes," Jenny agreed after the slightest pause.

"I hardly had the opportunity to judge the man's character from— Excuse me. The telephone."

But Miss Green had already answered it. "It's for you, Cousin Hilary."

"Thanks. I'll take it in the study." He walked into the other room and shut the door behind him.

Jenny Green put a hand to her mouth. "Oh . . ." she gasped. "Not in there. Not in that room. That's where . . ."

"Nuts," said D. Vance Wimpole. "Duncan is in his cell. Nothing can touch Hilary further."

"But we still don't know how anything could ever have touched him. Maybe you could do it even from jail. We ought to seal up that room, lock it and never let anybody . . ."

Wimpole puts his arm around her. "Tush, toots. There's no boogyman in there. Nothing can happen."

But his eyes, like Jenny's and Sister Ursula's, remained fixed on the door.

It opened, and Hilary came out intact. But it was a Hilary even more nervous and shaken than before. "You know who that call was from?" he demanded. "It was from him. Duncan. He's out on bail. He wants to come and see me. Says he wants to persuade me to drop charges, he's innocent. Innocent, he says. But he wants to come here . . . He'll kill me, I tell you. He'll kill me. He can go through locked walls and stab you with your own dagger and . . ."

His trembling hands could hardly hold the bottle.

5.

Lieutenant Marshall had his troubles with the draft board. "But Lieutenant," the bald and elderly clerk kept insisting, "we simply cannot allow you to look at an enrollee's statement. These statements are strictly confidential. If we allowed them to be used for police purpose, we might as well install a Gestapo and be done with it."

"Look," Marshall pleaded. "The man's dead. I'm trying to catch his murderer. The American Civil Liberties Union isn't going to jump on your neck for helping me do that."

"I'm sorry, but rules are rules. You can see for yourself, Lieutenant—"

"I can see. But I cannot see that you're contributing much to defense or civil rights or the welfare of society or whathaveyou by holding up a man who's trying to prevent more murders."

The clerk relented a little. "If you told me what specific information you wanted, I might be able to help you. If it's a matter of indentification, say . . . ?"

"That's it chiefly. But it's hell to ask specific questions. What I want is just a gander at the whole thing to get a picture. There's something nebulously nibbling about in my mind that won't take shape. But what I mostly want to know is did he have any family? If he did, they can help me."

The clerk returned with the filled-in form and kept it carefully out of range of Marshall's eyes. "No. No family. Father and mother dead, and no claim for dependents. What else do you need to know?"

"Could you . . ." Marshall groped ". . . could you tell me when and where he was born?"

"August 5, 1915. Here in Los Angeles."

"Handy. That can be checked . . . And what'll it prove when I've checked it? All right. One important thing—if this isn't too much on the confidential anti-Gestapo side: What does it say under that question about Have you ever been known by any other name?" He smiled as he wondered what Austin Carter's draft board had made of his collection of names. Probably called in the F. B. I.

The clerk frowned. "I'm not sure if that is information I could rightly give out. But as it happens, there isn't anything. Funny . . . Looks as though he'd started to write something and changed his mind. Probably was filling in an answer on the wrong line. They will do that."

"So?" Marshall leaned forward. "Could I see that?"

"This . . . this squiggle? Just that?"

"Just that. All by itself."

The clerk sighed. "Very well." He placed blotters over the sheet so that nothing was visible but the one line, then laid it in front of the Lieutenant. "It looks like a capital J."

Marshall stared at it:

"Thanks," he said at last. "You've been a help. I'll try to return the favor some day."

"I wish you were a traffic officer then. I'm not expecting to commit a murder."

"Cheer up," said Marshall. "You never can tell."

The nebulous nibbling was stronger now. It was a crazy idea, too wild to mention yet to anyone on the force, too wild probably even for Leona's taste. Sister Ursula was the only person he could think of who wouldn't hoot impolitely at the notion.

He took out the delayed telegram from Chicago, which had so perplexed him when he received it an hour ago, and reread it. It began to make sense now. It fitted in with this other. And if he could only get any direct proof . . .

His first stop was the public library. He flipped through the card catalog, read the entries under *Foulkes, Fowler Harvey (1871-1930)*, jotted down two call numbers, and went on into the history and biography department.

First he asked for a *Who's What* for 1928-1929. He read the entry there and nodded. Confirmation was nowise complete, but the idea was at least not disproved. He then settled down to a hasty leafing through two large books. The crazy notion looked better than ever.

His next stop was at the Bureau of Vital Statistics. When he emerged a half hour later he was beaming as brightly as he had after the birth of his son.

6.

Lieutenant Marshall was smoking his pipe in the patio when Sister Ursula returned to the convent. He sprang to his feet at her entrance and advanced eagerly toward her. "Sister," he cried, "I think I'm on to something! And if it works, we'll have Matt free and exonerated before that Pasadena halfwit can say 'Lieutenant Kello.'"

Sister Ursula smiled happily. "Tell me this great discovery," she urged. "But tell me other things first. Quickly, if you can, but do not skip too much. The patience of a saint and the ingenuity of a fiend could not have coaxed a coherent story out of Mary, poor child. Please give me all the background you can so that I can justly estimate your new find."

"Gladly. It helps get things straight in my own mind, Sister, to tell them to you. You ask the right questions, and you've got a sense of proportion. So here goes. Let's see; up through the locked room you know about. After that . . ."

Rapidly but fully he sketched over the later developments of this exasperating case, up through Matt's arrest. And as he spoke he kept marveling at the adroitly apposite quality of the nun's questions and the deft speed with which she took in all facts.

When he had concluded, she meditated in silence for a moment and then said, "It's all obvious enough, isn't it? All but one thing."

"That being the mere trifle of who's the murderer?"

"No. That locked room. The identity of the murderer is clear enough. But proving the case against him and freeing Matt will be exceedingly difficult with that 'impossibility' as an obstacle to overcome."

"And everything else is obvious? That's nice. Then listen to what I've been up to today: I'm on a trail that if it's right (and I'm praying it is) will prove that the death of William Runcible was no accident, but an essential detail of a well-conceived plot." He paused for sensation.

"But of course. That's been perfectly clear from the first. Tell me, though, how you intend to prove it."

Marshall gawped. "I'd sooner have you tell me why it's so all-fired obvious."

"But of course it is. There's a perfect chain of probabilities pointing directly to it. If you don't mind, however, I'd like to hold that back. It involves a serious accusation which I don't think it is quite time to make yet. Tell me your researches."

Marshall relit his pipe. "All right. It goes like this: How did this whole case start? With Jonathan Tarbell and a rosary. We had nothing at all on Tarbell—no connections, no previous police record, nothing."

"*Had* nothing, Lieutenant?"

"All right. I'll confess we have a little now, and it helps. But if you can hold out, so can I; that'll fit in better later. Let's go back to the beginning. We know nothing about Tarbell save that he had the phone number of the Foulkes' apartment house and a rosary which proved to be the property of the first Mrs. Foulkes Senior.

Now if his death was an irrelevant subplot totally unconnected with the attacks on Hilary, then the caprices of fate are becoming uncommonly outrageous. It's where we start from, and it has to fit in."

"I agree, Lieutenant. I'll go further and say that if you had not investigated the death of Tarbell there never would have been a locked room."

"For the moment I'm not sure I follow that one. But to go on: Tarbell ties in at another point too. Matt Duncan once met him at Carter's, probably with Runcible. A further checkup with Runcible's landlady and a fan friend of his shows that Tarbell was his most frequent and intimate companion. This pulls Runcible right into the middle of the case, as a protagonist and no innocent bystander. If Tarbell is connected with Hilary, and Runcible is closely connected with Tarbell, then no matter what all the Foulkeses swear there is a tie-up someplace."

"I agree."

"All right. So next I try to find out something about Runcible: who he is, where he comes from, what he does. The last is easy: he's a grocery clerk. The others are practically impossible. Nobody knows a thing about him except that he pays his bills regularly and is a purist in his tastes in fantasy. He lists no close relative for the draft board. But he does start to fill in the space about having gone under other names, and then changes his mind.

"Now getting confidential information out of a draft board is hell. Ask me, I'm an authority. But a draftee mightn't realize that. If it were at the moment exceedingly important to conceal his other name (true or false), if he were engaged on some enterprise that meant keeping that name secret, he might risk charges of falsifying his statement rather than make the information available."

"True, Lieutenant. And could you make anything out of what he started to write?"

Marshall drew out his notebook, found a blank page, and sketched the squiggle of William Runcible.

"It looks a little like a J," Sister Ursula mused. "Or it could be . . . yes, I think it is the start of a capital F."

"It is. I'm sure of that. And doubly sure because for once our murderer slipped. He went too far. Somebody had been in Runcible's room before I got there. It was unbelievably cleared of all personal papers, save for an overlooked note signed *J. T.* I'll come back to its contents later; at the moment it indicates just one more tie-in with Tarbell. No man could have lived in such an impersonal atmosphere. And last night the landlady saw a 'burglar,' who was wearing the good old familiar Dr. Derringer get-up."

"Curious," said Sister Ursula, "how that costume runs through this case. Is it simply macabre humor, or is there some psychological compulsion driving the murderer to use it?"

"I don't know. With Carter it could be a gag. But he's out now. With Veronica Foulkes it could be psychological; but could a woman get away with it? Which by the way, as Wimpole would say, that was smart work of yours at the Elite, Sister."

"I thought that a disguise used once might prove to be a habit. And now this burglar . . . you think the murderer searched Runcible's room?"

"He got there fustest," said Marshall sadly. "He did his best to destroy all evidence of who Runcible was. But in a way, he helped me. As I said, he went too far. He removed a picture from the wall.

"Now I learned later from the fan Waring that there was no secret about that picture. It was an autographed photo of Fowler

Foulkes, a naturally treasured possession for any fantasy fan. If the picture had been left in place, I wouldn't have given it another look. But it was missing; and it could only be missing because the murderer thought it was, not part of a fan's collection, but an element in the evidence which he was destroying. Therefore that evidence concerned Fowler Foulkes."

"Excellent!" said Sister Ursula admiringly. "Lieutenant, why should you waste your time submitting such notable work to me for criticism?"

"Largely," Marshall admitted, "because it's coming out better now. It wasn't nearly this clear and logical in my mind when I started. So. Now how did that evidence concern Fowler Foulkes? I had an inkling, and I looked up the Foulkes biography in *Who's What.* And there it's been, staring us in the face all along.

"Hilary has built himself up in the public eye as The Son of Fowler Foulkes. We know that he's the son of a second marriage, but we automatically think of the first marriage as childless. I imagine it's because Hilary creates such a touching picture of the relationship between him and his father that you can imagine Fowler Foulkes leaning out from Abraham's bosom and proclaiming, 'This is my only-begotten son, in whom I am well pleased.' If you'll pardon the sacrilege."

"The sacrilege, I think, is Hilary's. He turns his father into God, after which it is only natural to think of himself as the Son of God. But the flaw, you mean to imply, lies in the 'only-begotten?'"

"Exactly. There was a child by the first marriage. Roger O'Donnell Foulkes, deceased. I checked it up further in Fowler Foulkes' autobiography. Roger was born in 1894. There are plenty of close and affectionate references to him, even after the second marriage and the birth of Hilary, up until 1914. Then there's not another word about him save for one allusion to World War I as 'this great struggle for humanity, to which I gladly surrendered my time, my self, and even the life of my son.' The Wimpole memoir isn't much help. It plays up Hilary, of course, because of his marriage to the Boswell's daughter, but it hardly mentions Roger. There is one cryptic mention of 'that deep sorrow of Fowler's life, which death did not heal.' What does all this add up to?"

"A serious quarrel which estranged father and son, and drove the son off to die in battle."

"And what would be apt to provoke such a quarrel at twenty? Can you think of anything more likely than an ill-considered marriage, with the Honorable Patricia St. John as stepmother doubtless having her say as to the girl's unsuitability? Standard formula. Cut off with a shilling, beyond doubt, and all the rest of it. And so off to volunteer in the Allied forces, to win death or glory on the battlefield, dashing off on his metaphorical white charger without waiting to discover that his poor wife was pregnant."

Sister Ursula nodded. "Then you think that your Runcible is the son of this ill-considered marriage of Roger Foulkes'?"

"I'm certain. I figured it this way: He may lie to the draft board about his name. But only a professionally adept deceiver makes up a false birthplace and birth date. Nine chances out of ten that much is correct. So I checked August 5, 1915, in our records here. No Runcible. But William Fowler Foulkes, eight pounds ten ounces, father Roger O'Donnell Foulkes, mother Eleanor Runcible Foulkes. It's easy to see what must have happened. Pressure brought to bear by the family to relinquish her claims and resume her maiden name in return for a lump sum.

"Now you know Hilary's family pride. Look how he has taken care of that distant English cousin. And a Foulkes working in a grocery store . . . This is guesswork, but I think there can't be much doubt that Runcible was gently putting the screws on Hilary. It can't have been a strong pressure, because he'd have no claim on the estate from a disinherited father. Just a sort of moral suasion and appeal to pride. And that's where Tarbell comes in."

"But how?"

Marshall took out the telegram from Chicago and handed it over. Sister Ursula read:

REGRET DELAY FILES MISLAID PRINTS MARKED TARBELL CORRESPOND HERMAN JARRETT HELD SUSPICION EXTOR-TION WEYRINGHAUSEN CASE RELEASED INSUFFICIENT EV-IDENCE JUNE 1939.

"Do you remember the Weyringhausen case?" he asked.

"One of those missing-heir affairs, wasn't it? A meatpacking fortune and a son that was supposed to have been drowned at sea years ago and a claimant who was said to be that son. The Tich-borne case repeating itself."

"Right. And this Jarrett was a backer of the claimant's. Which would seem to indicate that he specialized in finding heirs. They weren't able to prove fraud on him in the other case, and I doubt if there's fraud here. The pickings wouldn't be rewarding enough to justify it. But Tarbell-Jarrett hasn't been doing so well, to judge from where he was living, and he doubtless wanted to keep his hand in.

"The note signed *J. T.* that I found in Runcible's room corrob-orates this. It read *He says maybe. Keep hoping, keed.* Or possibly that *He* might be *H period.* That indicates Hilary was nibbling, and indicates too that they must have been able to present some-thing of a case.

"What sort of evidence they had, we can't fully know. Most

of it has probably been destroyed by now. But we do know that Runcible had his grandmother's rosary, which Tarbell was using as evidence, he had his marked physical resemblance to Hilary and to old Fowler himself, and he had the arm trick."

"What on earth is that?"

Marshall explained and showed Waring's sketch. "Wimpole mentions it in the memoir, it was apparently the one good light parlor trick in Fowler Foulkes' dogmatic and dominant personality. Which is what Tarbell meant by saying it might be useful."

"These are amazing facts that you've uncovered, Lieutenant. But what sort of a pattern do you make out of them?"

Marshall paused before replying. "I've been looking at the works of that Charles Fort that Austin Carter and Matt loved to quote. It seems that a few years after the famous disappearance of Ambrose Bierce there was another disappearance—that of one Ambrose Small. Mr. Fort suggests, and I honestly think only half in jest, that somebody was collecting Ambroses. Well, in this case, somebody's been collecting Foulkeses."

"Then why Tarbell?"

"Because only he knew that Runcible was a Foulkes. Don't you see: If Runcible's death seems a mistake, then the whole plot appears aimed at Hilary. Your whole question of motivation is in another light. Anyone whom Hilary has antagonized becomes a candidate; and that's a wide field. But if Runcible's death is deliberate, then the murderer must be a man who profits by the three deaths of Tarbell, Runcible, and Hilary. His motive can be only one thing. And there's only one man who has that motive."

"And one woman," Sister Ursula reminded him. "Perhaps even two."

"Can you see a woman visiting the Elite Hotel as Dr. Derringer? It's the man all right."

"But he has a series of most impressive alibis."

"Which topple over at the touch of a finger."

"And the locked room?"

"There is still that. God knows there is still that. Other things clear up. The bomb, for instance. I didn't see how anybody in this kind of circle would know about Louie Schalk; but it's evident now that Tarbell must have known, and might easily have mentioned the picturesque profession of his neighbor to a visitor—a visitor with whom he was dealing professionally and who later killed him. But that—" Marshall broke off, and his eyes lit up.

"Yes, Lieutenant?"

"That means the screws weren't on Hilary. Tarbell's visitor, according to the clerk, was Dr. Derringer—that is, the murderer. A shady dealer like Tarbell wouldn't object to a person of some fame and position disguising himself for visits to the Elite. And that phone number links Tarbell, not with Hilary personally, but with the Foulkes apartment. Say Tarbell was double-crossing Runcible, selling out to the two people who had the greatest interest in seeing Hilary maintained in status quo—"

"But you said that this was not blackmail proper. Just a gentle pressure appealing to Hilary's family pride."

"All right. Skip it. It's a sideline. It'll come straight, everything will come straight, when we break down that devilish locked room. And that's what I most need your help on, Sister. You unlocked a room once. Can't you do it again? If I can clear that up, I can make an arrest today on attempted murder, force Kello to withdraw his charges against Matt, and turn the murderer over to him on the capital charge. But how, in the name of all the words that should never shatter the peace of this patio, how was that locked room contrived?"

Sister Ursula pressed her hands together tightly over the cross of her rosary. "I hinted to you before what I thought was the nature of the solution."

"The Invisible Man? And a lot that helped, aside from Leona's brilliant theory that it might mean Sister Felicitas." The nun laughed. But the laughter was nervous, strained, far from her usual free and full peal. "Sister Felicitas would be delighted by the joke, if I could make her hear it. But I can go further than a hint now. In this visit you have told me exactly how that room may be unlocked."

"I have?"

"And remember Dr. Derringer's dictum. Eliminate the impossible, and when nothing remains . . ."

"Sister!" Marshall's voice was harsh. "Are we playing games? Don't you realize that there may be a third murder while we—"

"No. There will not, there cannot be a third murder. Because, you see, you have neglected to mention yet another person who would profit by the death of a Foulkes."

Marshall emptied his pipe and filled it slowly. His expression changed from anger to doubt to amazement. "Sister," he said at last, "are you implying that . . . ?"

Another nun entered the patio. "Lieutenant Marshall?" she asked. "There's a telephone call for you."

Marshall's face was black when he returned. "So?" he grated. "That was Ragland. He's been phoning all over town for me. So there couldn't be another murder?"

"Lieutenant . . ." Sister Ursula's voice trembled a little.

"That was a bright suggestion of yours, that last. But I think this clears him. And," he added, heedless of the peace of the patio, "it's the same goddamned locked room."

7.

Veronica Foulkes stared at her brother curiously. "So it happened at last." She shut behind her the door to the study.

Vance Wimpole nodded his pale face. "It happened at last. They got Hilary."

"And it's the same as before?"

"The same as before. The night latch is on the hall door. Jenny here and I have been in this room ever since Hilary entered the study. No one has come or gone."

"You're very clever, Vance," Veronica said levelly.

"From one of your demonstrated ability, my dear, that is an impressive compliment"

"But possibly not quite so clever this time. Before, you had impartial witnesses. The two nuns. No one could suspect them. But who will pay attention to the evidence of your fiancée. And she is the only one who can prove that you did not enter that room."

"So that's how it's to be, Ron? I'm slated for the role of scapegoat this time? Come, that's hardly fair. Or necessary. You know that you've nothing to fear from my administration of the estate. You'll do better to keep me around."

"I don't know how you did it before. That was perfect. But this is too brazen, Vance. It's not that I want to turn you over to them. But they'll never believe this story."

"Marshall will. He's conditioned to locked rooms. That's probably what gave you the idea, isn't it?"

There was a tight circle drawn around these two as they stood there cold-bloodedly discussing the likelihood of their respective guilt. Vance's gay flamboyance had disappeared, and with it Veronica's rootless strivings for effect. They were naked now. The others with them, the brother's Jenny Green and the sister's newly acquired Joe Henderson, were silent and helpless and a thousand miles away.

"I wouldn't persist in that notion, Vance. I wouldn't mention it to Marshall. Or I might be moved to make some reference to airplane travel."

D. Vance Wimpole shrugged and reached for the bottle. When he had finished pouring two drinks, he was smiling. "Does it matter, Ron? Isn't it the main thing that Hilary is dead now? You are a free woman and I am the administrator of the Foulkes estate. If you care to pretend that you think me guilty of his death, well and good. It harms no one. They can never pin this crime on either of us. Come on, drink with me."

Veronica nodded silently and accepted a glass. They drank together.

Jenny Green shuddered. "I've never seen them like this before . . ." she murmured. "It's . . . they aren't human."

Joe Henderson blinked. "I know. It's . . ." He groped for words and found them in the only language in which he was truly articulate. "It's like watching something extraterrestrial, extragalactic even, across cold reaches of interstellar space . . ."

"And now," said Vance Wimpole, "now that that's settled, for the police." He looked up a number and dialed. "Police headquarters? I wish to report a murder. The murder of Hilary Foulkes."

The astonished voice of the desk sergeant crackled into the room. "What!" it exploded. "Again?"

"A total murder this time, officer. Please send your men at once." He added the address and hung up.

"Oh . . . !" Jenny Green gasped. "How can you be like this? Hilary's dead!"

Veronica paused in lighting a cigarette. "We know."

"But he was . . . He was so good to us all. He was so kind to me. And he was your husband, Veronica."

Wimpole leaned back against the table. "Don't be childish, Jenny. Hilary was good to you, yes, out of an odd sort of family pride. You may possibly regret his death. But surely you have enough sense to see that no one else can."

"But you might at least have the decency to—"

"To play the crocodile? There'll be time for that later, with the police and the press. Now there are only you, so much a part of the family, and Joe, who probably sees all, possibly knows all, but certainly tells nothing prior to 2500 A.D. We cannot afford to waste these moments in tears, idle tears. We need to think, to map our campaign."

Veronica leaned forward eagerly. "How about suicide?"

Jenny gave a little stifled gasp.

Wimpole laughed. "No, no, my dear. Ron is not proposing a romantic suicide pact to obliterate our guilt. Hardly. You mean we might suggest that Hilary . . . How should it go? Say that he killed Runcible and then committed suicide out of remorse?"

"Yes," said Veronica tensely.

"Inadvisable of course from the point of view of insurance. And otherwise impossible. Marshall's no fool, even if Kello is. He's seen enough of Hilary to know that no crimes on earth, nor any other conceivable cause, could drive him to take his precious life. Physical impossibilities may be overcome, but not psychological. Hilary could never commit suicide. Besides, I have no doubt that the medical examiner will find that the angle of the blow is inconsistent. Or were you more careful this time?"

Jenny rose. "I'm going to my room. I can't stand this. You talk about Hilary as though he were a . . . a *thing* . . . a . . ."

". . . a prime bastard, which he was, and whose passing can have none but good effects."

"It's too cruel. I'm going."

Joe Henderson rose indecisively as though to follow her. Then the doorbell rang.

"Alice still out shopping?" Wimpole asked. "I'll take it. Mustn't keep the police waiting when they're so prompt."

Veronica Foulkes sprang to her feet as the visitors entered. They were not the police. They were Matt and Concha Duncan. Veronica extended a graceful arm, index finger pointing straight at Matt. "You dare to come back," she declaimed, "after the evil that you have wrought here!"

Vance Wimpole nodded approvingly. "Yes, Ron, I think that'll do as well as any. And we'll have Kello on our side. Duncan, my friend, you're elected."

8.

Sister Ursula stood staring at the spot where Hilary's finally dead body had rested. "May God forgive me . . ." she murmured. "I never dreamed . . ."

Marshall paced about the room, glaring bitterly and abusing his pipe with hot and furious puffs. "There couldn't possibly be another murder. So you go off and leave Hilary here with his murderer."

"Yes," she confessed. "I did. I left him with his murderer . . . I wish that I could be a fatalist. I wish that I could shrug it off with a casual, 'It was written thus.' But I know that man operates through his free will, and that whatever end he may serve, he must bear the responsibility of his acts."

"The same damned business. Every detail repeated, down to the shirt sleeves. Pity the proud Hilary should die without his beautiful dressing gown . . . All the same but the knife."

"The knife?" Sister Ursula sounded distracted.

"Of course. The token of esteem from the Zemindar of Kota Guti is in our hands now. This time the murderer swiped a knife from the kitchen. Good idea, too; longer blade, more efficient. Everything the same—but at least this time we don't have to believe it. The locked room's out, thank God. We can discount the Green girl's testimony at once."

The nun's attention revived. "But no. You can't do that, Lieutenant. Then what becomes of the previous episode here in this same locked room?"

"Does that matter? If we've got him for murder, we're willing to waive a charge of attempted murder. I'll admit I would like to have all the threads tidily bunched up, but—"

"I waited too long to speak. And was it because it was necessary, as I convinced myself, or was it my devilish pride . . . ? At least save me from another mistake, and let me save you from yours. You must believe the Green girl's testimony, and you must let me show you how wrong you are."

Marshall hesitated. "I'll admit I've forced this case on you. I can't pull out without hearing what you've got to say . . . What do you want me to do?"

Sister Ursula frowned. "Simply this. Please, without any questions, call the surgeon who examined Mr. Foulkes' body and ask him to come out here again. Tell him . . . tell him you need fresh details that would be too hard to explain over the phone."

"Doc won't like that."

"It was the same dogmatic young man with the crouch whom we met before?"

"Yes."

"Please, Lieutenant. Bring him out here. Or do you wish to make a Kello of yourself?"

"All right." Marshall shrugged. "I'll take the chance." He used the study phone. Just as he was finishing, Sergeant Ragland came in.

"Hey, Lieutenant! There's a plain-clothes boy from Pasadena and he's got a warrant for one of the guys we're holding out there."

Marshall jammed down the mouthpiece noisily. "Kello!" he snorted, and made a peculiarly vicious swearword of the name.

It was indeed Sergeant Kello, and looking particularly pleased with himself. "Hiya, Marshall. This time I'm in your bailiwick, but it happens I've got authority with me. Look at this: bench warrant charging Matthew Duncan with murder. No more diddling around with manslaughter. We try to keep 'em safe in Pasadena, and your L.A. lawyers get 'em out to finish the job right under your nose. Soon's I got word of this, I talked the magistrate into changing the charge on the Runcible case. You can have him when we're through with him—us and the guy that runs the lethal gas chamber."

"I don't want him," said Marshall quietly. "He didn't kill Foulkes. He didn't kill Runcible either; but if you're set on making a fool of yourself, it's no skin off my nose."

"Thanks, Terence." Matt's voice was reasonably level. "I'd hate to see you fighting over me."

Vance Wimpole laughed. "Marshall's just jealous of your astuteness, Sergeant Kello. Carry off your prize and good luck to you. I'll be glad to see my brother-in-law avenged so promptly."

Marshall turned on him. "He'll be avenged. Don't worry about that. But not by Kello. You've got a few questions to answer first."

"I have? But Lieutenant! I admit that I have been present at a couple of the high points in this orgy of assassination, but the rest of the time I have been merely an offstage character."

"So? You didn't think you could keep Phyn's mouth shut forever, did you? Wouldn't it have been wiser to dispose of him too?"

"Vance!" Veronica cried out "I told you that nasty little man couldn't be trusted. I warned you—"

"You idiot!" Wimpole snarled at his sister. "Can't you see this police dolt was groping in the dark? And now you—"

"Which by the way," said Marshall mockingly, "your sister's exclamation was no more of a give-away than your turning on her like that. So Phyn has been blackmailing you. And I'll lay odds on the subject matter. He saw you in Los Angeles while you were supposed to be at the ends of the earth. Very pretty, that train-stub alibi, but very futile. After the first locked room, you had more than time enough to fly to San Francisco and take that train back. And Mr. Phyn is going to stop and think when he weighs the profits of blackmail against the power of the police and a possible perjury charge."

D. Vance Wimpole poured himself a drink. His self-possession was beginning to return. "Lieutenant, I have just realized the motive behind these attacks upon me. You are still vexed because I found your delightful wife so attractive that evening at Chantrelle's."

"Huh?" Kello did a slow take and finally guffawed. "So that's it, Marshall? Out for a little private revenge? Well, pin this one on him if you can. All I want's the Runcible murderer, and I've got him right here. So long, boys."

"You won't need those handcuffs, Sergeant," said Matt firmly.

"So I suppose you'd warn me in advance if I did? No, brother, you're going to wear the pretty bracelet and like it. We take good care of our murderers in Pasadena."

The sight of the flashing steel was too much for Concha. She had been standing beside Sister Ursula, sobbing dryly and quietly. Now she ran forward and threw her arms around her husband. "You can't!" she cried. "You can't take him away, Sergeant. I won't let you take him and kill him and be a Lieutenant. I'll—"

"Mary," said Matt warningly.

"He'll kill you, Matt. He's bad. He doesn't care about truth or anything but his old promotion. And he'll take you and—"

"Break it up, sister," said Sergeant Kello. "You can see him tomorrow—through the bars."

"Wait, Sergeant," Sister Ursula stepped forward. "Please let me speak."

"And who the sweet h— I beg your pardon, Sister. But who might you be?"

"Who I am is not important. The Lieutenant will tell you later if you care. But I must not let you take this man back to prison. He did not kill William Runcible."

"Yeah? And I suppose you know who did?"

"Of course. It was Hilary Foulkes."

The reactions in the room were predominantly of scornful disbelief. Only Veronica Foulkes sounded receptive. "You mean then that Hilary killed himself after . . . ?"

There were loud protests. "But the medical evidence . . ."

"But the psychology of the man . . ."

"But the other attacks . . ."

Sister Ursula held up a hand. There was something so quietly imposing about her small erect figure in its archaic robes that even Sergeant Kello fell silent

"No," she said. "No; Hilary Foulkes did not commit suicide. But please listen to what I know must be the truth."

9.

"The 'attacks' upon Hilary Foulkes," Sister Ursula began, "were suspicious from the first. They were too completely unsuccessful. The first two, the brick and the car, rest purely upon Mr. Foulkes' unsupported accounts. With the third, the chocolates, he 'happened' to notice a needle-prick in the coating and 'happened' to have been reading a novel which made him wary.

"The fourth, the bomb, was carefully timed for delivery at a certain hour; and Mr. Foulkes had made an appeal to the police for protection and expected an officer to be present at that hour. To be sure, coincidence helped here. The police were slow about answering what they took to be a routine crank complaint, but Lieutenant Marshall called at the right time on a then apparently unrelated matter. Even if he had not, the bomb was contrived to tick loudly; Mr. Foulkes himself could have noticed that ticking and called the Emergency Squad if no officer had been present.

"The fifth 'attack,' the locked room, I shall pass by for the moment, observing only that it was obviously impossible for anyone but Mr. Foulkes to have engineered it."

"Hold on there," Sergeant Kello protested. "The medical evidence . . ."

"Please be patient, Sergeant. I shall set your mind at rest on that in a moment. But if all these 'attacks' were framed, what could be the purpose behind them? Two possible motives occurred to me: a chain of preparations to make a suicide seem like murder and defraud an insurance company, or a schizophrenic condition in which one part of the mind tries to produce physical evidence to justify the delusion of persecution which obsesses the other part.

"I did not know enough of Mr. Foulkes then to realize that

neither of these hypotheses could conceivably fit him. He was sane, if a criminal can ever be called sane, and he was if anything abnormally tenacious of life. Neither mania nor suicide could possibly have motivated the feigned attacks.

"Not until it was too late did I see the third possibility: that the murderous attempts on Hilary Foulkes were preparation for the successful murder of another, apparently by mistake for Hilary Foulkes. There was only one person whose death could be contrived in that manner, and that was William Runcible."

"But why?" Matt Duncan protested. "God knows I want to believe this, Sister. I've got my reasons." He jangled his steel bracelet. "But why? Runcible was just a nebulous and negative fan. What should Hilary have against him?"

"Lieutenant Marshall, with an admirable persistence and refusal to accept the over-obvious, has established that Runcible was William Runcible Foulkes, son of Roger and grandson of Fowler Foulkes."

Veronica gasped. Her brother said slowly, "A lot of things are beginning to come clear now."

"But," Marshall protested, "the heir of a disinherited son couldn't have been any serious menace."

"Then manifestly, Lieutenant, Roger had not been disinherited. It will not do to say casually, 'Oh, Mr. Foulkes had no motive.' Only Mr. Foulkes could have planned the murder; only Runcible could have been the planned victim. Therefore Mr. Foulkes had a motive. Tell me, Mrs. Foulkes, did your father-in-law leave a will?"

"No." Veronica sounded puzzled and afraid. "No, he didn't"

"You know how old men feel about wills and death," Wimpole added. "And Hilary was all the family there was—we thought."

"Then William Runcible Foulkes had a claim, not only to the

money in the estate, but to a share in its administration. The blow to Hilary Foulkes was more than merely financial, though that might have wounded him deeply enough. It was a blow to his prestige, to his position as his father's sole heir, custodian, and steward. No longer would his faintest whim be firmest law. From an autocratic despot he would become a mere shareholder in power. The threat was intolerable; it had to be removed.

"It is possible that Runcible himself did not realize the full extent of his claim on Hilary Foulkes. It is quite likely that Jonathan Tarbell had concealed Fowler Foulkes' intestacy from him, and was promising Runcible merely some aid as a member of the family, such as Miss Green has received, while he threatened Mr. Foulkes with the loss of half the estate. This notion is rendered more plausible by the fact that Runcible was not scared off by Tarbell's death. He did not see that the threat applied to him. If he knew anything of Tarbell's past, or even from what he knew of where the man lived, he might assume that he had been killed for quite other reasons.

"Mr. Foulkes had strung Tarbell along with hopes, as the note found by the Lieutenant indicates, and killed him when his demands became too pressing, but the mistaken-identity murder of Runcible had to wait until Mr. Wimpole's arrival. Mr. Foulkes knew that Runcible, as a fan, moved in the circles of what Austin Carter calls the Mañana Literary Society. Once Vance Wimpole had arrived, it would be simple to contrive some occasion of being accidentally in such a situation that the mistake might seem possible. Chantrelle's rocket party was the ideal opportunity, and Mr. Foulkes took full improvisatory advantage of it. Almost every individual present was a likely candidate for the role of intended murderer of Hilary Foulkes; it was probably only chance, Matthew, that made him pick on you. But tell me, Miss Green, was Hilary Foulkes' account of the meeting by the shed correct?"

Jenny Green swallowed hard. "I don't know . . . They did talk about Cousin Hilary's father. But Runcible didn't sound quite like a fan. It did seem more . . . somehow more intimate. As though he were trying to show Hilary how much he knew. And once he said, 'I've lost the rosary, but I still have enough.' So you must be right about that; but I still can't believe that Hilary . . ."

"About that rosary, Miss Green: did you know anything about it?"

"Why . . . It was odd. When Veronica was being interested in religion, she read a memoir of the first Mrs. Foulkes that praised her as a lay saint, and she told me about that queer rosary devotion and the famous specially carved one. When the Lieutenant asked us about seven-decade rosaries, I started to mention it, but Hilary signaled me to be quiet. Later I spoke to him about it, and he said that he didn't intend to have the name of his father's wife bandied about in a criminous conversation."

"And that didn't seem peculiar to you?"

"No," said Jenny Green stoutly. "It . . . it still doesn't. I can't believe any of this. And anyway, Cousin Hilary couldn't have stabbed himself. The doctor said so."

Sergeant Ragland had answered the door. Now he said, "Here's the doc, Lieutenant."

The police surgeon strode in with his habitual swooping stoop. "Well?" he demanded. "What's all the fuss, my boy?"

Sister Ursula spoke. "Is it possible, doctor, that on either this or the former occasion, Mr. Foulkes could have stabbed himself?"

"Bosh!" he snorted dogmatically. "Rank physical impossibility."

There were puzzled murmurs, half of relief, half of fear. "If

Hilary did kill him," Veronica Foulkes began haltingly. "Mind you, I'm not admitting it, but if he *did* kill that fan . . ."

"Your nephew, darling," said Vance Wimpole.

She said no more, but the unasked question was loud in the room.

"One other point," Sister Ursula went on. "May I have that sketch of Runcible, Lieutenant? Thank you. Now doctor, would you say, from the characteristics you can see here, that this man could be a close blood-relative of Hilary Foulkes'?"

The doctor contemplated the picture and looked annoyed. "Hard to say," he snapped. "Out of my line. Very little known anyway about exact genetic details of physiognomy. Now if this showed coloration . . . But in pen-and-ink, no. Could be, certainly. Marked resemblance."

"Thank you."

But he went on staring at the picture. "Ridiculous drawing," he observed testily. "Position of those arms. Both back around the neck clasping the chin. Rank physical impossibility." He swept out of the room in a fast crouch more than ever reminiscent of Groucho Marx.

10.

"So you see?" said Sister Ursula quietly.

Marshall swore. He looked like a man whose solid earth has turned into quicksand.

"Remember the dictum of Dr. Derringer, Lieutenant. 'If nothing remains, some part of the "impossible" was possible.' Such dogmatic statements of physical impossibility apply to the normal man. But Hilary's father and his half-nephew were both double-jointed. Both were noted for this trick." She showed Kello and the others the grotesque sketch. "Your father, Mr. Wimpole, mentions in his memoir how those who had not seen the trick damned it as an impossibility. For Fowler Foulkes or for Runcible such a self-inflicted wound was perfectly possible. So we have no right to state flatly that it was impossible for Hilary Foulkes."

"Phooey!" Sergeant Kello snorted. "If a doctor says a wound can't be self-inflicted—"

The quiet Joe Henderson spoke up. "It's not just Foulkeses," he said. "Tony Boucher can do that too. I remember once he made an offer: Anybody could bring him a mystery novel where it was proved that death couldn't be suicide because of the direction of the wound, and if he couldn't get a knife or a gun into that position he'd pay out ten bucks. Nobody ever collected."

"We were all too ready," Sister Ursula went on, "to accept a verdict of 'impossible' as correct, when it really meant no more than 'unlikely.' In ninety-nine cases out of the hundred, such a self-inflicted wound would have been impossible. Perhaps the percentage is even higher than that. But here the evidence of the locked room clearly rendered any other solution even more unlikely—in fact this time quite truly impossible. That is what I meant by directing your attention, Lieutenant, to the Invisible Man, the man who is present but unnoticed: the victim."

"And I bit," said Vance Wimpole. "A good Fortean like me, and swallowing Science as gospel."

"The dressing gown," Marshall muttered. "That's why he was in shirt-sleeves both times. He had to take it off to get freedom of movement for his arm."

Sergeant Kello laughed heartily. "Nuts to L. A., Marshall. We may not be smart in Pasadena, but we don't swallow locked rooms like that. We'd've known right off that the only guy could've done it was the victim."

"You are wise after the fact, Sergeant," Sister Ursula smiled. "But at that, what you say might be true of the average policeman who had never met with an apparently impossible situation. Remember, however, that this crime was designed to meet the inspection of Lieutenant Marshall, who was confronted only last year with a murder committed, at first glance, in quite as impossibly locked a room. He was, as one might say, conditioned to such a situation. I can imagine that one of the Harlem detectives who investigated the Fink case might have reacted similarly here. I am certain that Superintendent Hadley or Inspector Masters would have done so."

"I suppose that excuses me?" said Marshall sourly.

"And this brings us to the reasons for the 'impossible' situation, and none of them seemed to apply here. But the reason in this case, we can see now, was to gain time. You will notice that none of the 'attacks' was designed to implicate a specific attacker, although one did by chance lead the Lieutenant onto a false trail. Mr. Foulkes had to avoid an arrest while keeping the police interested. Any possible suspect must be still at large when the opportunity for the actual murder presented itself. So the locked room was deliberately contrived as a tough nut for the Lieutenant to try to crack, with the certainty that he would still be chipping his teeth on it when Runcible was finally murdered.

"The method had probably been evolving in his mind ever since he learned that the Lieutenant was the man who worked on the locked room Harrigan case. That morning, when he heard on the telephone that Lieutenant Marshall had located an accidentally perfect suspect and was almost ready for an arrest on suspicion, he realized that he had to act at once. He groaned and dropped the phone. Then in the time it took the Lieutenant to arrive and investigate, he had ample opportunity to stage his locked room attack, knowing that none of the household ever dared interrupt him when he was shut up in his study."

"O.K.," Kello grunted. "O.K. You make a good story out of it—up to today. But who the hell killed Hilary Foulkes?"

"Kello," said Marshall, "for once I'm with you. We're agreed, Sister, that Hilary could never have committed suicide. All right, so even granting that he made the phony attacks on himself and killed Tarbell and Runcible—who killed Hilary?"

Sister Ursula clasped tightly the crucifix of her rosary. For a moment her lips barely moved in silent prayer. "I'm afraid," she said at last, "that I did."

11.

Even Sergeant Kello was dumb. Concha stared from the nun to the study and back again incredulously. Lieutenant Marshall's pipe fell from his teeth, spilling coals ' on the rug, and not even Veronica Foulkes noticed it.

"I knew," Sister Ursula went on, "even before Lieutenant Marshall had established the motive, even before I had seen the sketch of William Runcible's arm trick, that Hilary Foulkes alone was responsible for all these crimes and seeming attempts at crime. But I knew also that legal proof would be a difficult matter. This morning I visited Mr. Foulkes about another matter, and I contrived to plant in his mind the idea that it would seem markedly queer to the authorities if the attempts on his life should cease after attaining a mistaken objective.

"It was apparent by the increasing complexity and audacity of the 'attempts' that the man's vanity was running away with him. No, vanity is not the right word. It was his overweening trust in fate, his confidence that nothing could fail him, since he was acting to uphold his sacred stewardship. It was, in fact, this almost religious assurance of his that gave me the first essential clew to his character and potentialities. I might almost say that I began to solve his crimes by reading a psalm in the office of Compline.

"I hoped that now, in the nervous reaction from his success, this self-assurance would carry him too far, that he would perpetrate an 'attempt' so patently fraudulent as to convince the police that the whole series was a hoax. But I over-reached myself. And so did Hilary Foulkes.

"He had not been drinking in my presence. I did not realize how much he had taken, nor how unaccustomed he was to liquor. His fuddled imagination failed him; he tried the locked room trick over again. But this time he was confused and shocked (successful murder had proved more of a strain than he had anticipated) and very drunk. His Persian dagger was in the hands of the police, and he was forced to use a hastily chosen kitchen knife, with a longer blade. The carefully planned wound, convincingly dangerous but actually safe, turned with the slip of a drunken hand into self-destruction.

"Suicide was impossible to Hilary Foulkes. But he killed himself, and the fault is mine."

There was silence in the room. Jenny Green sniffled quietly. Veronica Foulkes finally glared triumphantly at her brother and said, "See?" Vance Wimpole made a resigned grimace. Concha extended a hesitant hand toward her husband.

"Well, Kello?" Marshall demanded.

Sergeant Kello fingered his warrant. "A lot of talk . . ."

"All right. You bring Duncan to trial. So. The defense proves

A: Hilary Foulkes had framed a series of faked attempts on his own life. B: Hilary Foulkes had the strongest of motives for killing Runcible. C: Hilary Foulkes died by his own hand. If we need to, we'll get Henderson's friend Boucher on the stand to demonstrate how it was done. We pile up all those items, and where are you? Hell, you won't even get an indictment."

Slowly Sergeant Kello's fingers shredded the warrant. "O.K., Lieutenant. Lieutenant . . ." He repeated, savoring the lost title wistfully.

Matt Duncan extended his hand (the steel links jerking Kello's up with it) and gripped Marshall's. "Thanks for the 'we,' Terence. It's the first time I've ever heard of a policeman presenting the case for the defense."

"It's a day for novelties," Vance Wimpole observed. "It's the first time that an action of Hilary's has ever saved anyone trouble."

AFTERWORD:
Saturday, December 6, 1941

IT WAS a Saturday night a month later, the last Saturday night of a nation nominally at peace. Lieutenant Marshall was hospitably mixing drinks for a company replete with one of Leona's noble dinners. There were present the Duncans and the Carters and Joe Henderson and Jenny Green.

"One thing," Marshall observed as he poured. "You've affected my taste in reading matter. You boys have got something here in this fantasy field." He gestured toward a bookshelf where two pulps stood beside the Greek Anthology. "At its best, it's fresh, vigorous, creative imagination, and the perfect escape literature. I never could find much escape myself in a mystery novel. Too close to home or too exasperatingly far from it. But in a space ship . . . God can I escape! Some of it, of course, can be pretty flat; but for instance in the two magazines that your friend Don Stuart edits, it's the McCoy."

The three writers bowed gratefully. "We'll prove that there's a market for fantasy yet," said Austin Carter. "Maybe even between book covers, though my novels so far haven't caused any partic-ular worry for the fire wardens along the Thames. And wait till you see Matt's latest novelet. I kicked around that time machine alibi I sprang on you, but it wouldn't jell. So I generously turned it over to Matt and he did a sweet job. Don's always maintained that a science fiction detective story was by definition impossible, but wait till you read that one."

"Thanks for the plug," said Matt. "I'll return it: How's your anthology coming?"

Carter made a face. "I'm doing an anthology of science fiction for Pocket Books," he explained. "And I've got the strictest instructions never to pay over fifty dollars for reprint rights on a story."

"So?" Marshall asked as he paused.

"So it doesn't contain any Fowler Foulkes. Vance wants a hundred or no dice."

Joe Henderson gaped. "Vance did that to you?"

"But," Matt objected, "I thought Metropolis reconsidered and bought your novel. Vance played ball on that."

"Sure. After I promised him a cut on the sale, or he'd repeat Hilary's trick of withholding the Derringer stories."

"Good God!" Marshall ejaculated. "All that trouble and what have we got in the end? Another Hilary."

"Please!" Jenny Green protested. "Oh, I know the things Cousin Hilary did. I know there's no excusing him. But he was good to me. Even in his will after he died. And I can't stand the way you all always talk about him . . ." There were the first wellings of tears in her eyes. Joe Henderson unobtrusively took her hand.

"Hilary's dead," said Austin Carter, "and the evil that he did lives after him very actively."

"A man is dead," said Marshall, "and the arrangement that allowed and all but compelled him to do wrong—in this case, the arbitrary administration of literary rights by a capricious individual—"

"Oxford," said Leona in a loud aside.

"All right. Anyway this arrangement allows and compels his successor to do likewise. A man dies, but nothing is changed unless the system dies too. You could work out some pretty metaphorical applications . . ."

"I don't know," Carter frowned. "I agree the system has worked badly on this estate; but what is one to do? When we eventually get into this war and the Navy calls me up for active duty, supposing I get killed? I certainly want Berni to enjoy whatever small income my stuff may still bring in."

"Thanks, sweet," Bernice smiled. "But don't be in a hurry to leave me holding the royalties."

"The income," Marshall said. "Of course a writer's heirs should enjoy his income, unless one wishes to attack the whole problem of hereditary fortunes. But should they have willful and unchecked control of his work? I can imagine something like a committee of the Authors' League of America which would pass on all applications for the use of material and fix a reasonable fee, which would of course be received by the estate. I—"

"You're getting out of your depth, dear, aren't you?" Leona suggested. "Tell these charming people your latest professional discovery."

"Oh." Marshall laughed. "Yes, this was one of my main reasons for having you over. Thought you'd all want to know. For my own satisfaction, you see, I've been checking up on loose ends on the Foulkes case. My report is in and done with, but there were things I wanted to know. Maybe they weren't my professional concern any longer, but I needed to know them.

"I went wrong from the start on this case. I'll admit that. I was too preoccupied with detail to see pattern. To Sister Ursula, it was clear from the start that the attacks originated with Hilary.

Me, the bright industrious professional, I go snooping around on little trails of detail, and end up damned near arresting you, Mr. Carter."

Austin Carter grinned. "Some imp kept prompting me to try to goad you into that, Lieutenant."

"I know. And I kept trying to figure if that was a sign of malicious innocence or brilliant guilt."

"What was it put you on to Austin, Lieutenant?" Bernice Carter asked. "The Derringer costume?"

"But if you'd only asked me about that," said Jenny Green. "Or if I'd only thought to tell you . . . Hilary always had a Derringer costume, even long before I knew him. He used to wear it for family masquerades and such."

"Mr. MacLeish was right," Marshall sighed and quoted: "'It is the questions that we do not know.' So I got beautifully lost on detail in those first attempts, and I got lost again toward the end. I got enough detailed facts to figure out two beautiful theories about Wimpole and Runcible, put them together, and thought I had everything. And all the time I kept worrying my eyes over these details, there was the grand pattern if I'd only step back a couple of feet and take it in.

"But even after we saw the big pattern, some of these details still bothered me until I realized that they were parts of incomplete sub-patterns. And I needed to fill in the rest."

"Skip the *mea culpa,* Terence," said Matt, "and tell us these sub-patterns."

"Well now, for instance, about Vance Wimpole. Most of my guess was right on that. He had been in Los Angeles from time to time during his supposed wanderings, and Phyn had seen him and was blackmailing him. But the whole set-up, including letters mailed by friends from distant points, was intended to circumvent detectives, not from homicide, but from a divorce-evidence agency. I managed to find out enough to set up in blackmail for myself; but I'll hold out the juicier details.

"And the other business is too bitterly good to be true. William Runcible Foulkes, I discovered by painstaking checking through records, was orphaned at an early age and brought up in an asylum. He learned a trade and grew up into a first-rate turret-lathe operator. He died in Chicago of natural causes in 1938."

The audience was duly and gogglingly petrified. "Then our Runcible . . . ?" Austin Carter ventured at last.

"Something we'll never know about this case is who did what and with which and to whom, or in less famous words, who was defrauding whom in what manner. Did a false Runcible put himself over on Tarbell, that specialist in lost claimants? Were Runcible and Tarbell collaborators in fraud? Or did Tarbell convince a young innocent that he was the missing Foulkes heir and use him as a lever on Hilary?"

"Tune in to this station tomorrow and find out," Leona murmured.

"I wish this station knew. But it can make a guess that the last of those assumptions is correct. Tarbell was in Chicago building up his Weyringhausen case at the time the real Runcible died. And he did have the rosary, and God knows what else that was destroyed either at the Elite Hotel or at the rooming house on Adams. Say that he knew the young man and was planning to press his claims when he up and dies. So Tarbell filches and preserves the evidence for future use. Finally fate is kind, and he runs on to a man with a marked physical resemblance to the Foulkes', even down to the arm trick. If this young man's own family background were hazy, it shouldn't be hard to persuade him that he was the descendant of the Fowler Foulkes whom he so idolizes."

"Then all Hilary's . . ." Jenny Green began. "It was all for nothing?"

"For nothing?" said Joe Henderson quietly.

"You and Bernice should be happy," Matt Duncan observed to his wife as they walked home from the streetcar. "It looks like you've finally got a nice girl for Joe."

"I like her."

"So do I. But she does seem mild for Joe's tastes. I'd have thought that bitch of a Foulkes woman was more his type."

"I think I know what happened there. Jenny says she and Joe were there when Mrs. Foulkes and her brother talked about Hilary's death, just before we came in. She says it was awful . . . like something inhuman. I think then Joe realized just how evil a woman can really be; and evil women sort of lost their fascination." Concha paused and removed a pebble from her shoe. "If we had a car . . ." she muttered.

"We're not going into that again!" Matt snapped.

"But I used my own money when . . . you know . . ."

"I know. Sorry, darling. I shouldn't have barked at you like that. You used your money, and it meant more than I ever thought money could mean. It meant that you loved me and needed me and wanted me free even when I was charged with killing a man. But still I . . . Damn it, my love, life is so confusedly much a matter of prides. Hilary had his own peculiar kind of pride. Sister Ursula has hers. Well, I have mine."

"I think," said Concha in a very little voice, "I've got a solution."

"Yes, dear?"

"I could spend the money on anything that was my own, couldn't I? I mean let's say I wanted to raise pedigreed chows. I could spend it on them, couldn't I?"

"I guess so. I wouldn't stop you. But I don't know as how chows—"

"Silly. That was just for example like. I don't mean *chows*. But I could ... oh I know I wouldn't be very good at it and not nearly so capable and admirable as Leona but then who is? And every time we go to the Marshalls' I get to thinking about it and ... I could spend it raising my own baby, couldn't I?"

Matt Duncan did a very slow take. Then, though they were at that moment right under a bright street lamp, he took his wife in his arms. "Darling," he said a little later, "let's get home and make sure of that."

Thirty hours later, in the white-and-gold chapel of the Sisters of Martha of Bethany, the chaplain had just finished saying the requested month's mind Mass for the repose of the soul of Hilary Foulkes. A nun moved slowly about the chapel. As she paused in devotion before each station of the Cross, she fingered a curious rosary which should by rights have reposed in the Black Museum of the Los Angeles Police Department.